JUSTICE INKED

COWBOY JUSTICE ASSOCIATION
BOOK SEVEN

by
Olivia Jaymes

www.OliviaJaymes.com

JUSTICE INKED
Copyright © 2016 by Olivia Jaymes
Print Edition

Cover art by Sloan Winters

Justice Inked

Sheriff Dare Turner is known for his ever-present scowl and general bad mood. Between a teenage sister who thinks she's all grown up and a killer on the loose he doesn't have much to smile about these days. He simply doesn't have time for fun and games.

Rayne Dunn is half free spirit and half workaholic. She doesn't mind the long hours in her tattoo shop creating works of art on skin but sometimes she'd rather be dancing in the rain with someone special. The trouble is she hasn't had a date in way too long. She needs to change up a few things or she's going to work herself into an early grave.

Every time these two find themselves in a room together they end up arguing. Rayne thinks the sheriff has a big stick up his posterior and Dare thinks the sexy little tattoo artist is too loud and mouthy. It's best if they stay far away from each other.

But when someone breaks into Rayne's shop and then winds up dead that probably isn't going to be an option. Whether they like it or not, they're going to be spending a great deal of time with each other.

And they're starting to really like it...

CHAPTER ONE

S heriff Dare Turner was a handsome hunk of man.

At least he was to Rayne Dunn. Since she'd moved to Valley Station months ago and opened her tattoo shop, she couldn't help but admire the head lawman in town. He was sexy, gorgeous, and absolutely, positively not interested in her. At all.

If he dated, and he didn't very often, he went for delicate little blondes who dressed conservatively and spoke softly.

And probably only when spoken to.

Rayne, on the other hand, had almost midnight black hair with a few purple streaks added in for fun. She had multiple piercings in her ears and sported a few visible tattoos.

And more that weren't visible.

She also talked. A great deal and loudly. When she was mad she let people know and when she was happy she sang it from the rooftops.

In other words, she wasn't Dare's type and couldn't even hope to be.

So it wasn't the easiest thing to sit here in her shop working on his latest tattoo. There was really no way to ink someone's body without getting close to them and touching. Rayne was so close she could feel the heat from his skin and smell the scent of his body wash. Kind of citrusy with a hint of spice. Clean and fresh.

Dammit.

Why couldn't he smell like a barn or a locker room? The only saving grace from making Dare Turner completely perfect – other than his questionable taste in females – was the fact that he was the grouchiest man Rayne had ever known. Nothing made him smile. Not catching a criminal. Not eating ice cream or pizza. Not hanging out at the local bar and seeing his favorite team win.

Nothing. Zip. Nada.

Rayne was certain that if Dare did smile his face would crack or melt off like those bad guys at the end of *Raiders of the Lost Ark*. He wasn't mean; in fact, he could be quite kind to the residents of Valley Station. But he wasn't a jolly, happy go lucky kind of guy.

Which only made her wonder if he smiled during sex. Or more specifically, could *she* get him to smile during sex? The challenge was beginning to become an obsession.

"How much longer?"

Dare's familiar growl pulled Rayne from her daydreams as she changed ink colors. It didn't take long but the sheriff wasn't the most patient of men.

"As long as it takes. I'm creating a work of art here, Sheriff, not rotating your tires. If you need to get back to work we can finish another time."

Dare had commissioned her to ink a phoenix rising from the ashes on his right shoulder blade. It was colorful and intricate and he was like a five-year-old getting a root canal. He tried not to fidget but clearly, he hated sitting still. There was no way they'd finish this today.

He growled again but Rayne didn't even flinch. At this point she was used to the sheriff's unusual mode of communication. He had different growls for various occasions and this one wasn't anything to be alarmed about.

"Can you at least change the damn channel on the television? This movie is ridiculous."

She didn't even have to rise from her chair. Picking up the remote, she simply held it out to Dare. "Knock yourself out. It's just background noise when I'm working."

This time he grunted in response, which seemed to be an improvement over the growls. He skipped through the channels until he landed on an all weather station.

"I'd pictured you as more of a sports channel kind of guy."

Dare peered over his shoulder, his brows pulled down in his usual half frown and half scowl as if he was shocked she had the audacity to try and start a conversation with him.

"I'm going hunting this weekend and want to see what the weather is going to be like."

That might be the longest sentence he'd ever said to her. She was on a roll, so why not push her luck? Something she did on a daily basis and it could really piss people off.

"What kind of hunting do you do, Sheriff?"

"Turkey."

She waited for him to elaborate but of course, he didn't. What a tool. What a sexy, gorgeous, alpha male tool.

"It's not even Halloween yet. I guess I only thought people hunted turkey for Thanksgiving."

"Turkey season lasts pretty much the entire fall." He muted the television and looked back at her as she worked on the piece. "You're not from here, are you?"

That was progress. He'd asked her a personal question although the answer should have been obvious. She didn't fit in all that well, but then she hadn't tried hard to.

"No. I'm originally from San Francisco, but my sister Camy married a man from Fairfield so I moved there when she got pregnant. To help, I guess. Then my shop burned down and this place came open, and it was such a good deal I couldn't turn it down. I'm still close enough to drive to see her whenever I want, but I really miss my friend Misty since she and Jared moved to Seattle."

Way more information than he'd asked for, but Rayne was a talker, which was normally a good thing in her profession. Most people wanted to chat and get their minds off the fact that she was injecting ink into their skin with needles.

"San Francisco, huh? That explains a lot."

Normally with a customer she'd have ignored the implied insult, but something about Dare made her mouth say things she shouldn't.

"That's not a nice thing to say, Sheriff."

His brows shot up in surprise and she didn't bother to hide her chuckle. "I meant no disrespect, Miss Dunn."

"Really? It kind of sounded like an insult from where I'm sitting. Usually people are nicer to me when I'm holding the needle, but I can see you're a man that doesn't mind a little pain as long as the end result is worth it. By the way, please call me Rayne. It's hard to stay formal when we've been this close to each other."

A fact that Sheriff Turner seemed to just be realizing. His shoulders, which had been relaxed, now stiffened and it felt like he was holding his breath. Or maybe his temper. She'd been known to rile a few in her time.

"I simply meant that you seemed unfamiliar with the local ways...Rayne. Not that there was anything wrong with that."

He wasn't mad but he was perturbed. The good sheriff didn't appreciate her comment. *Good.* She hadn't much liked his either.

It only underlined the sad fact that he didn't find her attractive in the least.

What was a single girl in the middle of Montana to do?

Annoy the crap out of the man she couldn't have, that's what.

There was a fire in Rayne's sparkling green eyes and Dare had to hide his chuckle that he was the poor bastard that had lit the fuse.

Inadvertently, of course, although he sure as hell liked to poke and prod at the dark-haired beauty. Despite her funny looking clothes and the purple streaks in her hair, she had an exotic air about her that he found very attractive. She wasn't his usual type, though. He liked his women quiet and shy, and she was far from that. Rayne was out there living her life loud and proud, which was great. Just not what he was looking for.

Not that he was looking. He wasn't. He had too damn many things going on in his life to be getting involved with a female. They needed time and attention. Plenty of it. He simply didn't have it to spare.

"Don't know the local ways? That's a polite way to say I don't fit in. Which I don't. I stick out like a sore thumb. But I thought you might be more tolerant than the local church ladies, who pray for my soul like I'm a harlot come to town to lead all the men astray."

Rayne looked capable of leading a male into temptation. The black bustier she had paired with a purple vinyl skirt showed off every God-given curve of her body. That skirt had scooted higher on her thighs as she leaned even closer, her glasses sliding down her nose as she worked, showing off several inches of creamy skin.

"I'm sure they don't think that, and I am tolerant. There's nothing wrong with your appearance."

Rayne snorted and not in a delicate manner. "Funny how I didn't mention my appearance but you did. Face it, Sheriff, I'm just never going to fade into the background of Valley Station or Fairfield."

"Do you want to?"

The question was out before he could stop himself, but then he wanted to know the answer. She didn't seem like the type of person who spent much time courting the opinions of others, but he didn't know her well. She could be hiding a huge inferiority complex with tattoos and funny clothes.

"Stay still," she scolded, pressing her palm to his shoulder. Her hands were small but capable, the nails cut short and painted a bright red that matched her lipstick. "And the answer to your question is not particularly. My parents weren't people that encouraged hiding your light under a bushel as you might say here. They stood out and they wanted us to as well. If you met our family, you'd remember it."

He believed it.

"What do your parents do?"

"They follow the Grateful Dead around the country and sell crystals out of their van."

Wha–?

Rayne was openly laughing at him and he felt heat rising in his cheeks. "That's what you expected me to say, isn't it? You don't think they're bankers or attorneys, right?"

"I suppose not," he said curtly, not enjoying the experience of being the butt of one of her jokes. Most people in Valley Station gave him a wide berth when it came to something like that. "Does it amuse you to laugh at me?"

"Kind of, yeah." Rayne giggled and he found it difficult to stay annoyed. The sound was simply too cute. "But if you must know my parents own a company that puts together adventure vacations. You know like hiking, mountain climbing, bungee jumping, white water rafting. They really like the outdoors."

"Doesn't sound like you do."

She wrinkled her snub nose and he noticed a smattering of light freckles. "Hardly. My idea of camping is sleeping with the windows open, but my parents had other ideas. I've been dragged along on every sort of family vacation they could think up that wouldn't get us all out and out killed. Someday I want to spend a week being pampered at a spa, but I don't know when that will ever happen. People complain when I close the shop on Sundays and Mondays."

The bell over the door rang and Dare turned to see his little sister saunter into the tattoo shop. Just turned eighteen, Sophie was really Dare's half sister from his father's second marriage. When his dad had a heart attack and passed away several months ago, Dare had left his deputy job with Griffin Sawyer and moved back to Valley Station to care for his sister.

A completely fucking thankless job.

While he and Sophie loved each other, they didn't exactly see eye to eye about how she should live her life. She thought she was all grown up and he still saw her as the tiny innocent girl with big blue eyes and blonde pigtails. It made for more than a few tension-filled conversations.

Just this morning they'd argued over how tight her jeans were. Sophie had told him they were "skinny jeans" and meant to hug the legs, but Dare had said they were simply too small. Then she'd reminded him she was eighteen and could dress herself however she wanted, and that had pretty much ended their heated discussion. Dare was afraid if he pushed her too much she'd move out and then he'd never know what was going on in her life. That was much worse than tight blue jeans.

"Hey, big brother, I thought I saw you through the window." Sophie came closer to inspect Rayne's work and a smile bloomed on her face. "That's so cool, Miss Dunn! The colors are so bright and the detail is amazing."

Rayne gave his sister a warm smile that she'd never given him. "Thank you. And please call me Rayne. All my friends do."

Did that mean they were friends?

"I'd love to have a flower." Sophie pointed to the top of her shoulder. "Right here. Something soft and feminine. Maybe pink. Could you do something like that?"

"No," Dare grated, not caring that he didn't let Rayne get in a word edgewise. This was his little sister. Emphasis on little. "No, she cannot. Ever. You are not getting a tattoo."

Sophie's chin jutted out, her eyes narrowed. "As I keep reminding you, big brother, I'm eighteen. That's the age of consent to get a tattoo. If I want one there is no way you can stop me."

His hands tightened into fists, Dare tried counting to ten before he replied but only made it to five. She was right, of course, but that didn't mean he was giving in. "You're too young. Ink is for life, little girl. When you're a few years older then you can decide."

He should simply be grateful she didn't want to get the name of her latest horn dog boyfriend inked on her shoulder, or worse…on her ass. But he wasn't feeling all that grateful at the moment.

"Says the man that's getting a tattoo as we speak," Sophie smirked. "You're a gigantic hypocrite, you know that? When did you get your first tat?"

"That's not the point. The point is—"

"Excuse me." Rayne had stood up and her voice boomed

through the small shop. "Can you have your family feud somewhere else? I need you to be still and I need to be able to concentrate, or you're going to end up with a sad-looking tattoo. Capiche?"

No one talked to Dare that way. Ever. And yet this five foot two Goth pixie had just laid down the law. After laughing at him.

What the fuck?

He'd had enough for one day. "Can we continue this another time, Miss Dunn?"

He didn't give a shit that he sounded curt or pissed or whatever. He was the goddamn law in this town, and he didn't appreciate being spoken to like he was a naughty teenager.

Rayne grabbed the appointment book from the reception desk and slammed it down on her chair, her scarlet lips pressed together in a tight line. She wasn't any happier than he was.

Tough.

"Fine. When?"

"Next Wednesday? About two?"

She carefully dressed his fresh ink before Dare slipped his shirt back on and she shoved a piece of paper in his hands. She wasn't happy with him, but proper care of his new tattoo was important. "See you then. Here's instructions on how to care for your tat. Let me know if you have any problems."

He knew how to take care of new ink. This wasn't his first rodeo.

"Thank you." He placed his hand on Sophie's upper arm to lead her out of the shop. "Shall we head home, sis?"

Rayne was standing there, her hands on her hips, looking very unhappy. Apparently she hadn't embraced the whole motto regarding the customer always being right.

The bell over the door rang as he and Sophie exited onto the sidewalk and she elbowed him in the ribs, her lips turned up at the corners in merriment.

"You are in so much trouble, big brother. Rayne told you off...but good. I don't think she's afraid of you in the least."

"She should be," he growled as he thought about how huffy she'd been with him.

The less he saw of Rayne Dunn the better. He'd get his tattoo and then forget she existed.

Women like Rayne were a menace and made a man's life a misery. He needed to stay professional and far away.

CHAPTER TWO

F riday night in a small town never changed much. If it was
football season, most of the population would be sitting in
the stands watching the game and freezing their asses off only to
head to the diner or pizza place afterward. Or maybe the local
watering hole if they were over twenty-one.

Louie's was a typical sports bar with pool tables in the back
and dart boards on the wall. Big screen televisions circled the
large room and there was even a tiny dance floor if a couple
became amorous. It was mostly just good fun, but every now
and then a few patrons got a little rowdy.

That's why Dare had been called in tonight.

He strode into the bar, his gaze scanning for trouble and
quickly found it. He wasn't all that surprised. Tim Wallace,
Sophie's latest heartthrob, was punching it out with his older
brother Duke Wallace over something stupid. At twenty-eight
the guy was living on his past glories as quarterback of the high
school team. Meanwhile in the present, he hung around bars and
worked odd jobs to make beer money.

Tim wasn't exactly Dare's favorite person either. He had a
job at least, but Duke had way too much influence on his little
brother and this brawl highlighted that fact. Tim hadn't been

dating Sophie long but he looked at her like…dammit…like he wanted her and that sure as shit wasn't going to happen.

Dare pointed to Duke, who had just taken a nasty punch and was leaning against a pool table, blood trickling down his chin. "Billy, grab Duke and I'll get Tim."

Letting his deputy handle Duke – all the cops in Valley Station had plenty of practice dealing with him – Dare grabbed Tim by the arm and spun the younger brother around. Tim needed an attitude adjustment and Dare was the man to give it to him.

"What in the hell do you think you're doing?"

Dare dragged Tim back, one hand on his arm and the other on his shirt collar. Tim struggled, but Dare had forty pounds of muscle on him and easily moved him from the fray.

"Dammit, Dare. Duke was asking for it."

"I don't doubt it, but you aren't required to give it to him. Just calm the hell down and keep your family feuds out of public places."

The younger man was breathing heavy, his lip swollen and his knuckles bruised. Dare could feel the waves of anger coming off Tim so he placed himself directly between the two fighters.

"He's a son of a bitch. He deserved it."

Probably, but that wasn't the point. "Start at the beginning. If your story is halfway decent, I may not have to throw your ass in jail tonight. How do you think Sophie will feel if you spend the night in my drunk tank?"

"I ain't drunk," Tim denied, his neck and face red with anger. "Just had a couple of brews."

Sadly, the same couldn't be said for Duke. If it weren't for Deputy Billy the man wouldn't be standing on his own two feet. He was wobbling but still belligerent as hell, barely letting Billy get a word in.

"Talk," Dare commanded, getting right in Tim's face. For

the life of him he couldn't see what his little sister saw in the guy.

"We were playing pool and things got heated. I told him he was a greedy bastard, always living off my hard-earned money and he called me a momma's boy."

"So that's why you hit him?" Dare asked, his voice deadly soft. Tim blanched at the unspoken anger in Dare's tone. The entire incident underlined how Wallace wasn't the man for Sophie.

"He–he said that I needed to grow up…"

Both men did, that was clear. Dare took a few deep breaths and tried to remember that he was the law in this town. That meant loudmouth punks like Duke and Tim were going to say stupid shit.

"Anything else?"

Tim's Adam's apple bobbed as he swallowed hard. "Yes. He said that paying for things was all I was good for. That's when I hit him."

So Tim had taken the first swing. For a semi-good reason, but he still shouldn't go around punching people. Even people that heartily deserved it. Dare believed in the karma universe. He'd seen it do its magic many times and he never ceased to be amused by how accurate it was despite its mystical origins.

"Stay here and don't fucking move."

Tim ran his sleeve over his bleeding lip and nodded, suspiciously watching Duke who was telling Billy his side of the story. Dare needed to hear it for himself. He strode the small distance between the two men until he was looking down at Duke almost nose to nose. The man reeked of booze, weed, and sweat, and once again Dare had to question his own wisdom in becoming a lawman. He should have gone into something else, anything else. That was better than dealing with fools and drunks on a regular basis.

"What's the story, Duke?"

Duke pointed to Tim standing a few feet away. "My brother swung first. I was just defending myself."

"Yep, you were just sitting in the corner reading scripture and minding your own business when Tim punched you, right? Is that your story? Or did you flap your gums and say something you shouldn't have to provoke him?"

Some of Duke's bravado seemed to slip and he hunched his shoulders, looking down at the sticky concrete floor. "I didn't say nothin'."

"Are you sure?" Dare pressed. "Is it your sworn statement that Tim Wallace punched you out of the blue? That you said nothing about him personally?"

"Shit, Sheriff, no one in this damn town can take a joke."

"Yeah, you're a riot, Wallace. A real comedian. Billy here is going to run you in for public intoxication, disturbing the peace, and anything else that comes to mind." Dare leaned down, using his size to intimidate the other man, who cowered back against the deputy. "Next time you and your brother decide to tangle keep it at home. Got it?"

Not one word fell from Duke's lips as Billy hustled him out of the front door of the bar and into the waiting cruiser. Dare turned back to Tim, who was standing there with a hopeful look on his rapidly swelling face.

Dare was about to dash that hope. The young man needed a lesson in reality. He drank too much, gambled too much, and generally made a mess of his life. He needed to get far away from his big brother's influence if he hoped to make anything of his future.

"You're going too. As much as I can see why you did it, you can't go around punching people who say shit you don't like. If you and Louie can come to some agreement on the damages then maybe we can drop any charges. But you're spending the night at the lockup."

"Fuck, Dare. I was defending myself."

The kid didn't have a clue what it took to be sheriff of this town. It was all Dare could do not to put a major hurt on both of them so they would wake the hell up and see that they were wasting their lives, but that's not what the good people of this town paid him to do. It was selfish and indulgent and Dare prided himself on being disciplined. He had plenty of things wrong with him but that wasn't one of them.

"And that's why I'm not going to cuff you or put you in the back of the SUV. You can ride up front with me and sit in the office while I do paperwork tonight. By morning Louie will have calmed down, and as long as you pay for what you broke he'll forget this ever happened."

Tim nodded and Dare let the young man lead him out of the bar. Billy would come back later and talk to Louie, hopefully smoothing the entire situation. A bar fight wasn't anything to ruin someone's life over.

But Dare wouldn't pass up this opportunity to have a man to man chat with Tim.

CHAPTER THREE

"**J**ust you and me, Spartacus. Again."

Rayne scratched behind the ears of the tabby cat, eliciting a soft purr as she sipped her glass of red wine. Sprawled on the couch with the feline perched on her lap, she flipped aimlessly through the channels, barely paying attention until she finally settled on a chick flick.

The heroine seemed to be having issues with her love life, something about choosing between two men. One looked perfect on paper but didn't light her fire, and the other made her tingle but didn't make a lot of money. Or something like that. Having trouble deciding between two men didn't seem like much of a problem to Rayne. In fact, she'd like to have issues like that.

It had been months since her last date and she was beginning to feel downright pathetic.

Taking another gulp of her wine, Rayne closed her eyes and let the fruity liquid warm her abdomen. It had been a long week already and it wasn't over. Saturday was always a busy – and long – day at the shop and all she really wanted to do was crawl between the covers of her bed and sleep for a week. She really did need to think about that vacation seriously. She hadn't had much time off in the last two years and the stress was beginning to wear her down. She'd been close to losing her temper yesterday with Dare Turner when he'd decided to have an argument with his sister while she was trying to create a masterpiece on his shoulder blade.

Asshole. Heaven help the woman he ended up with. Sure, he was hot and sexy but his personality left plenty to be desired. Bossy and high handed, he was the kind of guy that wanted to be in charge all the time even if they didn't have a freakin' clue of what to do. She didn't need a Neanderthal. She simply needed one really nice man. Preferably one able to support himself with a kinky side in the bedroom. She was getting tired of dating her vibrator.

Hating herself for what she was doing, Rayne slid her phone off the end table and dialed her best friend in the world. With a husband, a baby, and a career, Misty Foster Monroe really didn't have time to hear all of Rayne's problems but she needed more than a cat to talk to tonight. She needed someone to smack her hard and tell her to stop feeling sorry for herself.

Rayne wasn't about to call her sister Camy either. Camy would only somehow turn everything around and make it about her and how everyone had disappointed her. Camy truly believed that the people in her life simply didn't do enough for her and it made her difficult to be around at times. Mostly Rayne ignored her sister's whines and complaints, but there would be no way she could do that this evening.

Misty picked up on the second ring.

"Hey, girl. What's going on in Valley Station?"

Groaning, Rayne situated herself more comfortably on the sofa, tossing a wool throw over her legs. "Not a thing, but that's not different than any other day, is it? Another week in a small town. Why don't you tell me what's going on in Seattle? That has to be more exciting."

"Diaper rash."

"What? I'm not sure I follow."

Misty's laugh rang clearly through the phone. "Lizzie Rose has diaper rash. We've been battling it for the last few days and she's been miserable, which means all of us are exhausted. I think we finally have it beat and she's fast asleep now. Hopefully she'll stay that way for several hours. Neither Jared nor I have had four consecutive hours of sleep in two days."

"When you put it that way Valley Station sounds pretty good. I'm sorry she wasn't feeling well. It makes my piddly ass problems seem small and petty."

"Tell Dr. Misty what ails you. I'd love to hear about something else besides diapers and red butts. I love my baby girl, but talking to a grownup is certainly needed tonight."

Rayne hated to whine when she really didn't have much to complain about. She had a good life and was lucky in so many ways, but every now and then she felt a little sorry for herself.

"It was a long week at the shop and tomorrow is shaping up to be even worse. I have a full day scheduled and then some."

"That's because your work is amazing," Misty declared firmly. "From what I hear you're attracting business from all over, not just locally. You're a wonderfully talented artist."

Rayne snorted so hard she had to put her wine glass down on the end table. "Tell that to the grouchy sheriff. He and his sister decided to have an argument in my shop the other day while I was working on him. It's not easy to create a masterpiece when two people are sniping at one another. Then he had the audacity to get nasty with me when I called him out on it. That man is never happy about anything and he wants the rest of us to feel the same."

Except that she'd seen Dare Turner being quite sweet and

friendly more than once, especially to children. He had a gentle quality to him but at the same time, he was strong and reassuring. He wasn't going to be playing Santa at the community center anytime soon, but he was well liked all over Valley Station by pretty much all the residents.

"Jared says he's a hell of a lawman, if that helps any. I asked him once why Sheriff Turner was so grouchy, but he said he didn't know but that maybe Griffin did. I do know his father passed away not long ago and he took up guardianship of his little sister until she turned eighteen. That says a lot about him. He didn't have to do that."

Rayne had the feeling the sheriff didn't do anything he didn't want to. "He's just a difficult person to be around. I'm happy most of the time and I like to be around others that feel the same."

"I don't think he's unhappy. I just think he doesn't smile much. There is a difference."

"Not much of one," Rayne grumbled, wanting to change the subject. Dare shouldn't get to live in her head rent-free. "So when do I get to see you again? It's been ages."

"Glad you asked that. You're going to get to see me very soon. Next weekend, as a matter of fact. We're coming into town to see Jared's family and let them spoil Lizzie Rose for a few days."

"And you and the handsome hunk will get a night to your-selves," Rayne finished with a chuckle. "I know how this works."

"I'm ready for a night on the town and so are you. Jared has an old friend that is reentering the dating scene after a divorce. I'm told he's smart, handsome, and successful. How about I fix you two up? We can double date so you won't have to be alone with him right away."

Rayne exhaled noisily, and it came out as half whine and half groan. Overly dramatic, yes, but she wanted to get her point across. Being fixed up on a blind date was simply too pathetic.

"I am not so lame that I cannot find my own man."

"When was your last date?" Misty shot back, clearly not intimidated.

Rayne fell back on the cushions with a sigh. "Shit. Okay, it's been awhile."

Images of Dare Turner floated through Rayne's mind and she ruthlessly pushed them away. He might be gorgeous but he wasn't her type.

She wasn't his type.

They weren't for each other.

Although the way his shoulders made his shirt strain at the seams was certainly a fine sight to see, not to mention the way he filled out his worn blue jeans.

"Jared said he's a nice guy. What's the harm in having dinner? I promise you don't have to marry him and have his baby."

"Is he a cop too?"

A picture of Dare in his uniform sent a flush of heat through her body all the way to her fingertips.

"He's a veterinarian. You can't go wrong with a guy who likes animals."

That was true. Rayne had never met an asshole vet. If anything, they were always smiling and friendly.

Unlike Dare Turner.

Stop thinking about the sheriff!

"Just dinner. That's it. No movie. No inviting him in for coffee. Just one meal."

"Agreed. One meal. No commitment. Now go buy a new outfit to wear. Something sexy but tasteful."

"Do those two things even go together? Are you thinking

more pole dancer or debutante?"

Not that it mattered. Rayne didn't have either one in her closet. Although she usually wore edgy outfits to the shop, when dressing up she preferred floaty romantic attire.

"Very funny." A baby's cry in the background interrupted their conversation. Poor Lizzie Rose was awake again. "Listen, I need to go. I'll text you when we get to town with all the details."

Rayne bid her best friend goodnight and placed the phone on the coffee table. Although the idea of being set up with a complete stranger was galling, Misty had a point. Rayne needed to get out of the house and live. She'd become a prisoner of her own success, something she swore would never happen. She needed to make time for herself and the things she enjoyed doing.

She had the awesome career.

Now it was time to find the love of her life.

✧ ✧ ✧ ✧

"I can't believe you put him in jail last night."

Sophie elbowed Dare in the ribs – hard – as she passed him in the kitchen to grab a soda from the refrigerator. She was dressed to go out in a pair of black jeans and an eggshell colored knit sweater. Her long blonde hair was curled and she was wearing too much makeup. Which was any at all, if he were honest. When had she ditched the pigtails and braces?

"He threw a punch at another human being, Soph. I had to put him in jail. Luckily Louie calmed down and didn't press charges. He and Duke busted up the back room and caused some damage."

Sophie's lips tightened in distaste. "Duke's an ass."

Hell, everybody knew that except Duke and a few of the

floozies he spent time with.

"He went to jail as well, so it's not like I gave him a pat on the head and sent him home with a cookie." Dare took a deep breath to calm his temper. Sophie had been digging at him about this since he got home. "Maybe if you dated a different kind of guy this wouldn't happen."

Slamming her soda can on the counter Sophie rounded on him, poking his chest with her finger. "You'd hate any boy I dated. Why don't you just admit it? Nobody would ever be good enough for you so I might as well date someone from the Manson family."

His sister could be incredibly dramatic.

"That's not true," he protested. "I liked that one guy. What was his name? The one that brought you flowers and books. Gordon someone or other. He seemed like a decent guy."

Sophie rolled her eyes and groaned. "Gordon Shell? You think he's a great guy because he brought me flowers and books? That's your criteria? Let me tell you about Gordon, dear brother. Gordon likes to liquor up his dates, take naked pictures of himself with them, and post them on the Internet for strangers. He also thinks he's smooth as butter with the ladies and that the word 'no' doesn't apply to him. How's that for decent?"

It was hard to tell about some people. Now that he thought about it the kid had seemed kind of pervy. "That just proves my point that most men are scum and you should stay far away from them."

"I see you're a fan of the crazy cat lady lifestyle. Too bad for you I'm not." Sophie held up her hand and shook her head sadly. "I love you but you need to back off. I mean it, Dare. It's my life and I'm going to live it as I see fit. You can have an opinion but that's all it is. I'm not making my decisions based on votes. There is no democracy here. I'm the queen."

"I'm just trying to protect you."

His fingers flexed on the edge of the counter, sadness making his heart squeeze painfully. He was going to lose Sophie. Soon. She was talking about leaving Valley Station, and if she was anyone else's sister he would say that was a good decision. But they'd grown closer this last year and he simply didn't want to lose the last family he had.

It made him hold on too tight.

"I know you are and I love you for it." Sophie laid her hand on his arm. "I trust you to run your own life. Can you trust me to run mine?"

Every cell and molecule in his body screamed that she was way too young, but saying those words aloud were only going to get him in trouble. She didn't want to hear about his fears of the future.

"I'll try," he said grimly, pulling her into a hug. "Just be careful, dammit. There's a lot of crazy people in this world that don't give a damn about anybody else."

"I promise."

The sound of an engine outside had a smile on Sophie's lips and a sigh on Dare's.

"That's Tim. I've gotta go. Don't wait up. In fact, maybe you should go out tonight too. Ask a woman on a date or something. Live a little."

It was a sad day when his eighteen-year-old sister had a better social life than he did. But a woman? He needed a female in his life like a hole in his head. They were nothing but trouble and he didn't have the time or patience.

He was fine on his own.

CHAPTER FOUR

D r. James MacMillan was everything Misty and Jared had promised. Charming, intelligent, nice, plus handsome enough to be pleasing to the eye without being so good looking that women would be hanging all over him. He'd been divorced for about a year and spent his free time hiking, camping, and rock climbing.

Dear heavens, an outdoorsman.

Jared and Misty must have warned him because he didn't bat an eyelash at her ink or purple streaked hair. She'd tried to dress as conservatively as possible for the evening in a sleeveless black dress with a scooped neckline and a flared skirt that ended about two inches above her knees. She pulled out her one expensive pair of shoes – black pumps with four inch heels – that made her feel taller, which wasn't an easy feat. A silver simple necklace and earrings completed the ensemble. From the admiring gaze he gave her and the approving look from Misty, Rayne must have done something right.

The restaurant was lovely but not too fancy. Valley Station wasn't a mecca for foodies so they'd driven to Springwood, which was still a small town but large enough to have something that resembled fine dining. James ordered them all a bottle of wine, which Rayne had sipped as she ate her filet mignon with a parmesan crust and a twice-baked potato that melted in her mouth. Misty had been right. It was good to get out of the house once in a while.

"So I'll be hiking the Grand Canyon in the spring. Have you done much hiking?"

Rayne fidgeted with the stem of her wine glass as the waiter whisked their dinner plates away. She had to give James credit. He was really trying but they didn't have much in common.

"Quite a bit actually. I…uh…I'm not a big fan of the great outdoors though. Every time I've tried something bad has happened."

His brows pulled down in a frown. "Bad? Like what?"

Shifting uncomfortably in her chair, she glanced over at Misty and Jared who were deep in conversation. They weren't going to come to her rescue.

"That's how I discovered I was allergic to bee stings. I was stung by a bee and had to be rushed to the hospital."

"That's terrible, but you shouldn't let it keep you from enjoying this beautiful land of ours. There's so much to do and see."

He didn't seem to get it.

"I was chased by a gang of chickens. Or is it gaggle? Anyway, a bunch of chickens chased me."

"It's a flock."

"I thought that was seagulls."

"That's a band."

"Wait. What?" Rayne had lost track of the conversation.

"You were chased by a flock of chickens," James prompted. He was starting to get that look on his face that she knew so well. The one that people got when they thought she was crazy, or at the very least strange. "Did you get hurt?"

"No. We were visiting a friend of my mother's who owns a

farm in Wisconsin. They had chickens. I went out to explore and they ended up chasing me back into the house. So I stayed there for the next three days."

Rayne's father had tried everything he could to get her to go outside but she wouldn't budge. Those chickens had ignored everyone else in the family and come after her like she owed them money. She wasn't going to make the same mistake twice. The next time she'd set foot out of the house had been to take the dozen or so steps to the car so they could get on the road and head home.

James looked down at the table and then up at her, his smile hopeful. "How do you feel about puppies and kittens?"

A topic they could agree on. "I love them. I think they're the cutest things ever."

His smile widened. "You should come by my office. We're fostering a litter of Golden Retriever puppies and their mother. The owners had to move and couldn't take them along so I agreed to take her in. She gave birth about four weeks ago and they really are adorable."

Rayne couldn't help but wonder how Spartacus would feel if she came home with a puppy one day. It probably wouldn't be a happy sight.

"Maybe I will," she agreed, giving herself a silent lecture that she would look, cuddle, and kiss but not adopt. "Actually I already have a cat. Spartacus."

James burst into delighted laughter. "Spartacus? I don't suppose there's a story behind that name?"

Like most things in Rayne's life, it was a silly one.

"He looks like Kirk Douglas."

His brows shot up and his mouth hung open. "Your cat looks like Kirk Douglas? I've seen hundreds, maybe thousands, of cats in my lifetime but I've never seen one that looks like Kirk

Douglas. I don't suppose you have a picture?"

She was a doting pet parent; of course she had a picture. Her phone was filled with them. She dug it out of her purse and swiped at the screen only to see she had several missed calls and texts.

"What the—"

Quickly paging through them, she shook her head as her anger began to boil.

"What's going on?" Misty asked, leaning over to whisper in Rayne's ear. "You're making a face and not an attractive one."

"The alarm at the shop has gone off and the security company has been trying to call me. I need to get to the shop and see what's going on."

Misty straightened in her chair and tossed her napkin on the table. "Then we'll get the check and leave right away. I hope it's a false alarm. Do we need to call the sheriff?"

Dare Turner. Rayne couldn't catch a break and stay away from that guy. "No, the security company will have notified the police. I'm hoping they'll get there before I do, honestly."

"Jared will go with you if you want," Misty offered. "He's hauled in a few burglars in his time."

"I'll be fine. I just need to get there and see what happened."

Misty and Jared signaled for the check and Rayne murmured her apologies to James.

So much for romance. Her life always came back to business.

With any luck she'd still have one.

✧   ✧   ✧   ✧

Grumbling under his breath, Dare surveyed the damage to Rayne Dunn's tattoo shop with dismay. She'd relocated to Valley Station after her shop in the nearby Fairfield had burned to the ground because some crazy bitch was trying to kill Misty. Now less than a year later her new shop had been burglarized and reduced to what appeared to be a fucking mess. The little lady was not going to be happy and neither was Dare.

He might not get along with the sarcastic brunette, but she was a resident and business owner in this town and that meant she deserved the best from her law officers. This wasn't Dare's best. He took pride in his job and this didn't reflect well on him. He was determined to bring whomever did this to justice.

"Has anyone called Rayne?" Dare asked Deputy Billy. "Does she know yet?"

"The alarm service that called us said they notified her. I'm guessing she'll be here any minute."

And madder than a wet hen. Rayne could certainly get upset over little things so this big thing was liable to send her into orbit. He only hoped he could keep her calm so he could ask her some questions.

"Keep an eye out for her arrival. I need to talk to her."

Everywhere Dare looked around the shop there was mayhem and destruction. Carts and equipment overturned, drawer contents tossed aside, and paperwork strewn as far as Dare could see. The backroom hadn't fared any better, and if anything was worse. Every file cabinet had been pilfered and the lockbox in the desk had been broken open. If there was anything of value in this building it had been taken.

"Oh my God. What the hell?"

Dare heard Rayne before he saw her. She'd come in the front door and he had to step over the contents of a bookshelf to get to her. Pale and shaking, she was flanked by former sheriff Jared Monroe and his wife Misty. They each had a hold of one of her arms as if keeping her from crumpling on the messy floor.

"Rayne, it's not as bad as it looks."

Dare tried to sound reassuring, but the withering look she gave him said that she didn't believe a word out of his mouth.

"It looks bad. How did they even get in? Shit, is there anything not destroyed?"

There was pain in Rayne's voice but a deep strength as well as she squared her shoulders and lifted her chin as if waiting for another roundhouse punch. She took a few tentative steps forward, her arms wrapped around her torso as she took in the damage.

"It looks like they broke in through the back door. Then they looked through the shop for any valuables such as cash or electronics. Things they could sell. Probably a meth head looking for a quick score. I'll need you to tell us what's missing."

Rayne turned to look at Dare, tears shimmering in her eyes. The tough little cookie that told him off without a thought didn't look all that confident at the moment. Dare wished there was something he could say to comfort her but that wasn't his forte. He had teddy bears in the trunk for small children but he didn't think a stuffed animal was going to fix this. Whoever did this hit her where she lived.

"It could take days of cleanup to figure that out."

"How can we help, Dare?" Jared asked, his own grim glance sweeping the room. "Lizzie is with my brother tonight so we can stay to help Rayne sift through this and see what's been stolen."

Rayne's hand was pressed to her cheek and she was looking around as if she didn't even know where to begin. "You guys don't need to stay. I'll be fine. But I don't know what they would have taken. I don't keep cash on the premises and the only electronics are the television on the wall and the alarm system. The most valuable things are my tools and although thrown around, they're still here."

"We're not leaving you alone," Misty replied, wrapping an

arm around Rayne's shoulders. "We can help you start cleaning this up once Dare is finished with the investigation."

"Maybe the robber got pissed when there wasn't anything to steal so they busted the place up," Jared suggested. "But of all the businesses on this block it seems strange they chose this one. There's a cell phone store two doors down that might have been easier pickings."

Dare had been thinking the same thing. Rayne's was the only store on this block that didn't accept cash so it didn't make much sense that she was broken into.

"We checked the other businesses and it doesn't look like they were hit." Dare picked up a chair that was on its side and set it upright before guiding Rayne by the shoulders into it. Her skin was still pale and her hands still shaky. He didn't need her passing out on him tonight on top of everything else. "Have you had a dispute with a customer lately by any chance? Anyone not satisfied with your work and not want to pay?"

Smoothing down the skirt of her dress, Rayne shook her head. "The closest I've come to a dispute is when you and your sister argued here in the shop. It's been busy but professional. Except for...you know...you."

Jared quirked an eyebrow at Dare. "Want to tell us about that?"

Dare coughed a few times, heat rising in his face. Even at a moment like this, Rayne couldn't leave it alone. He was here to help her and she was poking the bear. He could admit that he was in the wrong that day but he wasn't going to admit it at this very moment.

"No, I do not," Dare retorted. "It's not pertinent to this investigation. Well, as soon as we're done getting fingerprints you can start your cleanup. It shouldn't take much longer."

"Jared and I will help you clean up, sweetie. We'll get this place ship shape before you know it." Misty patted Rayne on the shoulder and grabbed her husband's hand. "We can call in some help if you like. I bet Royce would help us."

Jared was already on his cell talking to someone in a low voice.

"Caffeine."

Dare leaned down closer to Rayne, not sure he heard her correctly. "I'm sorry. What did you say?"

Rayne stood resolutely, her lips a mutinous line. "I said we're going to need some caffeine. Lots of it. This will probably take most of the night and I'm hardly dressed for it. I think I have a change of clothes in the closet by the restroom."

"I'll make a coffee run," Jared offered as he hung up the phone. "Royce is on his way and everything is set for Lizzie. She'll be fine. Now what does everyone want?"

The sound of shuffling feet and the clearing of a throat pulled Dare's attention from Rayne.

"Uh...Sheriff." Deputy Billy stood uncertainly in the doorway between the front and back rooms. "I have a situation here."

"What is it?" Dare had sent Billy outside to check the perimeter. The thief might have dropped a piece of evidence as they made their getaway. This strip of shops backed up to a wooded area that went all the way to the main road. A nice, easy drive away from Valley Station.

Billy's eyes were wide and he was fidgeting on his feet. "I kind of found something."

"Then *kind of* bag the evidence."

The deputy didn't move from his place in the doorway.

"Do you have a problem with that?"

Billy had been a deputy when Dare had been hired and he was a good kid but a tad green. Little things tended to shake him up that wouldn't faze a more seasoned officer.

"It's just..." Billy trailed off, staring at the floor before trying again, his eyes glistening with unshed tears. "It's just that I can't bag it up. I don't think I should touch it, Sheriff."

Dare didn't need this shit. It was okay to feel empathy for a victim, but Billy was taking it too far. Rayne hadn't been attacked or anything. She'd been robbed of material things. They could be replaced.

"Fine. Then tell me what and where it is and I'll do it."

Billy pointed over his shoulder. "Outside just about twenty feet inside the woods. It's—it's a body, Sheriff. He's dead. Or at least I think he is. I called for an ambulance."

Rayne gasped and fell back down into the chair and Misty's hand had flown to her mouth in shock. Dare exchanged a glance with Jared, who had immediately put himself between the women and the door.

Suddenly things looked a whole hell of a lot different than they had a few minutes ago.

CHAPTER FIVE

Rayne's earlier numbness was beginning to wear off, and now she was fighting an overwhelming wave of emotion that was part rage, part horror, and a big dose of helplessness. The events of the evening had quickly spiraled out of control, and she was being forced to stay in her shop while Dare and his deputies made sure there wasn't a killer roaming around outside waiting to pounce on her or any other citizen of Valley Station.

There was a dead man outside her shop. She could only hope that he didn't have anything to do with her robbery but it was probably a long shot. It seemed too much of a coincidence.

"They've finished dusting for prints. We can start cleaning up this mess." Jared placed his hand on her shoulder and she reached up to pat it, grateful for the support he and Misty had shown this evening. "Do you want to do the front room first?"

She wanted to curl up in the fetal position and cry until morning. She was tired of the universe kicking her ass whenever things were getting too good. She'd been happy, and apparently that simply wasn't acceptable.

Of course, things were going better for her than the guy lying in the woods. His day really sucked.

"Yes," Rayne sighed, standing and starting to sift through a pile of rubble. She'd already changed into an old pair of jeans and t-shirt that she'd left at the shop for those just in case moments. She hadn't thought she'd be using them to clean up a robbery. And murder. "I need to see how much of this equipment will need to be repaired or replaced. I may not be able to even open for a few days."

"Rayne, can I speak to you for a moment?"

Dare had appeared in the back doorway, a tentative expression on his face. She'd been pretty crappy to him earlier and she felt badly about it. As frustrating as he was to deal with he didn't deserve to be her whipping boy when things went wrong in her life.

"Of course, Sheriff. What do you need?"

She stepped out of the back door to join him but he didn't answer right away, appearing to struggle for words.

"I need you to take a look at our murder victim," he finally said. "See if you know him or why he might have been here. Can you do that for me?"

It was the last thing she wanted to do but she couldn't say no. This was a serious investigation and someone was dead. This wasn't about her comfort level or lack thereof.

Her answer stuck in her throat so instead she just nodded. He seemed to understand her reticence and placed his arm loosely around her middle to guide her back toward the woods behind the building. The area was lit up by several mobile spotlights and a lone figure was covered by a black tarp. She stumbled taking in the scene but luckily Dare caught her, pausing long enough to steady herself before moving forward.

"Are you sure you can do this?"

No. I am not sure at all.

Lips pressed together tightly, she took a deep breath and exhaled slowly, trying to will herself to relax. "I don't think I have much choice."

He didn't argue, instead leading her over to the tarp-covered body and reached down to take hold of a corner of the plastic. "Are you ready?"

Fuck no. How am I supposed to prepare myself for this?

Rayne had a feeling that her life was going to be separated into two sections from this moment on. Before seeing a dead body and after seeing a dead body.

"Let's get this over with."

"You know him?" Dare pressed, once they were back in her shop. Rayne's stomach was churning at the sight of a dead man, his face still and ghostly white. She was sure to have nasty nightmares tonight.

If she slept at all.

The young man's name, according to his driver's license, was Patrick Moulton and he was twenty-nine years old. He wouldn't be getting any older. That thought had Rayne's stomach twisted into painful knots. The delicious dinner she'd eaten earlier was in danger of making an untimely reappearance.

"I don't know him but I've seen him before."

Sitting shakily down onto an office chair in the back room, Rayne pressed her clammy hands to her cheeks trying to make some sense out of the night's events. She knew there were people out there that were violent. She'd been hit in the head by a homicidal woman who wanted Misty dead after all, but for some reason this felt closer to home. This wasn't about Misty. Did that mean it was about her? And if so, why?

"Do you remember where? Anything you can tell us will be helpful," Dare urged, settling into a chair across from her, their knees bumping. For once she didn't mind his close proximity.

His strong, no nonsense demeanor was comforting and oddly reassuring despite the fact that he got on her nerves. He had taken charge of the situation since the moment he'd shown up and every detail looked to be under control.

"He came into the shop about a week ago," Rayne explained, sipping the coffee that Jared had placed in her trembling hand. "He wanted a tattoo of course, and he'd brought in a drawing. We chatted about it and then he left without making an appointment when my next client showed up. He said he'd stop back by when I had more time."

"Go on. What happened when he came back?"

"He didn't. Come back, I mean. He said he'd return the next day but he never did so I kind of forgot all about him. The only reason I really remember him now is because I recognized that tat on his neck."

The man had a devil's pitchfork inked on the side of his neck in red and black. It had been a simple design but she'd never seen one like it.

"What did he say when you talked to him? Did he ask any questions about the equipment or how much money the shop takes in?"

"We only talked about the design, the colors. The usual things. He didn't act strange or out of the ordinary and he didn't ask me anything personal."

It had been like any other consultation and he had been like any other customer.

Dare tapped his pencil against the small notebook in his hand. "Did he say anything about himself? Anything at all?"

Rayne wracked her brain to remember the details of their all too brief conversation. Nothing about it had seemed strange so it had been filed under "Just Another Day", which meant the retrieval of the memory was shaky at best.

"Not that I can remember. He'd had tattoos before obviously, so we didn't have to have the usual first timer discussion. He knew what he wanted and I suggested a few tweaks since it was going to be on his upper arm." Rayne blew out a breath. "That's it, really. He said he'd come back to talk more but he never did."

"And no one was with him?"

Rayne shook her head. It had been just another day.

"I'm really sorry, Dare. It was a normal client interaction. Nothing out of the ordinary or strange. He was a nice guy who didn't trip any creep out wires. But we kept the conversation to business. He didn't tell me anything personal and I didn't ask."

"It's okay." Dare didn't smile but he wasn't scowling either. He was actually trying to be nice, which was a switch. "The fact that you remembered him is great. He may have been here casing the joint and never had any intention of getting a tattoo."

The guy had seemed genuine, but perhaps she wasn't as good a judge of character as she had thought. She'd had Dare pegged as an asshole but he was acting more than decently at the moment.

"If his plan was to break in and steal then how did he end up...dead?" Rayne asked, still seeing his dead body before they'd pulled the tarp back over his face. "Do you think he had a partner?"

"There's no honor among thieves, Rayne." Dare stood and shoved the small notebook into his chest pocket. "There's a good chance he had an accomplice. They might have argued and then a shot was fired. I certainly don't think this was some sort of tragic accident."

Jared stepped in between Rayne and Dare. "Is that all you need? She's been through the wringer tonight."

Please let him be done. Her head hurt, her stomach was nauseous, and she wanted to sleep for a week, only waking up when this nightmare was all over.

"For now," Dare conceded. "Once I get the ME's report and the forensics I may have more questions."

"That's fine. I'll see what I can pull for you on your victim's background. It might be some help."

"I'd appreciate that. I wouldn't say my computer research skills are all that strong."

Dare turned on his heel and strode out the back door toward the second crime scene. Rayne huffed and crossed her arms over her chest. Just when she thought Dare was a good guy he did something crappy.

"You're welcome, Dare," Rayne said sweetly to his retreating figure. He was too far to hear her but that wasn't the point. "Please don't give it a second thought. Jerk."

Jared laughed and wrapped his arm around Misty who was chuckling as well. "That pretty much sums up Dare Turner most of the time. Kind of a jerk. His bedside manner sucks but he's a good lawman, Rayne. If whoever did this can be found, he'll find them."

"I swear his tightie-whities must be two sizes too small. He has such a sour puss all the time. It doesn't seem like his life should be that terrible. He has a job, a home, family, friends. What is he lacking that makes him so cranky?"

Jared smiled and pressed a kiss to the top of Misty's head, his entire demeanor one of love and protection. "Maybe the love of a good woman."

"She might start out a good woman, but by the time he was done with her she'd be at her wit's end," Rayne declared. "Dare Turner could drive a saint to the bottle."

"He is handsome," Misty observed. "Some might even say sexy. Not me because I married the sexiest man in Montana. But some might say it."

"He's good-looking but it isn't enough to offset his personality. The man is downright difficult. I'll happily keep my distance."

Heaven help the woman who fell in love with the sheriff. She'd need all the help she could get.

Chapter Six

"Everything is fine. I'm fine and the shop will open again on Monday. I'm okay."

Assuring Rayne's sister Camy of anything wasn't an easy task. Once she had an idea in her head it was difficult, if not impossible to change it. Rayne had known that her sister's breakfast invitation was a not so subtle ploy to question her about the body and break-in, but she couldn't think of a decent reason not to go.

She loved her sister. She truly did. But Camy was wound tightly. Too tightly sometimes. She could make life a nightmare for those around her without breaking a sweat. The only person who could handle Camy was her mother, and she was hiking the Appalachian Trail at the moment.

Camy eyed her sister up and down while holding baby Blair. Blair Christina had pretty golden brown curls and bright blue eyes just like her mother but a dimpled chin like her father. She was going to be a looker when she grew up. Not that Camy would ever let her daughter out of the house.

"You're not telling me everything," Camy shot back, holding the bottle in Blair's mouth, the infant sucking hungrily. "There's more to the story."

"There isn't. I swear." Rayne held up her hand as if testifying in court. Camy was tougher than any prosecutor. "My shop was broken into by an almost customer who then ended up dead a few feet away. Shot in the chest. End of story."

"Do they know anything about him? Who would want to do this?"

Rayne stood from the table where they'd eaten breakfast and picked at a piece of leftover bacon. Was it too early in the morning for wine? Her sister made drinking look attractive.

Refilling her orange juice, Rayne counted to ten before she answered. It wouldn't do to lose her patience. "I haven't talked to Dare since last night. He said he might have more questions later after the autopsy and forensic reports, but I haven't heard from him, which isn't a surprise. It's only been a few hours. As to who would want to do this, I have no idea. I don't fraternize with killers, sis."

"There is a certain…element…that frequents a tattoo parlor," Camy sniffed with a tone of disdain. "I'm sure you get your share of criminals."

Rayne had been dealing with the attitudes of closed-minded people for years. To many, tattoos equaled trash or at least someone lesser than. Rayne's own sister often looked at her as if she was only one rung above a carnival worker. How Camy got so stuffy Rayne would never figure out. Their parents were completely open-minded, almost hippie-like, and then Camy somehow became priggish and judgmental.

"Every business probably has customers with less than stellar pasts. It's not my job to judge them. Besides, I've also done artwork for what you would call pillars of the community. I'm in the process of working on the sheriff's latest ink and he seems trustworthy. Or do you think he's the killer? He does look kind of shifty. Maybe he's a serial killer in disguise."

Camy slapped the empty bottle down on the table, luckily not waking her now sleeping daughter. "I'm being serious here. Sheriff Turner is not a serial killer. But I am surprised he's getting a tattoo. I wonder why."

"This isn't his first ink. Maybe he simply likes the artwork on his body."

Which of course made Rayne think about Dare's body, which was very fine indeed. Too bad his personality lacked a certain something. Like friendliness.

Camy grimaced and stood to place Blair in her playpen. Mark would be along in a few minutes to change Blair's diaper and put her to bed for her morning nap.

"He seems more conventional than that."

"He's a grouch," countered Rayne. "Whether that is conventional or not I don't know, but it is unpleasant. Actually, I just feel sorry for him. It must be terrible to be that unhappy every single day of your life. It's sad when you think about it."

Maybe Rayne needed to be extra nice to Dare next time she saw him. She'd always assumed that everything was fine in his life but it could be an emotional hell for all she knew. Instead of bitching about him, she ought to try being extra special friendly to him. Everyone thought he was the invincible sheriff of Valley Station but that could be a front for a soft, sensitive heart.

"I hope he finds this person soon," Camy replied, settling herself again at the table. "I don't like to think about you at the shop while this person is running loose. Maybe they'll come back and shoot you too."

That was Camy…always thinking of the bright side of life.

"If they wanted me dead, sis, they would have come in the daytime while I was there. No, I don't think I'm the target here but I appreciate your concern." Rayne glanced at her watch and then drained her juice glass. "I need to get going. I have several loads of laundry piled up and they won't wash themselves."

Camy grabbed Rayne's wrist. "Will you call me tomorrow and let me know you're okay? And if you hear anything from Dare? I really am worried about you. When I told Mom—"

The tenuous thread that Rayne held on her patience snapped. "You talked to Mom? When? Why? Shit, Camy, she doesn't need this kind of worry when they're out on an adventure and she can't do anything about it. This will just make her worry over nothing."

Color flooded Camy's cheeks and her hand fluttered to her throat nervously. "I sent her a text and she called me back. They have cell towers everywhere now, you know."

Rayne pressed her fingertips to her forehead, trying to hold back every word that threatened to spill out of her lips. Not nice words. Mean words. She didn't want to be nasty but Camy was making her crazy. Her sister needed to get a life and stay out of Rayne's. It was becoming a habit. A bad one.

"You went too far," Rayne said between gritted teeth. "I don't want to worry Mom and Dad about something that isn't a big deal. I swear your life isn't dramatic enough so you have to stir shit up. You'd probably be in heaven if they'd shot at me. Would that be dramatic enough for you?"

"That's not true," Camy protested. "It's just—"

"What?" Rayne shot back. "It's just what? You've blown this entirely out of proportion. Like you always do and then you sit back and get all pissy when people call you out. Just stop it. I moved here to Montana to help you when you were sick and pregnant but now I wonder if I've made a huge mistake."

"If you feel that way maybe you should leave."

"Maybe I should," Rayne agreed, knowing that they both would apologize later for the nasty things they'd said. "Stop trying to interfere in my life and for the love of God, stop judging it. I know things about you, Cameron Elizabeth. Things that would horrify your friends but you have apparently conveniently forgot about. Let me remind you that people who live in glass houses shouldn't sing opera."

There were too many stories to count that Camy wouldn't want her husband to know about. They had major dirt on each other.

Camy's eyes had gone wide with fear. Good. Her sister needed to remember that she wasn't a perfect angel. She'd lived life to the fullest for many years before settling down.

"You wouldn't," Camy whispered, her hand over her trembling lips. "That's cruel."

"I don't intend to, but you need to stop acting like you're Mother Theresa. You're a Dunn whether you like it or not, and that means you've lived on the edge. Embrace it, sis."

"This town…" Camy's voice trailed off, shaking her head. "Since moving here…"

Valley Station and Fairfield could kick anyone's ass. Rayne had learned the hard way how a newcomer could be treated in a small town. Especially a person that stood out as much as she did. She'd chosen not to buckle under and dealt with the gossip and stares, but Camy had gone another route deciding to blend in. Neither one was right or wrong, and they needed to stop harping at each other about it.

"Come here and hug me." Rayne held out her arms and Camy flew into them, sniffing delicately without any actual tears. "I love you. I know it's tough here. I feel your frustration. But the way to deal with it is not to become one of the *Stepford Wives*. You can fit in but still be true to yourself. And not be a pain in the ass to me."

"I swear I'm not trying to be. But you might have a point about my life being a little boring. I love Blair, but I feel like every day is the same and they are all starting to blend together."

"You need to get out more. You know I could use a receptionist at the shop. It's not that far of a drive between towns and you could bring Blair. I'll set up a play area for her and everything."

Camy's mouth hung open. "Work? In a tattoo shop?"

Rayne's smile grew at her sister's shock. "Who knows? You might enjoy it. Maybe you'll even decide to get some ink of your own."

Camy was uncharacteristically speechless so Rayne took full advantage, slipping her purse on her shoulder and heading straight for the front door. "Think about it. The offer is open. If you need me I'll be at the house."

Rayne climbed into her vehicle and headed back home. She had a million things that needed to be done today but she had to admit her mind was filled with questions. The main one?

Why was that man killed at her shop and what did they want?

CHAPTER SEVEN

Yawning from no sleep, Dare pulled his SUV into a parking space at the roadhouse. One Sunday morning each month the head lawmen in the area met and traded information regarding cases in process or any other major events. It had made them exponentially more effective at their jobs and Dare was grateful to be a part of the group.

As quiet as Valley Station normally was, he rarely had much to report to the other men. But today was a different story. He hoped someone might know of his victim or even if there was a circle of thefts in tattoo parlors.

It was doubtful but despite his reputation as a curmudgeon, Dare was an optimist. It was hard to do this job unless you were. Just because he saw the realistic side of life didn't mean he had no hope of things getting better.

"There better be hot coffee. I've had zero sleep," he growled as he strode into the roadhouse, taking a seat at the table with the other men. As usual, the roadhouse smelled like beer, sweat, and vomit the day after a raucous Saturday night and Dare's empty stomach churned at the stench. They really needed to find another place to meet that didn't stink to high heaven.

The group had changed over time – Logan and Jared had

moved on to different challenges with Jason Anderson – but new members such as himself, Knox Owens, and Evan Davis had made up for the loss. As always, Tanner Marks was the unofficial leader of their loose association and as such had the honor of calling the meeting to order.

"There's coffee on the table, Dare." Tanner banged his fist on the table. "Help yourself. There's also sodas and some snacks."

Seth had taken to bringing in food that Presley made since she was trying to learn to cook better. As far as Dare was concerned, she was already a pretty damn fine cook already. Her double fudge brownies were delicious and there was a new pan of them in the center of the table.

Maybe today wouldn't be so bad after all.

"Any new business?" Tanner asked, his gaze rounding the table as the men helped themselves to food and drink. "Dare, did I hear you had a murder Friday night?"

Taking a large gulp of coffee, Dare readied himself to tell the story to his friends. "One Patrick Moulson, age twenty-nine, was found with a bullet in the back about thirty feet from the back door of the local tattoo shop. The shop had been broken into and tossed. At this point, the owner says that nothing appears to be missing which I find strange."

"He must have had an accomplice. You can't shoot yourself in the back." Seth Reilly asked, munching on one of his wife's brownies. "If there was a second person there that means you still have trouble in your town, my friend."

Dare knocked back the rest of his coffee and didn't hesitate to refill the cup. He might just drink the whole damn pot before this meeting was over. "We'll know more when the autopsy is done about the angle of entry. From what I could see at the crime scene he was being chased out of the back door of the shop and shot, probably in the back. There was broken foliage and matted down grass that indicated running and even maybe a struggle."

"So the big question is why was he killed?" Tanner sat back in his chair and rubbed his chin before quickly checking his phone. His wife Madison, after a few years of fertility issues, was finally pregnant with their first, and probably their only child. The cocktail of pregnancy hormones was playing havoc with her stomach and she was throwing up on a daily basis despite passing her first trimester. Tanner had gone into major protective mode. "I take it he's not from Valley Station."

"Never seen him before. He had a Billings address on his driver's license but that doesn't mean anything. When I leave here today I'm headed there to take a look around his place. See if there is anything that might give a clue as to who he was with or why he was at Rayne's last night. Jared also said he'd look into the guy's background. Who knows? Maybe we'll get lucky."

Most police work didn't involve car chases and shootouts. The work was in the details and was accomplished with good old-fashioned detective skills. Wearing out shoe leather was a hazard of the job.

"So he didn't want money?" Griffin asked from the end of the table. "Or was there no money to take and then everything fell apart?"

"That's a possible theory. Rayne doesn't even take cash, let alone keep any around. They must not have realized that her tattoo equipment was pretty expensive, so they trashed the joint looking for something to steal then maybe they argued. It got heated and one pulled a gun on the other. They struggled. Moulson ran and then was shot. Second guy makes a run for it."

Knox popped open a soda, foam spraying onto the table. "So he didn't know she doesn't keep cash around? Guy didn't do his homework. Sounds like an amateur."

Dare shook his head. "That's the one problem with that theory. Moulson did know she didn't take cash. He came in to talk to her about getting ink and she says she gave him the details. That it's part of the standard introduction she gives everyone. I should know because she gave it to me when we talked about doing a shoulder piece."

Evan scowled as he rubbed the back of his neck. "Then he knew she didn't have cash. Maybe he was after credit card numbers? Those are big business and easy to sell."

Tanner shook his head. "Why go to a shop that has only a few customers a day? This woman can only give so many tattoos in a given period. Maybe eight a day? More or less, I would imagine. They could get more credit card numbers down at the local tavern or diner. Dozens, if not hundreds. It doesn't make much sense."

Reed hadn't said anything so far, which wasn't unusual. The lawman didn't speak unless he had something to say so everyone paused when he leaned forward, his gaze intent on Dare.

"They wanted something," Reed stated. "Something specific. Something worth killing for. Your job is to find out what it is."

That thought had been rolling around in the back of Dare's mind this morning but he hadn't wanted to entertain it. If it were true then this was a bigger mess than just a dead body.

"Drugs?" Knox offered. "Is the shop owner doing some side business?"

Dare coughed in shock at the mere thought. "Rayne? No way. She's strange, but she's as honest as the day is long. No, it isn't that."

"Have you checked into her background?" Evan asked. "Not everybody is what they appear to be."

"Not Rayne."

As crazy as she made Dare, as much as she drove him up a wall, she was as transparent as glass. Her thoughts and feelings were out there for everyone to see and she didn't care who sat back and played judge and jury.

He actually admired her more than a little bit.

"You've known her a long time then?" Griffin asked. "She's a good friend?"

Well, shit. "Not really. I wouldn't even say we were all that friendly. I've known her less than a year but she's Misty's best friend. She was the maid of honor at the wedding."

Seth's brows shot up. "The one with the ear piercings and the blue streaks in her hair? She was cute."

"That's her. If she's friends with Misty I have no doubt that Jared has checked her out."

The conversation lagged and Tanner redirected. "Any other business? No? I have something. Did you hear there was a bank robbery in Springwood last week? Four masked men armed with heavy weaponry killed a teller and the bank manager and made off with two hundred thousand dollars. The four men are still at large and there's a big reward for them from the company. I'm letting you know in case you see anything suspicious or perhaps someone spending a large amount of cash. You may also want to warn your local bank managers to be extra vigilant and call you if they see anything out of the ordinary."

Knox snorted and shook his head. "Do people still rob banks at gunpoint? I can think of ten different ways to steal money and not one of them involves leaving the comfort of my own home and laptop. These guys sound old school to me."

"Interesting theory," observed Reed. "Do you have any leads, Tanner?"

"Not much," Tanner sighed. "I have half a dozen witnesses with a half a dozen different stories, none of which are even close. I also have some footage from the bank cameras but there's not much to work with. They were all dressed identically in black from head to toe. They even wore gloves."

"I wouldn't mind seeing that video," Reed said. "Maybe I'll recognize a mannerism of one of the men. It's a long shot, but you never know."

"I can arrange it for anyone who wants to view it. I wouldn't mind some more eyes on this one. I don't want this to become a crime spree."

Dare didn't need the complication of a bank robbery to go along with a murder. He had little to go on for his own case and not enough resources to deal with the crime the town already had.

What he needed was a big break in the case. A good night's sleep. And maybe a full rack of ribs with steak fries on the side.

He'd start with lunch just as soon as the meeting was over.

CHAPTER EIGHT

Rayne flipped through the horticulture book until she found the photo she was looking for. Sophie Turner, Dare's sister, had come into the shop to talk about the ink she wanted and since it was a slow day, she and Rayne were working on the design.

"What do you think of this?" Rayne asked, pointing to the delicate purple petals of the wild violet. It was small and feminine, and a good way to pop the young woman's tattoo cherry.

"Oh, it's pretty! I really like that. Can you do that right here?"

Sophie pointed to the front of her left shoulder.

"I can. Let me draw out what I think would work."

Rayne quickly sketched out the flower, keeping it on the smaller side since this was her first. If she liked it, then Rayne could add on to the design at a later time.

"Dare is going to lose his mind when he finds out," Sophie laughed, clearly not bothered in the least by the prospect of angering her brother. "He still thinks of me as a little girl and it makes me crazy. He'd lock me in my room with dolls and a tea set if he could get away with it."

"You are only eighteen. That's not exactly old and gray."

Sophie rolled her eyes and giggled. "Dare acts like an old man and he's only thirty-four. He doesn't even like to drink in front of me. He says it doesn't set a good example. Dad never worried about that."

"I'm sorry about your father. You must really miss him."

Her father had passed on several months before, which was why Dare had come back to his hometown and taken the job as sheriff.

Shrugging, Sophie shook her head. "I loved him, but he wasn't much of a father. Mom ran the household and then when she was gone he just sort of withered away slowly. He loved her very much. I don't think he had a very happy marriage to Dare's mother at all, and Dare never talked about her either."

"I didn't realize you had different mothers."

Rayne didn't really know that much about Dare at all and she couldn't figure out why that bothered her. The details of his life were none of her business and never would be.

"Mom was much younger than Dad. I don't think Dare ever approved but I think it was romantic. It was like their love was taboo but they couldn't stay away from each other. Such passion."

Depending on the actual age difference, Rayne wasn't sure that the love was so much taboo as it was simply unconvention-al. But it was funny that Dare didn't approve. That man had a giant stick up his ass and it had to be uncomfortable. If anyone in this world needed to relax and let go, it was Sheriff Dare Turner.

"It sounds like your older brother doesn't approve of too many things."

Sophie rolled her eyes and groaned with typical teenage dramatic flair. "I could spend all day listing all the crap he thinks

I shouldn't do. He hates Tim, my boyfriend. Dare's constantly handing me pamphlets about safe sex and the virtues of abstinence. When he first came back home he told me that penises were dangerous."

Rayne could imagine Dare saying exactly that if it meant scaring his little sister into celibacy. He might be sex on legs but he was probably a bore in the sack. A man as uptight as he obviously was probably only did it on Saturday nights with the lights off and in the missionary position.

"All brothers are supposed to hate their sister's boyfriends," Rayne said instead of what she was really thinking. "I think it's a federal law or something. They may have a point, actually. My taste in males has certainly improved as I've aged and I imagine yours will too. The guy you think is perfect now won't be all that wonderful in a year or two."

Sophie sighed, a dreamy, faraway look on her pretty face. "Tim is amazing. He's cute and funny. He's smart too. And when he kisses me…" A grin and a giggle. "My knees actually go weak and I tingle all over. Just like in those romance books. That's true love."

"They have medication for those symptoms," Rayne teased. "If you start to get dizzy as well you may want to see a physician."

"You sound like one of those drug commercials on television." Sophie slapped her hand over her mouth to stifle a laugh. "When they list all those horrid side effects that are worse than whatever it is they're trying to cure."

"So," Rayne began, trying to keep the conversation casual. "Has your brother said anything about the break-in of my shop and the man that was killed?"

Dare hadn't said a word to Rayne and honestly, she'd been put out by his behavior. Since she was the victim of the crime she'd expected to be kept in the loop, but apparently that wasn't the procedure.

Or maybe Dare was being a prick and not telling her anything on purpose.

Sophie shrugged. "Nope, but that's not unusual. He only talks about work with me when he's using it as a moral lesson of some sort. Like don't drink and drive or don't take drugs. Stuff like that. I'm pretty sure he knows I'm not going to break into a tattoo shop and shoot someone. God love him, he's trying so hard to be a role model for me. Were your parents overprotective like this?"

"Hardly," Rayne snorted. "My parents felt that my sister and I should be free to express our individuality and to explore our boundaries. We didn't have too many rules when I was growing up except that we should explore our feelings."

Though her parents had taken the whole "free love" idea a little too far, Rayne appreciated that she'd been given enough latitude to make her own decisions. And her own mistakes.

Sophie's eyes bugged out and her mouth fell open. "You didn't have a curfew or anything? Even now Dare tries to tell me when to come home although I just ignore him."

"I didn't have a curfew, but do you want to know a secret?" Rayne leaned forward as if to whisper it in Sophie's ear. "If you're the only one without a curfew there's no one to hang out with after midnight. Everybody has to go home so you might as well have a curfew too."

"That blows. I would have loved not to have a curfew in high school."

Rayne smiled, remembering her school years. She hadn't been super popular, but she'd had close friends and that time held mostly pleasant memories.

"As I said, all that freedom is overrated. Be glad that you

have someone that cares if you come home. All I have is a cat named Spartacus."

Sophie licked her lips nervously and drummed her fingers on the table between them. "Can I tell you a secret? You won't tell Dare, will you?"

Rayne wasn't sure she wanted to get in the middle of Sophie and her brother.

"Maybe you shouldn't tell me if it's a secret."

The young girl was practically vibrating she was so excited. "It's only a secret from Dare. I mean, I'll tell him eventually. I just need to find the right time, that's all. I'll tell him when he's in a good mood."

They'd all be putting on parkas and ice skates in hell when that happened.

"Still…if it's a secret…"

"Tim and I are planning to move to Denver together." The words burst from Sophie's smiling lips. "I've been accepted to an art school there and Tim's going to get a job. I can't wait. Freedom from this stuffy little town."

No wonder Sophie hadn't told Dare yet. He was going to freak, and not in a good way.

"Have you lived here all your life?"

"Every long, tedious day." More sighing and eye rolling. "I've wanted to leave since…well…forever, really. Now that I've graduated there's nothing here holding me back."

Except one six-foot-three, two hundred plus pound big brother with a protective streak a mile wide.

"You might want Dare to have a drink or two before you tell him. I don't think he's going to be a happy camper."

Rayne wasn't sure what he would be more pissed off about – his little sister leaving town or the fact that she'd be living with a guy.

"I'll make him his favorite dinner of fried chicken and mashed potatoes along with a big chocolate cake. He has a major sweet tooth. Then I'll make sure he has a couple of whiskeys before giving him the news." Sophie's chin lifted. "He can't stop me. I'm eighteen."

To be that young again.

Everything seemed possible. Blue skies and clear sailing. Happiness, kittens, and rainbows.

"No, he can't," Rayne agreed readily. "But he can make things difficult for you. I'm sure he just wants you to be happy. You're very young to be living with someone. Sharing the same home can knock the romance out of a relationship faster than you can ever believe. Trust me on this."

"You're starting to sound like Dare. You won't tell him, will you?"

Rayne couldn't imagine a conversation where the topic would come up. In fact, she didn't know when she would even be seeing the handsome sheriff since he didn't see fit to update her on his investigation.

"I won't tell him. It sounds like this is your news to deliver. But can I give you a word of advice? Don't wait too long. If other people know he's going to eventually find out. He'll only be more upset if he hears it from anyone other than you. Tell him as soon as you can."

The sooner Rayne wasn't a secret keeper for Sophie the better. The last thing she needed was to get Dare on her bad side. She'd stay far away from the brooding lawman.

But she still needed to find out about the break-in. Maybe one little phone call to the station wouldn't be so bad. Or she could stop in. Either way, she had a feeling she – and her questions – wouldn't be welcomed in the least.

Too bad.

CHAPTER NINE

"Dare asked Jared about you."

Misty's statement had Rayne setting her half full wine glass on the nightstand. After another long week she'd been happy to take a long hot bath and curl up with a good book and some vino. Getting to talk to her best friend had been icing on the cake.

"Like what did he ask?"

Was this some adult version of passing a note in history class? If the sheriff was interested in her romantically he had a funny way of showing it. She'd left several messages at his office, all of which had been ignored. Finally, she'd tried showing up at the station a few times but he'd been conveniently out when she had. The deputy had promised to have Dare call her, but she was still waiting and likely would be until her bones turned to dust. It didn't take a genius to figure out that he was ducking her.

"About your family, background, finances. Basically he wanted to know if Jared had ever done a full check on your past."

Anger crept up the back of Rayne's neck and her fingers dug into the soft down of her comforter. "My finances? He asked about that? Shit, I'm going to kick him in the balls next time I see him. Oh wait, I'll never see him because he's been avoiding me for over a week now. Asshole."

"He's avoiding you? Passive aggressive isn't Dare's style. He's full on confrontation. Did you scare him or something?"

Rayne grasped the glass of wine and tossed half of it back in one gulp. "I dunno. Maybe I smell bad or he thinks I'm funny looking. Dammit, he's investigating me. That's bullshit."

Misty sighed into the phone. "That's pretty much what I told Jared, and then he said that Dare was just doing his job or some crap like that. Anyway, I said that if he was going to make excuses for Dare he was sleeping on the couch."

Rayne groaned and banged her head against the stack of pillows she was using to prop herself up. "That makes it even worse. I don't want to come between you and Jared. This is Dare's issue, clearly. That man doesn't have an ounce of tact. If he wanted to know about me all he had to do was ask." Another thought occurred to her and she couldn't stop herself from expressing it out loud. "So…had Jared investigated my background?"

"Hell no. He'd be sleeping in the barn if he had and he knows it. He told Dare he'd do a full check on you but that he wouldn't do it without your knowledge. Dare said it wouldn't be necessary."

Rayne was still pissed. For all she knew, he'd simply asked someone else to do it.

"Rayne? Are you still there?"

Rubbing the back of her neck, Rayne tried to calm the ever-growing anger in her belly. She hated that Dare Turner could get under her skin like this. The fact that she found him physically attractive only made it worse. Someone that hot looking shouldn't be such a jerk.

"I'm here. I'm just mad."

"He really is just doing his job like Jared said. He had to investigate you to see if there was some sort of link between you and the murder. He'd be remiss if he didn't."

"Sounds like Jared didn't have to sleep on the couch."

Which was a good thing as the couple were completely perfect together. Rayne had never seen truer love than Misty and Jared. They were disgustingly happy and still hot for each other, even after having a baby. She could only dream of finding someone to love her half as much as Jared loved Misty.

"He didn't," Misty giggled. "He explained the process of looking into a murder, and honestly it sounds terrible for the people closest to it. A lot of poking into your private life and nosing around which is awful, but I guess something that has to be done. I know Dare gets on your nerves, but you might want to cut him some slack on this one."

She wanted to do that, and then he'd do something that made her change her mind. He'd had a tough time of it and she'd hoped to be able to be extra kind to him when she saw him, but then he went and dodged her for days. She couldn't decide whether to kick him in the shin or give him a great big old hug.

"Gotcha. Slack. I'll get right on it."

Dare did have a thankless job that she wouldn't want for all the money in the world, so maybe she would let it go. She wasn't the type to hold a grudge.

"I don't suppose Dare said anything to Jared about the case when he called? I don't have a clue as to what is going on with it."

"Not that I know of, but Jared said it takes time for the autopsy and forensics to come back. Dare may not know anything."

"I simply want to know why someone broke into my shop

and then shot someone."

"You may never really know the truth, even after Dare finds who did this. Criminals aren't known for their veracity."

Rayne shivered at the thought that the person who perpetrated these crimes might get away scot free. That meant they were still around and could come back. Perhaps to finish what they started.

The disturbing thoughts didn't make for a good night's sleep. For her own peace of mind, she hoped Dare caught whomever had killed that man.

And put him behind bars for good.

Dare slammed his fist down on the scarred wood of the old desk. Sitting in his office at the sheriff's station, he had the file in front of him from the tattoo shop break-in and murder, and to say that there wasn't much there was an understatement.

The fingerprints hadn't matched anything in the system.

The footprints out back of the shop had turned out to be a common hiking boot, size ten.

The autopsy revealed the victim had been shot in the back from about five feet away with a .38 caliber revolver. The bullet didn't match anything in the system either.

Dare had no witnesses and barely any evidence. Jared and Logan were working on the background of the victim, but they'd been spending all their time on a different case so Dare was in waiting mode.

He fucking hated waiting for anything.

There had been no other break-ins since then and crime had been light, except for a couple of teenagers spray painting graffiti and a rumble down at the local watering hole. Nothing that was going to lead him into finding out why someone would break into Rayne's shop and then shoot another human being after chasing them out of the back door. He didn't have the patience to put puzzles together one piece at a time. He was no Sherlock Holmes.

Speaking of no Sherlock Holmes…

Deputy Billy was lumbering into the sheriff station to take the late shift. Dare was ready to go home, pop open a beer, and sit in front of some mindless television. He wanted to forget this frustrating case even if it was only for one night.

"Hey, Sheriff. Sorry I'm late."

Again. Billy must have been an overdue baby because he'd been running late since then. Time seemed to have little to no meaning in his world.

"It's been quiet. Call if you need me. I'm heading home."

With any luck it would stay quiet.

"Will do. By the way, tell Sophie I really like her new tat. I saw her and Tim at the diner and she was showing it off, but I didn't have a chance to tell her myself. I was already running late for here."

Ink? No fucking way.

"Sophie was showing off a tattoo?"

Billy shrugged out of his jacket and hung it on the peg next to the door. "Sure was. On her left shoulder. Pretty purple flowers. Rayne sure did a good job. She's got talent."

And nerve. Dare had already told that woman not to ink his little sister. He'd known Rayne was trouble and this simply confirmed it.

He needed to have a talk with Miss Rayne Dunn.

Right now.

CHAPTER TEN

Another boring Saturday night at home.

Despite what seemed like the longest week of Rayne's life, she wasn't asleep and drooling before nine o'clock at night. The mere thought of having the next two days off from work had given her a second wind. Now she was prowling her house looking for something more exciting to do than the laundry.

I am the most boring woman on the planet.

A cursory inspection of the contents of her refrigerator revealed a slab of baby back ribs and a half-eaten slice of chocolate cake. They were leftovers from dinner a few nights before and she congratulated herself on remembering to eat them before they grew a layer of fuzz like most of the food in her kitchen did. Recently she'd thrown away a plastic container of pudding that had been in her refrigerator so long she was shocked it hadn't learn to speak and drive.

Settling in at the kitchen counter, she poured herself a glass of wine and bit into the tender ribs, the barbecue sauce firing up her taste buds with just enough sweet to take the edge off. She'd worked through the whole rack and was digging into the cake when she heard banging on her front door.

Not knocking. Pounding. Like the person outside was drunk

and she'd insulted their mother.

Quickly running her sticky fingers under the faucet, she hurried to the door hoping the jerk hadn't grabbed the attention of her nosy neighbors.

"Just a second. Hold your horses."

Rayne swung open the door and had to take a big step backwards. Dare Turner stood on her front steps looking mad as hell. His brows were pulled down and a muscle was working in his jaw, his teeth gritted together. His arms hung loosely at his sides but his shoulders were tense and his hands were furled into tight fists. From what she could tell, he was barely holding himself back from punching her right in the face.

What the hell did I do to deserve that?

Forcing herself to stand her ground, she didn't move any farther to let him in. Instead, she squared her own shoulders and braced herself for incoming fire.

"How may I help you, Sheriff?"

"We need to talk," he snarled, although it didn't make him one bit less handsome.

Jerk.

"It's a little late in the evening for that," she replied, keeping her voice even despite her curiously knocking knees. She didn't think he'd truly take a swing at her but he was damn intimidating in this mood. "I'm guessing you got all my messages then and want to discuss the case?"

"No. Are you going to let me in?"

Not yet. She wanted to piss him off a bit more first.

"No, you didn't get my messages or no, you aren't here to talk about the case? Either way, it isn't really the best time for me. You should call first."

His face and neck were red and there was a distinct possibility he might explode all over her front steps, leaving a gooey mess.

"We need to talk," he said between gritted teeth. "We can do it out here for all your neighbors to hear or you can let me in. Your choice."

With a put upon sigh, Rayne stepped back so he could enter. "You can come in but you need to leave your attitude outside. This is my home, Dare, and I reserve the right to kick your ass right out of it."

He clomped through the entryway and into her living room, his narrow eyes taking in the bright colors and comfortable surroundings. She had a flair for decorating and this room was one of her favorites, second only to the bedroom.

"People don't usually kick the sheriff out of the house. They're usually more respectful."

Rayne couldn't stand this passive-aggressive shit. If he was pissed off he just needed to damn well say so, although she had no idea what he could be angry about.

Life? Ice cream? Good friends? Delicious food? Kitten whiskers?

The man was mad all the time and that was his issue, not hers.

"When I'm treated respectfully I return the favor. Sadly, banging on my door unannounced on a Saturday evening and then growling at me doesn't seem very respectful, but then I'm from out of town. Maybe it's different here in Montana." Rayne perched on the edge of her couch trying to appear completely calm. "Why don't you sit down and tell me why you're here?"

Another scowl but he sank into the cushions of her leather recliner. His icy blue gaze rested on her and she had to quell the urge to squirm in her seat under such scrutiny. She wasn't going to allow him to intimidate her, although with his imposing frame it wouldn't be difficult.

"I've been trying to get in touch with you all week. You're a hard man to pin down."

A good offense was the best defense so she threw the first salvo, hoping to get her own questions answered before he went into some diatribe about an imagined slight.

"I got your messages. I'm not here to talk about that."

"Then why are you?" she snapped, her temper simmering under the surface. "You came to me, remember?"

He hopped up from the recliner and paced the small space between her coffee table and the television before finally turning back to her, his gaze stormy. "I told you not to ink Sophie."

That's what this was about?

"Yes, you did. What's your point?"

"My point is that I told you not to do it. She's too damn young."

"She's of age—"

"Fuck that." Dare leaned down, his hand on the arm of the sofa and his face inches away. She could feel the waves of anger coming off of him, the fury mixing with the scent of his skin and giving him an otherwordly vibe that messed with her head and made it hard to concentrate on his words. "She's a kid. She may be eighteen but that doesn't mean she's ready to make a decision like this. Is that how you run your business? You prey on the young and naive?"

Oh no, he didn't just go there.

Rayne poked her finger at the wall of muscle he called a chest, her own eyes narrowed and her lips twisted with anger. She stood up and moved so close to him he stepped back, perhaps not as sure of himself as he had been seconds ago.

"Just so we're clear here, Sheriff, I provide a service. A service that can be purchased by anyone sober and over the age of eighteen. It would be bad business to pick and choose only those people I think should have a tattoo. In fact, some people might even call it discrimination."

"She's a little girl." Dare's voice had inched up several decibels but her own had gone almost to a deathly whisper.

"She's a grown woman and you are a big baby. I've never seen a man so petulant every single hour of the day. Is your fucking life so bad, Dare, that you have to be an asshole all the time? Is it? Just what do you have to complain about? Good health? A job? A roof over your head? Just what is your fucking problem? Hemorrhoids? My advice is to take that gigantic stick out of your butt. You'll be a lot more comfortable."

The hiss of his breath was the only indication he'd heard her, his features a mask of stone. She didn't feel sorry for her outburst because God almighty, somebody needed to tell this man a few home truths.

"You're treading on dangerous ground, woman."

At the moment, Rayne didn't give a flip. She was on a roll and it felt amazing to let loose. She was tired of everyone in this town scowling at her like she was the Antichrist.

I'm just a woman trying to make a damn living. Jeez.

"Am I? How will I know, Dare? Will you hold up a sign? Because you only have one expression and that's pissed off, so I don't think I'll be able to tell the difference. Are you ever happy? Does anything make you smile? Are you going to go to your grave with that sour puss because, let me tell you, it's not a good look for you."

Dare took two strides forward until he towered over her. "Do you want to know what makes me smile, Rayne? Do you really want to know?"

Rayne practically vibrated with anger and she looked up at him with a smirk. "Yes, I do because I'm not sure that you really can. Your face might peel off."

Rayne barely had time to suck in a breath before his lips came crashing down on her own. She squeaked in shock even as her hands curled around his rock hard shoulders to keep herself from falling in a heap on the floor. His tongue ran along her bottom lip seeking entry, and to her utter shame she found herself opening up and allowing him to explore her mouth thoroughly.

Skillfully. Arousingly. Achingly.

Clearly she'd been too long between men. Her body was pressed against the hard planes of his and she could feel the outline of his cock against the softness of her belly. His tongue was sweeping her mouth, teasing and playing until she was a mass of desire in his arms. Her panties were soaked and her nipples were peaked and he was the last man she wanted to be doing this with.

Dare Turner was the devil in disguise and here she was handing over her soul with barely a whimper of protest.

One huge hand was at the base of her spine and the other cupped the back of her head, tangling in her long hair. He lifted his lips briefly to change the angle on the kiss and she could have pushed him away at that moment or told him no, but her body had other ideas and most of them involved the shedding of clothes. He tasted like coffee and oranges and the mixture was intoxicating, making her head spin with arousal.

Her heart was racing and her breath ragged when he finally lifted his head. Those icy blue eyes were dark with desire and she felt an answering tightening in her pussy. Despite his outwardly sullen appearance he was a gorgeous man and he awakened every biological need deep inside of her.

His own chest was rising and falling rapidly but he still didn't move away, seemingly content to stay close. The heat of his skin burned through the thin fabric of her t-shirt and his manly scent teased her nostrils – a mixture of clean sweat and something woodsy. If he bottled it he'd make a fortune.

The silence stretched on and it played on her already frayed nerves. She couldn't take it.

"Why did you do that?"

Instead of the strong confident woman she'd wanted to sound like, the words came out soft and tentative. They mirrored her current emotional state but that was the last thing she wanted Dare to know.

"Because I couldn't help myself. I apologize." He paused for a long moment. "Do you want to slap me or something? I'll stand still and let you."

She was tempted but her innate honesty wouldn't allow her to blame him for something she'd enjoyed. A heck of a lot. The man was a veritable kissing maestro and she'd been the willing instrument in his hands.

"I want to smack you all right, but not for kissing me. Is this how you court a woman? Accuse her of crappy stuff and then kiss her breathless?"

His eyebrow quirked and by all that was holy, his lips actually turned up a little. It wasn't a full smile but it was close.

And it was glorious. He'd been handsome before but now he was downright sexy. Completely gorgeous. If he ever truly smiled at her she'd probably slide down the wall in a dead faint, overcome with the beauty that was Dare Turner.

Well, crap.

"Breathless, huh? I think I kind of like that." He leaned forward, his lips next to her ear. "I was breathless too. For a little thing, you pack a wallop. You ought to come with a warning label or something."

"You're smiling."

Rayne groaned inwardly, her brain still not firing on all cylinders since the kiss. She sounded like an idiot and he already didn't have the best opinion of her.

"You asked what made me smile," he reminded her, his expression going back to its usual neutral position. "But this doesn't solve our problem. I'm still pissed off, Rayne. I wish you hadn't done it."

Dare's hands were gentle so he wasn't as angry as before. Now he seemed to be more disappointed than anything else, which did nothing to soothe all the emotions churning in her gut. She'd done nothing wrong.

"I didn't–"

"I know," he interrupted. "And I get it. Sophie's eighteen and she has a legal right to get a tattoo. I just wish you hadn't done it. My sister is still naive and rather impetuous. She doesn't think about the long term consequences of her actions. She's been rather sheltered most of her life and this Tim guy is her first real boyfriend. Ever since she started dating him she's acted different. I think he's a bad influence on her. I've tried to be a role model but obviously I've failed."

Rayne sighed as she placed her hands on his wide chest, his heart beating under her palm.

"I have no idea what kind of role model you've been, but knowing how stiff and uptight you are I'm sure you've been a good one. But I need you to listen to me, Dare. Just for one minute. Can you do that? You keep interrupting me."

"I'm not uptight," Dare muttered but nodded his head in agreement, staying silent. Rayne took it as a good sign.

"Now listen to me very carefully." She spoke slowly and clearly so there would be no misunderstanding. "I didn't give Sophie a tat."

Dare took a step back and Rayne immediately missed the heat of his body under her fingers. "But she has a tattoo. Did she go somewhere else?"

Dropping her arms to her side, Rayne sat back down on the couch. "She has a temporary tattoo. It should last a few weeks or so. I wanted her to get used to the idea before she did something permanent. So yes, she has a tattoo and I did it. No, it won't last a lifetime."

"Shit, I just assumed..."

She could imagine what he'd assumed. "The worst. Not sure what I did for you to think so little of me but thanks for that."

His cheeks were stained red but she didn't feel a bit sorry for him. His highhanded behavior and ingrained stubbornness had brought all of this on. He wasn't in charge of everything and everyone.

He needed to get over himself.

The kiss had been amazing but already she could see he regretted it. Their attraction to one another was tempered with mistrust and disrespect. There didn't appear to be any future pursuing it unless they both wanted to do something about it.

"I'm sorry. For everything. Are you sure you don't want to punch me?"

"I don't think violence is the answer." She heaved a sigh and stood, walking to the front door. She opened it wide and stepped back so he could exit. "I think it's time you took your leave, Sheriff."

Dare shifted uncomfortably while staring at his boots. "I really am sorry, Rayne."

"I know you are and I'm not mad. I just think that you and I probably shouldn't spend much time together. One of us is going to haul off and smack the other or we're going to end up taking that kiss a whole lot further. I don't think I'm ready for that. Are you?"

"No, ma'am. I don't think I am." Dare looked up this time,

looking quite abashed about all that had happened here tonight. "I'm trying to set a good example for Sophie and I really fucked up. I don't normally press my attentions on an unwilling woman. I swear I'm a good man, Rayne."

Aw, hell. She couldn't take his puppy dog eyes.

"I know you're a good man. Everyone in town knows it. And I wasn't unwilling. What I am is someone who doesn't go around kissing people casually. Unless this is a thing then I'd just assume we move along and forget it happened."

"A thing?"

Some men needed an instruction booklet to romance and it looked like Dare was one of them.

"A relationship. A couple. Or even a couple-to-be. Do you want to kiss me again?"

He didn't say a word so Rayne had her answer. Instead he shoved his hands in his pockets and moved to the door, stepping out onto her front porch. He kept his wall-like back to her staring out into the night.

"Good night, Rayne."

She watched as Dare climbed into his truck and disappeared into the darkness, his red taillights becoming smaller with each passing second. Chilled by the cooler air, she closed the door and locked it, leaning back against it, her fingers brushing her still tingling lips. Sheriff Dare Turner was a good man.

But he would never be her man, and that thought made her sad indeed.

CHAPTER ELEVEN

"Jesus, big brother, what the hell is your problem lately? You're acting like a big old bear with a sore paw."

Sophie tossed her wadded up paper napkin across the dinner table, hitting Dare in the middle of his forehead. He'd normally be annoyed by his little sister's behavior but he couldn't argue with her sentiment. He'd been a gigantic pain in everyone's rear end the last few days and he knew exactly why.

The damn kiss.

He hadn't been able to get the kiss – and Rayne – out of his mind. The way her sweet lips has surrendered under his, the way her tongue had sensuously explored his mouth, and the way her full, round breasts pressed against his chest felt like sweet, sweet heaven. He'd been hard, horny, and frustrated ever since while she had probably forgotten all about it and had moved on effortlessly with her life.

"I've had a lot on my mind. You could be more understanding."

Sophie blew him a raspberry as she picked up their dirty dishes and placed them on the kitchen counter. It was his night to do dinner clean up and normally he didn't mind, but tonight he had a yearning to drink some whiskey and listen to classic rock music in the bed of his pickup truck. He could lie there and look at the stars thinking about anything but Rayne's smooth skin or the curve of her jaw that begged to be kissed.

Fuck. He had it bad.

"I could, but then that wouldn't really be us, would it?" Sophie smirked, wiping her hands on a dishtowel. "What's got your knickers in a twist? Is it the murder case?"

Dare grabbed onto the excuse with both hands, not ready to admit he was all strung out over a female. "It's got me pretty wound up. I haven't been able to make much progress on the case at all."

"Have you updated Rayne about it? It seems like you should keep her in the loop or something. It was her shop. It had to have shook her up."

Dare had been exhausting himself trying to stay out of Rayne's orbit. In a town this small that wasn't an easy task. When he saw her in the diner he turned and left. When she was walking down the street, he crossed so he was on the other side. He'd ducked her calls about the murder until she'd finally stopped contacting him. He was a jerk and an asshole doing it but he wasn't in the head space to do anything else.

What had Dare's daddy always said? The best way to get one woman out of your mind was to put another in it.

Dare stood and grabbed his hat from the peg on the wall. "I'm heading out for awhile. Don't wait up."

"Wait! It's your night to do the dishes. You can't leave this for me to do."

Sophie had that look on her face that said she might short sheet his bed or put pudding in his shoes.

"Leave them. I'll do them when I get home or in the morning. They aren't going anywhere."

Climbing into his truck, he pointed it toward the local watering hole. Time to find a distraction. Preferably blonde.

Rayne Dunn wasn't his type and the sooner he remembered the better. He'd acted like a total asshole that night and she wasn't likely to forget it.

He certainly hadn't.

Rayne slid into the booth, her gaze darting around the bar. It wasn't as loud as a weekend night but she wouldn't describe it as mellow either. The jukebox played the latest Blake Shelton song while a few couples hung out on the dance floor. A few groups of guys were in the back area playing darts and pool while the bartender wiped down the bar.

"Just one drink," Rayne warned her sister Camy, who was desperate for a night out of the house sans husband and baby. She'd insisted Rayne accompany her and hadn't let up until she'd won. "Then I'm going home. I have to work in the morning."

"Fine, but I think you need more than one. In fact, we should find you a man tonight. See anyone in here that you like?"

Sighing, Rayne let her head fall back onto the vinyl seat. "I do not need a man."

"No one needs a man but they're fun to have around. They can kill spiders and rub your feet." Camy pointed to a dark-haired cowboy playing pool. "How about Emmett? He's good looking and he's got a nice butt. Do you have anything against a man who's divorced with kids?"

"Not if he's the right one, but I don't think Emmett is." An image of Dare in his uniform flashed through her mind. He'd been there constantly since their kiss the other day. "Can we just have a drink and leave?"

The waitress came and took their order of two white wines

and an order of cheese fries. Camy continued scoping out the local talent while Rayne tried to slump down in the booth and not be seen. It was mortifying to have her sister ogling potential boyfriends like they were a piece of meat.

"Will you stop that?" Rayne hissed, her cheeks warm. "People are starting to notice you staring. I don't want a man, okay? Just let me live my life in peace."

Camy snorted into the white wine that was slid in front of her. "If your life was any more peaceful you'd be in a coma. You need something to shake you out of your workaholic mode."

Rayne couldn't seem to stop the bitter words from tumbling out of her mouth. "Since when are you so worried about how peaceful my life is?"

Her sister's mouth turned down and she set her glass on the table. "Listen, I know I haven't been the best sibling ever. I mean, I get really involved in my own life and sometimes I forget that other people have feelings too. But I do love you and I do want the best for you. I hope you believe that."

Rayne had never doubted her sister's love. She *had* doubted that Camy saw much outside herself. "I love you too but I can't help but wonder what brought this on."

Camy traced patterns on the wood surface of the table. "It's something Mark said. He reminded me that guy who was shot could have been you. That really shocked me because I hadn't thought of it that way and it scared the shit out of me. You came all the way here to Montana to be with me when I was pregnant and I haven't been all that grateful. In fact, I've been pretty much a bitch."

"Did Mom say something to you?"

Their mother was one of the few people who could put Camy in her place. She had a way of speaking only a few words but saying a whole hell of a lot.

"She might have." Camy played with the stem of her glass, her gaze on the floor. "Does it matter? I know that I haven't been appreciative. You've done so much for me and Mark and I haven't done near enough for you."

Rayne's brow shot up. "So you want to find me a man? That's seems extreme even for you."

"You deserve to be happy. Any man would be lucky to get you even with those streaks in your hair."

Some things never changed.

"I like the streaks in my hair and any man that likes me will too."

"I'm sure you're right. It's not something I would do but there are probably tons of guys who would go for that sort of thing."

"That sort of thing?" Rayne groaned and took another gulp of her wine. "It's hair dye, not animal sacrifice. I fail to see what the big deal is. This town has too many people that like to clutch their pearls and bemoan the fact that not everyone thinks the way they do. They have to be exhausted. It's a wonder anything gets done."

"I know you're used to San Francisco…"

"You used to live there too. How can this not be a culture shock for you? Does this not make you a little crazy every now and then?"

Camy fidgeted in her seat. "I'm not like you. I actually care what people think about me."

"Don't let Mom and Dad hear you say that," Rayne warned. "They didn't raise us like that but I think you're brave to admit it."

Camy laughed nervously as the waitress slapped their cheese fries in the middle of the table.

"I'll never tell and you better not either. You won't, will

you?"

Rayne made a pretend "X" over her heart like when they were children. "Your secret is safe with me but these cheese fries aren't. I'm going to demolish them and you're going to help. Damn the diet, sis."

They munched away at the gooey cheese and fried goodness, chatting about the upcoming holidays. Rayne had gone home to San Francisco last year but she doubted she'd be able to get away again, as busy as the shop had been lately.

She'd stuffed a huge mouthful of fries and cheese in her mouth when the front door of the bar swung open and Dare Turner strode through it, his usual surly expression in place. Despite his grouchy demeanor Rayne could see almost every single girl in the joint perk up, retouching their lipstick and smoothing their hair. He was a sexy devil but still a demon. She hadn't been in the best of moods since he'd left the other night. Getting kissed within an inch of her life and then having the gentleman not want to do it again wasn't what she called a terrific Saturday evening.

Choking on her snack, Rayne held a napkin up to her lips as her gaze met Dare's. He simply stood there for a long moment before turning toward the bar and ordering a drink.

Camy's eyes were wide as she took in the spectacle. "Um…that was interesting. Is there something you want to tell me?"

Not a single, solitary thing. Camy would blow the entire situation – such as it was – out of all proportion and make it into something it wasn't.

"Not particularly. Dare's been ducking my calls about the break-in and he probably feels guilty or something."

"Or something," Camy echoed, her gaze on Dare as he joined the men in the back of the bar playing pool, his jeans stretched over his taut ass as he bent over to take a shot. "If I wasn't a married woman, I'd go for him."

"He's hot," Rayne conceded. "But he's kind of unpleasant to be around. He's always growling at people like every day is his worst on earth."

Camy shrugged and dug another fry from the cooling cheese. "He does have a tough job but I've seen him be nice."

Nice and happy were two different things. Rayne wasn't sure she could be with a man that was as sad – or mad – as Dare was all the time.

"Did he smile?"

"Well…no. I don't think I've actually seen him smile but I'm sure that he does. Maybe when he's alone."

"That's not a creepy thought at all, sis. Dare sitting by himself grinning like the Joker in *Batman*."

"All I'm saying is you could do worse. He seems like the kind of guy that wouldn't cheat on you or hit you or anything."

Rayne knocked back the last of her wine. "I hope my standards for a man are a little higher than someone who won't slap me around and screw my friends. That bar shouldn't be that hard to clear, honestly."

"And yet, it is," Camy sighed. "Remember Paul? I think he slept with every girl in my study group."

Of all Camy's loser boyfriends, Paul had been particularly loathsome. He'd even made a pass at Rayne one night at a family party.

Asshat.

"Paul was a jerk, plain and simple. He seemed to revel in it too. He enjoyed cheating on women and being an asshole. There's a whole lot of screwed up inside him, that's all I'm saying. The fact is, I shouldn't have to beg a guy not to be a horndog. Is that too much to ask?"

Camy patted Rayne on the hand and gave her a sympathetic smile. "It shouldn't be but it can be. Some guys just never grow up. Everything is a party. The real challenge is telling between the boys and the men. That's the hard part."

Dare was one of the men, of that Rayne was sure of. But there was no way she was going to chase after him. He'd made his position clear on Saturday night.

He wasn't interested. Period.

CHAPTER TWELVE

"Are you okay to drive, Rayne?"

Dare's large hand pressed over hers as she pulled on the door handle of her car, his touch sending a streak of heat through her veins and a tremble to her knees. She'd spent the last hour and a half trying not to watch him, and doing a pretty decent job, but now here he was talking to her in the deserted parking lot of the bar. Not another soul around as she'd parked on the outskirts to keep anyone from door dinging her rather new vehicle.

"I'm fine. I had one glass of wine and then I drank water. Are you okay to drive?"

With his massive body mass he could probably drink a hell of a lot more than she could and still stay under the limit.

"I could use a ride home. If you're offering."

She hadn't expected that answer. Was she offering? If she didn't give him a ride home there were others inside that could, but it would be churlish to refuse. She didn't hate Dare after all. It was just embarrassing that he'd kissed her and never wanted to do it again.

"Sure. Get in."

Rayne didn't bother to turn around, his nearness making it

hard to take a deep breath. Instead, she climbed into the driver's side on trembling legs while he punched something into his phone before swinging in beside her. Suddenly she wished she'd purchased a giant SUV instead of the low-slung fire engine red coupe. Dare was sitting a scant few inches away and she could smell his cologne and feel the warmth coming off of his skin.

It was the last thing she wanted. The sooner she dropped him off at home the better off she'd be.

Starting up the car, she flipped on the heater and backed out of the space before turning onto the main road. She kept her eyes forward but couldn't help but take a quick glance as his profile. He appeared relaxed, content almost, if not happy. Whatever alcohol he'd consumed must have done the job.

"Is this new?"

His question pulled her out of her reverie and she shook her head as if to shake away the cobwebs. "I'm sorry. What's new?"

"The car," Dare explained, sniffing the air. "It has that new car smell."

It certainly did and Rayne loved it. It was the first new car she'd ever purchased. All the others had been used, and she couldn't help but feel the thrill of ownership whenever she drove her new baby.

"It is new. Less than a month old. My old car needed to be put out of its misery."

"It's pretty but not very practical."

Was he talking about the car or Rayne? Probably both, she conceded.

"I didn't want practical. I wanted sexy."

"You got it then. Do you know where I live?"

Rayne laughed at the question. "Everyone knows where you live. The town isn't that big."

"I guess not. I appreciate the ride home, by the way."

Shit, he was being nice. She didn't want him to be nice. If he was an asshole this whole drive would be much easier.

"Just how many did you have?"

"A few too many. Not enough that I'm drunk but enough that my reflexes are slightly slower. I have to set a good example for the town."

He stretched out his long legs and she had to concentrate to keep her attention firmly on the road and not on those muscular thighs.

"I'm sure you do. How are you going to get your truck in the morning?"

Shit, she needed to keep her mouth shut or she'd be dragging her ass out of bed tomorrow extra early to give him another ride.

"Billy or Sophie can bring me back for it. It's not a big deal."

She turned onto his street and then into his driveway. The two-story home with an inviting front porch was dark, as were most of the houses on the street. Sane people were already in bed, which is where Rayne should have been over an hour ago.

"Thank you. I appreciate the ride."

Dare's fingers were on the handle but he didn't move to get out of the car.

"No problem. Have a good evening."

Get out. Move along. Nothing to see here.

"Listen, I think we need to talk about the other night."

It was the last thing she wanted to do. Rehashing how he hadn't enjoyed kissing her was pretty low on her to-do list. If anything, it was an absolute to-don't.

"I don't think that's a good idea. Maybe we should just forget about it."

His hand captured her own and he was suddenly even closer than before, leaning toward her over the console in the middle.

"I seem to be having trouble with that part. I've been thinking about it since it happened. Are you doing any better?"

"You didn't have any trouble running out the door after it happened," Rayne snapped, unable to keep a lid on all the emotions that had been torturing her the last few days.

"I…regret leaving the way I did. I didn't plan on kissing you and I sure as hell didn't plan on liking it was much as I did."

She wasn't sure she believed him.

"You didn't act like you enjoyed it. I asked if you wanted to do it again."

"I did want to, but I'd acted so incredibly fucking stupid about Sophie's tat that I was embarrassed. I figured you wouldn't want me to kiss you again."

So he had wanted to. If she were brutally honest with herself she wanted to do it again as well. She'd been distracted and there was really only one cure. More Dare. It was almost laughable when she thought about it. They were complete opposites. Two people that should never be together, but damn if that kiss hadn't lit something inside of her that she hadn't felt in a long time. Too long. She wanted to feel it once more.

Rayne sucked in a breath and gathered her courage. What was the worst that could happen?

Deep, grinding humiliation with a side of Oh my God, why did I do that? She'd have to move, leave Valley Station. Maybe even change her name. Possible plastic surgery to modify her appearance. She could talk to Presley about witness protection.

"You could kiss me now."

She couldn't help herself. She was a romantic at heart and the thought of making this giant man smile or even laugh was too heady to pass up no matter what the cost.

Dare leaned in until his lips were just millimeters from her own. He could probably hear the wild thumping of her heart and the whoosh of blood singing through her veins. His hand cupped her chin as his other arm slid around her waist to land on the small of her back, right under her jacket.

When his mouth touched her own it was as if she had been struck by a stray lightning bolt, and the sensation sizzled through her limbs until her fingers and toes tingled. His probing tongue brought a heat that settled in her belly and she clung to his shoulders as the universe spun around them. She lost herself in that kiss, her eyes tightly shut to keep out all the thoughts of why she shouldn't be doing this. It wasn't smart or wise and it was probably going to end badly but dammit, she needed this. Just one more. Like a junkie with her next fix, she wanted Dare's lips on her own.

So amazingly good.

When he finally pulled back, his breathing was ragged and his blue eyes were dark with passion. He might not want to like the kiss but he did anyway. There was something between the two of them that simply could not be denied.

"That was good." Dare's voice was low and gravelly as if he'd just woken up. "Real good."

"Yep. Good," she echoed, not knowing what else to say.

She stared out of the car window for a few moments waiting for him to speak…say something. Anything.

"What do you think we should do about this?" he asked, his gaze trained on his hands which were fiddling with his house keys that he'd dug out of his pocket at some point. "I mean, do you think we should do it again?"

I don't think I can help myself.

"You mean like a relationship? Like dating?"

The thought of getting to kiss him whenever she wanted, and perhaps even do more made her stomach twist into nervous knots. Happy, nervous knots though. The idea wasn't an unpleasant one, which came as a shock. A week ago she'd been cursing his name and now she was contemplating letting him have use of her girl parts. It was a quick turnaround.

"Yeah, maybe like dating, I guess. Would you go on a date with me if I asked?"

Christ, were they thirteen years old? He needed to know what she'd say before he asked.

"You could ask me and find out. Isn't that usually how it's done?"

Dare's thumbs were tapping out an unheard rhythm on the faded denim covering his knees. "We've kind of gone about this backwards so I'm not sure. So, would you go out with me, Rayne?"

Her head said no but every other part was saying yes. "Sure. I will."

Dare nodded, still not looking at her directly. "Good. That's good, I mean. How about we see a movie and then have dinner on Saturday night? Sound good?"

"Fine." This was awkward. Hopefully the date wouldn't be this bad.

"Sophie sure will be surprised," Dare observed. "Your sister probably will too."

Craptastic. Rayne hadn't really thought this through. The whole town, including Camy, was going to be all up in their business. Asking nosy questions and generally being busybodies.

Rayne slapped her forehead and groaned. "Camy knowing about this is kind of a nightmare. She'll be a pain in the butt when she finds out. She'll have you measured for a wedding tux before our first date is over."

Rubbing his temple, Dare grimaced, shifting in the leather seat. "Sophie might not be much better. She's always telling me to get a woman. Says I won't be so grouchy."

"I hope you'd be less grouchy," Rayne retorted with a giggle. "But we do need to think about this. If this...thing...between us doesn't work out it's going to be tough to explain to everyone. Heck, if it does work out it's going to be difficult to explain. Maybe we shouldn't tell anyone for awhile. Just until we know how this is working."

If the truth were known, Rayne wasn't sure they'd get past the first date. She might clobber Dare during dessert for being crabby or just plain uptight.

"You mean, sneak around?" Dare sounded incredulous and she didn't blame him. Everybody in Valley Station, and its close by neighbor Fairfield, knew pretty much everyone else's business. There weren't many secrets, or at least the salacious stuff was out in the open. The boring crap no one cared about.

"We could date out of town," Rayne suggested. "Drive separately. That kind of thing. Not for long. Just until we figure out whether we'll kill each other or not."

"I guess we could give it a shot. If people find out then we're no worse off than if we hadn't tried. It might help not to have any pressure for the first few dates. I think it's a good idea."

So it was settled then. They were going to sneak around like what they were doing was horribly wrong. It said too much about her that it gave her a small thrill to think of the subterfuge.

Rayne needed help. Deep therapy, apparently. Surely she was psychologically damaged in some way to get a kick out of the situation.

"So you can call me and let me know where to meet you. Or can you? Because you've been ducking my calls for over a week."

Dare held his hands up in surrender. "I swear I'll fill you in on the case completely on Saturday night. How does that sound?"

"Like the best I'm going to do," Rayne sighed. "I'll see you then."

The chances were high she'd see him before that, but they were going to pretend they barely knew one another.

"See you."

This time Dare did exit her vehicle before bounding up his front porch steps two at a time. She waited until he was inside then backed down the driveway, heading for home. Camy didn't realize how successful the evening had been.

Rayne had a date with Sheriff Dare Turner.

She better pick up those ice skates for hell. It had to have frozen over.

Chapter Thirteen

D are scrolled through the background information he'd been able to piece together regarding his murder victim Patrick Moulson. The man was born and raised in Lexington, Kentucky before he joined the Army after high school. Four years later he was discharged and never seemed to find his place in civilian life. He'd drifted from one job to another while dating one girl after another, never settling down. That wasn't against the law of course, but it spoke of someone who might be troubled or easily swayed into crime, especially if money was hard to come by.

Moulson's bank account was as bare as his apartment in Salt Lake City. Hardly any furniture, a closet half full of clothes, and an empty refrigerator were all he'd left behind when he'd come to Montana. Dare still hadn't been able to find where Moulson was staying while he was here. He'd checked every hotel and motel between here and Billings, turning up nothing. If the man had slept in his truck that too had disappeared without a trace.

Unless Patrick Moulson was a magician, personal belongings like clothes and vehicles didn't generally just fade away. They had to be hidden or disposed of. That meant an accomplice. It was a good bet that the accomplice was the shooter and had hidden any evidence that Moulson was in the area, but that simply challenged Dare all the more. Unless they'd dug a gigantic hole somewhere that truck could still be found. It might have a clue as to the identity of the killer. Or even just the why of the situation. He'd settled for that right now.

The forensics team hadn't done much better. Fingerprints confirmed Moulson's identity but all the other prints had led to a dead end. Rayne kept her shop clean and neat but there were still prints from at least half a dozen people, none of which were in the system.

Ballistics were run but the bullet hadn't matched anything in the database. It was beginning to piss him off.

His phone vibrating in his pocket pulled him from his thoughts. "Turner."

"Hey Dare, it's Tanner. Got a minute? It's important."

Tanner Marks didn't use that word lightly so Dare was all ears. "Of course. What's going on? Is there something I can help you with?"

"I think you and I need to start working together, my friend. You know I've been working on this bank robbery, right?"

Dare had looked at the footage but hadn't seen anything that would help the investigation, so he wasn't sure where Tanner was going with this.

"I do. Have you found something?"

"We did. Remember our two victims from the bank robbery? The ME pulled the slugs and ran them through the system. When the ballistics came back this morning it matched your unsolved murder. How's that for a strange coincidence?"

The hair on the back of Dare's neck stood straight up. "I don't believe in coincidences."

"Neither do I," Tanner agreed with a short laugh. "Somehow your break-in and murder are connected to my bank robbery. I'd bet on it. I'd like to get together and compare notes if you don't mind."

This was the first positive news Dare had received in days. "Absolutely. I can drive over there if you like. You name when."

"How about tomorrow around ten? We can go over the evidence and then have some lunch and catch up while we figure out our next steps."

Dare quickly agreed and ended the call. Finally, a break in the case that might lead to solving Moulson's murder once and for all.

Rayne hadn't wanted anyone to know about her date with Dare tonight, but keeping anything a secret from her best friend Misty Monroe was almost impossible. Within just a few minutes of their phone call, Misty had known something major was up and didn't relent until Rayne confessed.

In truth, she was glad to have someone to talk to about the forthcoming evening. She was incredibly nervous and not at all sure she'd done the right thing by agreeing to this date. Sexual attraction didn't necessarily equate to any sort of real compatibility, so this whole endeavor could be headed for a failure of massive proportions the likes which few had seen before.

"So what are you wearing tonight?" Misty asked. Rayne had her friend on speakerphone as she stood in her bathroom making up her face. "That red dress always looks nice on you."

"Way too dressy," Rayne protested, slowly and carefully drawing on eyeliner. "He mentioned dinner and a movie which says casual to me. I was thinking black jeans and a sweater. It's chilly tonight and I don't want to freeze my fanny off."

"Hmmm...black jeans say casual and dressy. That's good. What sweater? And what shoes? Boots or heels?"

Rayne held up the two sweaters she was deciding between – one cream and the other purple. "Purple with the three-quarter sleeves. And black flats. I want to be comfortable tonight. I'm already short so heels wouldn't fool anybody. Dare is about seven feet tall so anything I wear would be just a drop in the bucket anyway."

Misty giggled on the other end of the line. "Dare is a big one. He's taller than Jared so that makes him around six-three or four."

And every inch muscle from the looks of him. Rayne wondered how many hours in the gym he had to put in to keep that mouth-watering physique.

She sat down on the edge of the tub with a groan, almost ready to call Dare and cancel the whole darn evening. "I think this is a mistake."

"No. No, it's not," Misty pressed. "You two are attracted to each other. A date is the next natural step. You'll just wonder what could have happened if you don't go."

"Nothing is going to happen tonight. Just dinner and a movie. No happy-naked-fun-time. Not on the first date."

"This from the same woman who told me I needed to get laid. You were right, by the way—now it's my turn. Don't say never. If it happens tonight, it happens. Since when have you become the morality police?"

It truly wasn't Rayne's normal attitude about sex. She'd always been of the live and let live persuasion and didn't believe that women should be slut shamed for enjoying something men clearly did. It was a natural biological function, not to mention fun as hell with the right partner. She'd had long-term and short-term relationships along with a couple of one-night stands, and she was okay with her sexuality.

But with Dare it was different.

Not in a bad way. He was smoking hot and devastatingly handsome. He was also something else, something that made her wary. He would never hurt her or force himself on her. That wasn't it. It was something else that she couldn't quite put her finger on, but she knew she was right to be cautious.

"Maybe I'm becoming more careful in my old age," Rayne smirked, standing to finish putting on her makeup. Right now she had eyeliner but no mascara. "I just think that this relationship might not work out, and sleeping with him tonight might make ending things that much harder."

"Do you realize that you haven't even gone out with him yet but you're already planning on how to break up with him? That's a bit harsh, not to mention pessimistic. Dare's a nice man. Grouchy as all get out, but nice."

"We're just so different."

"Maybe, maybe not. But you'll never know unless you go out with him. Go finish your face and have fun. Just relax and have good time. Worst case scenario you get to see a movie tonight. That's not so bad."

Rayne had been on some terrible, no-good dates. The kind that made you want to crawl out of the restaurant's bathroom window so you could escape. She doubted tonight with Dare was going to be that bad, although there was a better than average chance they'd end up sniping at each other about something.

"I'm sure everything will be fine. I'll call you with the details."

"Call me in the morning."

"I'll call you sometime tomorrow."

"In the morning. If Dare doesn't spend the night you don't have any excuse," Misty laughed delightedly. "Call me or I'll call you."

"Fine—in the morning, but late. I want to sleep in."

"You'd sleep better with a handsome hunk of man in your bed."

So very true, but still quite scary. Rayne had a feeling one night with Dare wouldn't be enough.

Chapter Fourteen

The date was going well.

The movie had been better than Rayne expected. Dare had chosen an action-thriller and it wasn't her first choice in entertainment with all the shooting, blood, and guts, but it had ensured that the date wouldn't get too amorous.

Add in the fact that he'd chosen an out of town theatre and seats in the back row, all the way in the corner, and it felt like they were sneaking around, cheating on imaginary spouses. As thrilling as it had seemed at first, now it felt kind of icky and dirty. Not in a good way.

"I hope you're hungry."

Dare led her to a back booth in a rundown diner on the outskirts of Springwood. The old linoleum floors were dingy and the soles of her shoes stuck as she walked, making a sucking sound with each step. The smell of fry grease hung heavy in the air along with the remnants of what she thought might be motor oil. Not the most appetizing combination, but she'd had a strong stomach since the summer she'd spent at camp eating what had been essentially prison cuisine along with the three hundred other kids sweltering in ninety degree heat.

Rayne still gave her mom and dad a hard time about that

summer. They'd swore that the brochure looked much better than the reality and had been so apologetic she'd scored a new computer from the debacle.

Sliding into the booth, her rear end came to a quick halt and she winced at the thought of what was gluing the material of her jeans to the vinyl. More grease? She had to lift up to be able to move farther into the booth, shuddering as she placed her handbag on the oily bench seat.

One look at the table didn't tell a much different story. It looked and felt like it had been wiped off with a rag that hadn't been washed or rinsed in days. She could certainly suck it up and eat here, but she wasn't sure why she should when there were literally dozens of restaurants within a fifty-mile radius.

"Do you come here a lot?" Rayne decided to answer his question with another question. If he said yes this was definitely a strike against him.

Dare squirmed in his seat under her steady regard. "Actually I've only been here once. I met an informant here about a drug deal."

Oookay.

Looking at the clientele that made sense. Everyone in the joint looked like they were hiding out from the law, a bill collector, or their jealous husband. There was a sense of desperation and secrets in the air, and Rayne had to admit it made her uncomfortable.

"You don't like it here," Dare stated flatly. "It is kind of a greasy spoon. I chose it because it was out of the way."

She could go two ways on this. Get pissy with him because he'd brought her to the "no tell diner" or laugh at the entire situation. She chose the latter.

"It's certainly out of the way," she giggled, letting her gaze wander across the room. "I hope you're packing heat tonight because it looks like most of the people in here are. I don't think I'll see anyone I know here, so excellent job."

Smacking his forehead with his palm, Dare groaned and shook his head. "Shit. This is really awful, isn't it? I was only here once and I guess I didn't really notice how bad it was. You must think I'm a total bonehead. I swear I'm not usually this stupid."

"I know that." Rayne gave him a warm smile to show she wasn't mad or even perturbed. He was trying his best, but she doubted he'd ever had to sneak around before in his life. "Listen, I have an idea. Why don't we go back to that drive thru chicken place we saw a few miles back? We can pick up some dinner and find a place to have a picnic. I bet you know some out of the way and really peaceful spots around here."

The corners of his lips turned up ever so slightly, and she felt her chest tightening and her heart skipped a beat. "I do know just the spot and that's sounds like a good idea." Dare stood and held out his hand to help her out of the booth. "Shall we go?"

Rayne placed her hand in his, already anticipating the streak of heat that would travel from her fingers to parts more intimate. If she continued to date Dare, she hoped she would get used to it eventually. Because if not, she was going to be a hormonal mess every time he touched her. She needed to get herself under control.

"Another biscuit?" Rayne offered Dare, holding out the plastic tray. "I'm stuffed like a turkey."

She'd put away a surprising amount of food for such a tiny woman. Not much more than five foot two and a hundred and ten pounds soaking wet, she eaten two chicken breasts, a large helping of mashed potatoes and gravy, plus three biscuits with butter. There was a chocolate cake as well for dessert but that would have to wait. Dare couldn't have forced another bite past his lips.

They were sitting in the bed of his truck by a lake he used to fish in when he was a kid. Dare had found a blanket in the back and he'd tucked it around them as the temperature fell. Rayne hadn't complained and Dare wouldn't either. She was tucked up under his arm, the entire length of her right side pressing into his left from shoulder to ankle. Despite the disparity in their sizes, she seemed to fit as if she were made for him.

A dangerous thought under such a starry and romantic sky.

"I think I'm full," he groaned, stretching his arms over his head. "This was a great idea. But I know you're not fond of the outdoors so I'm wondering why you suggested it."

"If it's a choice between contracting food poisoning at that dingy diner or sitting out here and enjoying deep fried goodness, I know what I'm going to do. I ate some bad chicken once and it was the worst twenty-four hours of my life. I don't want a repeat."

"It was shrimp for me and I agree. Worst night of my life. I think I actually expelled my intestines."

It was funny how he could talk to Rayne about anything, including gross stuff. He wouldn't have had this conversation with any of his former girlfriends.

"We shouldn't talk about puking right after eating a bucket of fried chicken. Tell me about the investigation instead. You said you would."

He had promised but they'd been sidetracked most of the evening. "There has been a major development in the case. Tanner Marks—he's the sheriff in Springwood—had a bank robbery a few weeks ago. The ballistics from that robbery match the ballistics from Patrick Moulson's murder. It looks like the two crimes are related in some way."

Rayne frowned, a cute wrinkle forming between her brows. "How does the shop break-in fit into all this? If they were smart enough to rob a bank and get away with it, why would they bust into my shop, knock things around, and then not steal anything? It doesn't make sense."

"No, it doesn't. Reed suggested it and I think he's right. They were looking for something specific and the question is, did they find it?"

"Nothing was missing."

"Then that means they don't have what they were looking for. Probably, anyway. I just wish I knew what or who to watch for."

"Did you find out anything about the victim? You asked Jared to investigate him."

"That didn't help much." Dare pulled Rayne closer, the air growing damp and chilly. Her skin was fragrant and warm and he rested his chin on the top of her head, rubbing the silky strands. So far this evening they hadn't clashed once. He was getting to know this woman, and so far he liked what he saw. Very much. "He was an average guy with an average life. Not much going on personally or financially. Sounds like he fell in with the wrong crowd. I've seen it happen dozens of times."

"He paid the price for it. Dying young and all. It's still creepy that there's a person out there capable of taking a human life. It freaks me out a little, honestly."

Dare hated to rip Rayne's rose colored glasses from her eyes but the world was a cruel place. "I can guarantee you on any given day you talk to more than one person capable of killing. Whether they were provoked, pissed off, defending themselves, or simply like doing it, they're out there, everywhere. I wish it weren't true but it is. It's the fight or flight response. If your life is threatened or the life of someone you love, what would you do?"

"I see what you're saying," Rayne sighed, her breath warm on his arm. "But I don't have to like it. It's weird, though. You go through life not thinking about it all that much until something like this happens, then you think about it all the time. Life. Death. Nothing seems simple these days."

Dare ran his fingers down her satin-soft cheek before tickling her behind the ear and eliciting a small giggle. "You want simple? It doesn't get much more simple than a picnic under the stars and a little George Strait."

The radio played softly in the background and crickets chirped in the distance. Dare couldn't think of a more pleasant evening than tonight. It was the best date he'd had in a long time and it was with a woman he'd vowed to stay away from. Typical. He knew she'd be trouble and she was. He was liking this way too much and it was only the first date. He was already thinking about kissing her – and maybe more – when he took her home later.

Would she invite him in? Would they make love?

It had been months since his last relationship and Dare couldn't deny he was horny as hell. It wasn't just a physical need, though; he had his own right hand, although it was a piss poor substitute. It was everything about Rayne that made him want to get to know her – carnally and otherwise.

A splash of something wet plopped on his hand and he scowled down at it, his mind trying to piece together where it came from just as another drop landed on his head and arm. Within seconds the single drops became a shower, the cool water raising goosebumps on his skin.

"Shit." Dare jumped up and began to pack away their dinner. "We need to get out of this before we're soaked. Go on and jump in the truck and I'll get this."

He gathered up the food and stowed it in the paper sack, checking the truck cab to make sure that Rayne was warm and dry. Frowning when he couldn't see her, he stood to get a better view and that's when he caught a glimpse of her from the corner of his eye.

The sweet little brunette with the purple streaks in her hair was standing in the rain, her arms outstretched and her head thrown back. She twirled around, a brilliant smile on her face as the gentle raindrops caressed her skin. Her flesh seemed to glow in the moonlight and Dare had a sudden strong compulsion to reach out and run his hands down her damp arms and tangle his fingers in her rapidly curling tresses.

Fuck, she was gorgeous.

"Come dance with me, Dare."

Rayne beckoned to him, her clothes now clinging to her curvy figure. For a small woman she had an amazing body, large round breasts and hips made to fit a man's hand. With her unconventional looks and untamed attitude she called to something deep inside – something wild and primitive. Joyous. Normally he kept that part of himself locked down tight but in her company he was tempted to let go.

For just a minute. Maybe two.

He didn't realize he'd moved until he was standing in front of Rayne, his hands pulling her body closer to his own. She was smiling up at him as if they didn't have a care in the world, and he supposed at that moment they didn't. It was just a man and a woman dancing under the sky, completely cut off from the rest of the world.

They began to move in concert to a song only they heard. Closing his eyes, he let himself relax and forget all the problems and issues he shouldered each day. Her delicious scent wafted around him, a combination of vanilla and rain. His body responded instantly, the blood pounding in his ears. This wouldn't last forever but he'd enjoy every single second of it that he could, committing every detail to memory. The way her soft skin felt slick under his fingers. How her body brushed his with each step. The sigh she made when he pressed his lips to the spot just under her ear.

The rain had cast a spell over them but he could already feel it slipping away, like sand through his fingers. He didn't try to grab at it, knowing its rarity was what made it special. Rayne ran her hands up his arms to his shoulders, her face still radiant with happiness.

"I guess we better get out of this or we're going to catch pneumonia. I wish we didn't have to, though. I love playing in the rain."

The rain was coming down harder now, pouring, and they were both soaked to the skin. Reluctantly he moved away, instantly chilled as he lost the warmth of her body pressed to his. He quickly helped her into the truck before grabbing their picnic and stowing it in the backseat. Swinging into the driver's seat, he directed the vehicle toward the main road, the heater blasting and the radio playing Luke Bryan.

With his right hand on the steering wheel, he reached up to touch his face with his left, running his fingers across his lips, the heart in his chest tightening painfully.

All be damned.

He was smiling.

CHAPTER FIFTEEN

R ayne could have sworn she saw Dare smiling when they were driving away from the lake. He'd covered his lips with his fingers but she would have bet everything she owned that his mouth was curved upwards...with happiness. For all she knew he might even have dimples in those cheeks, and that was a sight she'd pay big money to see.

"Are you okay? The blanket is wet and the heat is going full blast."

"If I'm cold it's my own fault," Rayne laughed. "It was my idea to dance in the rain. I should be asking you if you're okay."

Dare shrugged his wide shoulders. "I'm fine. This isn't really all that bad. I just don't want you to get sick or anything." That was sweet. She liked having him fuss over her. It had been a long time since anyone had. "You need to do the finishing touches on my tat, after all."

Rayne burst into laughter at his self-serving statement. "So I do. When do you want to come in and finish it?"

"Things are so crazy right now I can't commit to a time. Hopefully soon. I really like the way it's turning out. If I haven't already told you, you're very talented."

This night was turning out differently than she'd ever pictured. He had been nice and attentive, even adventurous. She hadn't expected him to play in the rain with her. If anything she'd thought he would scold her for being childish. But instead he'd held her as they danced, his warm, muscular body so close. She'd felt so safe and protected in those moments and she'd allowed herself to be vulnerable.

"Thank you. That means a lot to me, Dare. It really does."

The silence grew as he drove through the storm, finally pulling up in front of her house and putting the truck into park. Climbing out the driver's side, he came around to open her door, a gentlemanly touch he didn't need to perform but she found that she liked quite a bit. Without speaking he walked her to her door, the silence stretching between them and amping up her awareness. His wide shoulders. The soft rise and fall of his chest. The leashed power she could feel as he stood next to her at her front door. He towered over her, at least a foot taller, but she didn't feel one ounce of fear.

She took a few deep breaths to calm her libido, which was making itself a freakin' pest after months in hibernation. He was too damn handsome and she was a pushover for a pretty face.

He'd smiled.

He would probably never admit it and she didn't really know for sure, but she'd felt his happiness. He'd felt joy and she'd helped with that. It made him more approachable and infinitely more attractive.

Dare took a step closer and leaned forward so his lips were inches from her own. She resisted the urge to press herself closer to the heat of his body still trying to play it cool and safe. "Normally at the end of a first date I'd try and get a goodnight kiss. If I tried to steal a kiss right now would you let me, Rayne? Or would you slap me across the face?"

Rayne had zero self-preservation at this moment in time and

her next words showed it.

"You wouldn't need to steal it."

He didn't give her the opportunity to second-guess her answer. Wrapping his arms around her waist, she felt herself pulled onto her tiptoes as his lips descended onto hers. Her own fingers anchored into his shoulders, digging into the hard muscle while his tongue gently swept her mouth, playing tag and tickle and driving her slowly crazy with want.

She didn't feel the chilly wind or the dampness of their clothes. Her world had narrowed to the two of them and the wild beat of her heart beneath her ribs. Dare's kisses were pure sin and she didn't want salvation.

When they finally pulled apart, his cheeks were flushed and his blue eyes dark with desire. His hands were splayed, one on her back and the other behind her head, his fingers tangled in her hair. The heat from his fingers seeped into her flesh despite the layers of clothing between them and it was all she could do not to throw herself at him again, taking his mouth with her own until they couldn't remember their names. Or why it was too soon.

Too soon. Too fast.

A few days ago she hadn't even liked him much, and now she was planning how to get him out of his clothes with the precision of a military offensive. Slow down. Savor the buildup. She'd had too many relationships that rushed to bed but only ended up at the finish line.

Dare's palm cupped her jaw and his thumb caressed her swollen lips. "So...tonight was...good."

"It was. Thank you for dinner."

She sounded breathless but then again, she was. He'd kissed the heck out of her and she was still recovering.

"Thank you for being so understanding. Would you maybe

want to go out again?"

He sounded unsure and nervous, which was laughable really. He'd turned her knees to jelly.

"Sure, give me a call." Neither one of them seemed to want to end the evening but eventually she reluctantly pulled away, unlocking the door. "Well…good night. I'll talk to you soon."

"Soon. Good night."

She entered her home and slid the deadbolt into place before peeking out of the front window. He must have seen her because he gave a brief wave before climbing into his truck and driving away.

Shedding her wet clothes, she quickly drew a hot bath, adding some fragrant oil before sinking down into the water and letting the heat chase away the cold that had settled into her bones.

Dare Turner had turned out to be someone different than she'd thought. Someone sweeter. Kinder. Not to mention their chemistry was off the charts. She hated to hope – she'd only been let down in the past – but he might be a man she could fall for.

This relationship just might have a future.

CHAPTER SIXTEEN

D are drove up to the old barn on the outskirts of Harper where Tanner and Seth were waiting for him. Moulson's truck had finally been found in an old abandoned building and Dare was hoping there might be some clue as to the identity of the shooter. He was tired of coming up to one dead end after another.

Exiting the truck, he found Seth and Tanner standing in front of the wide open doors of the dilapidated barn that was practically falling down around their ears. One stiff breeze could have collapsed it and Dare wasn't so sure he wanted to spend much time inside. Search it and then have it taken into custody.

"Good job finding it. I was beginning to think it had disappeared into thin air." Dare slapped Seth on the back. It was only due to the cooperation of the local sheriffs that he'd made any headway on this case.

The smiling blond lawman led the way into the barn. "Glad I could help. I had one of my deputies out checking for a missing teenager and he came upon the truck. Looks like they intended to come back for it. The keys are still in the ignition."

Hesitating a few feet from the vehicle, Dare gave Seth a questioning look. "Has the forensic team finished?"

"They dusted for prints and everything they found was bagged for evidence." He pointed to the tailgate of the truck. "They put the items there. I figured you'd want to get a look and maybe some photos before they take them back to the lab."

Dare and Tanner perused the small bags, pretty much what Dare would have expected. Vehicle registration. Truck manual. Fast food and gas receipts. A parking ticket from Salt Lake City. A set of keys on a bottle opener keychain.

Tanner picked up the bag with the keys to take a closer look. "Looks like his truck key is on here but there are three other keys. They might be helpful if we could figure out what they open."

Dare peered over Tanner's shoulder. "I'd guess at least one is to his home."

Tanner held up a small silver key through the plastic. "This one is different. Smaller. Maybe a safe deposit box or a locker of some sort. Those are good hiding places for stolen cash."

"You think they hid it?"

"I would if I stole it. Lay low and wait until the cops move on to another case." Tanner placed the keys down on the tailgate and picked up the receipts. "Looks like he liked junk food. There are at least a dozen receipts here for hamburgers, fries, and soda. The first one is dated, coincidentally, five days before the bank robbery."

"Based on the dates and times, we could see if the restaurants in question have any surveillance tapes," Dare suggested. "We might be able to see if he has any friends. Your bank robbery had four men. so that means if Moulson is one of them there are still three to find."

Tanner nodded grimly. "And at least one of them is probably your killer."

Dare heaved a sigh and shook his head. "Nothing here gives

any indication why Moulson would break into Rayne's shop."

Tanner placed the evidence bag down on the tailgate and rubbed the back of his neck. He seemed to be struggling with his thoughts. "Listen, I don't want to tell you your business but I agree with Reed. I think Moulson was looking for something specific in Rayne's shop."

"I think so too. But what?"

"That's a good question. I only wish I had the answer because I think it would go a long way as to solving this case. But at least now we have something to investigate. I'll have one of my deputies start working on these receipts right away."

"I don't mind telling you, Tanner, this one's got me stumped. What does a bank robbery, a tattoo shop break-in, and a murder all have in common? I can barely sleep. It's driving me crazy. What am I missing?"

"I'm not sure, my friend, but I think when you have the answer to that question we'll have your murderer. And my bank robbers. We'll find the connection."

Dare only hoped it was before anyone else ended up dead.

Rayne sipped her iced tea and perused the menu of the local Italian eatery. She had a two-hour break in her schedule today and she'd decided to spend it having a leisurely lunch and then doing some grocery shopping.

Never go food shopping on an empty stomach.

She'd done it too many times to count but today she'd do better. She'd written out a list. A *list*, for cripe's sake. It was tucked inside the pocket of her jeans and not left on her kitchen counter as usual. It made her feel organized and put together today. Her earrings even coordinated with her sweater. She was hitting on all cylinders. She ought to buy a lottery ticket.

She was deep in thought deciding between chicken parmesan and lasagna when a shadow fell over the table.

"Rayne?"

Looking up, her eyes widened in surprise. James was the last person she'd expected to see today. Or ever, actually. She'd run out of their date abruptly without exchanging phone numbers, so she'd figured she'd never see him again which was fine since she'd started to see Dare.

"James! Hello. What are you doing in Valley Station?"

"Consulting with another vet. I was heading back to Spring-wood but my hunger got the best of me and I decided to stop for lunch. I'm really glad I ran into you. I've been worried about you since that night."

The concerned way he was looking at her, the plain sincerity on his face, made her do it. Later when Misty asked, Rayne would tell her friend that her brain hadn't been functioning correctly. Hunger had made her delirious and she'd used up all her common sense making a list for the grocery store. This was why being organized was overrated. Rayne waved her hand toward the other side of the booth. "Would you care to join me?"

His face split into a huge smile and he nodded eagerly, scooting onto the padded bench.

"What's good here?"

They discussed the merits of different dishes, and when the waitress came Rayne settled on the chicken parmesan and he ordered the cannelloni. With lunch business squared away she couldn't delay speaking any longer.

"It was a robbery," she offered. "And then they found a dead body out back. So it was a nasty business all the way around. But I'm fine. They didn't steal anything except my apparently false sense of security."

James's brows shot up. "A dead body? That's terrible. Was it a friend?"

"No, I didn't know him. He was from out of town but I still felt terrible for him. He was shot down like a dog in the street. That's no way to go."

"I'm just glad you're okay." He looked down at the table and then up at her. "I've been wanting to call you, ask you out. I was going to call Jared and get your number but things have been pretty busy at the clinic."

Months without a glimmer of a man in her life and now she had two that wanted to date her. When it rains it pours. That's what her mother used to say.

James was a nice man. A good guy. He didn't turn her on in the least. Her feelings were more friendly or brotherly than lover-like. She couldn't picture herself kissing or having sex with him. She needed to let him down gently. This wasn't his fault.

It was Dare's.

And that sexy son of a gun was walking in the front door of the restaurant at this very minute, his sister Sophie right beside him. His gaze quickly settled on Rayne and then those steely blue eyes narrowed as he took in her dining companion.

James's gaze followed her own as she watched Dare and Sophie settle into a table on the other side of the restaurant.

"He's the sheriff?"

Rayne dragged her attention from Dare back to James, who was giving her a quizzical look. "Yes. Dare Turner. I was just wondering if he had any new information on the case."

She wasn't the best liar and James's expression said as much. He glanced at Dare and then back at Rayne. "Is that his girlfriend? She looks young for him."

"Sister, and she is young. Just eighteen. She wants me to do a tattoo for her."

It was a desperate gambit to change the subject but James seemed to take pity on her.

"Eighteen seems awfully young. Tattoos are for life."

"You sound like Dare," Rayne laughed. "He was livid when he thought I had given her one. I thought he was going to blow a blood vessel in his head."

I can't go two seconds without talking about that man. What is wrong with me?

"I'd say I have to agree with him." The waitress slid their entrees onto the table. "This looks delicious. I'm glad I ran into you today. I hate to eat alone."

Rayne was used to it. All through lunch she kept sneaking glances over at Dare and Sophie, sometimes catching him looking right back. Glaring would be a better word for it. He didn't look happy which wasn't all that unusual, but right now he looked grumpier than usual. With his job there was no telling what his problem was today. Or perhaps Sophie was finally telling him that she was leaving town. Rayne wanted to be far away when that happened. Dare was going to go ballistic. And then he'd get really upset.

The waitress brought the check and she reached for it, but not as quickly as James. He held it up and shook his head. "Please let me get this. I have a feeling this is my last chance to buy you a meal."

"I don't understand."

James looked over at Dare, a rueful smile playing on his lips. "A man knows when a woman isn't interested. I'll be graceful in my defeat."

Heat rushed to her cheeks and her hand flew to her throat. Hopefully everyone didn't see through her this easily. "I'm sorry. I just…oh crap. I'm just really sorry. It's not you. You're a great guy."

"You're a nice woman." James placed some bills on the check. "I'd offer to be your friend but..."

Wrinkling her nose, Rayne groaned. "Believe me, I get it. Can I apologize again?"

James patted her hand. "I wish you wouldn't. It's no one's fault. It just wasn't meant to be. But I'm still glad I ran into you today. I truly was worried about you."

Now she really felt guilty. She'd barely given James a thought since that night. As a person, she sucked.

"Thank you. I'm really fine. I'm just so—"

James held up his hand. "Really. Stop. It's just one of those things. I'll survive. Hey, maybe you have a cute friend you can set me up with."

That pulled a smile from her. "Most of my friends are married but I'll keep it in mind."

James slid out of the booth. "Then we're good. Thanks for having lunch with me. It's my turn to apologize but I do need to get going. Maybe we'll run into each other again."

"I'll walk you out. I have a few errands to run before I head back to the shop."

Rayne and James exited the restaurant and she would have sworn an intense blue gaze followed her the entire way, boring a hole into her back. It was a relief as she bid James goodbye and headed down the sidewalk.

She didn't owe Dare an explanation about her lunch with James. It was completely innocent and she and Dare had only had the one date. They hadn't discussed being exclusive either. Besides, the jerk hadn't even bothered to call her yet.

And that hurt more than it should.

CHAPTER SEVENTEEN

"Are you listening to me?"

Sophie smacked the table, dragging Dare's attention from Rayne's retreating figure. He'd come here with his sister to have lunch only to run smack dab into Rayne...and her date. The man looked like a decent guy, too. Well dressed and nice looking. Probably educated and successful. The man had paid the check and then they'd walked out of the restaurant with his hand on the small of Rayne's back, guiding her out. It had to be a date. Dare didn't buy lunch and then put his hands on women he wasn't dating.

"Of course I'm listening to you." Dare struggled not to sigh in frustration. "Tim's wonderful. Tim's amazing. I get it, sis. He's the greatest. Who are you trying to convince? Me or you?"

Sophie's cheeks colored but she looked more annoyed than embarrassed. "I know how wonderful Tim is and that's what I'm trying to tell you. He's great and he takes good care of me."

Snorting, Dare bit into a breadstick, trying to concentrate on his little sister instead of thinking about Rayne and that guy. Dare had searched his memory banks but he was positive he'd never seen her lunch companion before today. He also couldn't help but wonder why she'd gone out on a date with him when she had a guy like that on the line.

"You're not listening again," Sophie hissed. "What is your problem?"

"I don't have a problem."

Rayne Dunn wasn't a problem. He didn't care that she was having lunch with another man. It was fine. Okey dokey. No issue here.

"I'm trying to tell you something important. That's why I suggested we have lunch."

"Then spit it out. I'm not getting any younger."

Sophie laughed and pointed at him, her finger wriggling playfully. "You certainly aren't my *older* brother. One foot in the grave and the other on a banana peel. You practically creak when you walk."

"I'm a geriatric, now talk."

Dare dug into his fettuccine with an enthusiasm born of clawing hunger. He'd missed breakfast and Sophie's idea to meet for lunch had seemed like a godsend at the time. Now he was annoyed as hell.

"Like I was saying...Tim is a great guy and we have so much fun together. He makes me really happy and we get along well. I think we have a real future."

That wasn't the best news Dare had heard today, or even this week. He wanted Sophie to get over Tim as soon as possible. The guy could barely take care of himself, let alone Dare's sister.

"Your future is wide open. It doesn't have to have Tim in it."

"But I want it to." Sophie's chin lifted in defiance. "I'm trying to tell you something and you're interrupting me."

"You keep hemming and hawing. If you have something to say you should just say it."

Sophie's eyes bugged and she emitted a long, pissed-off

groan. "You are such a butt. I knew you'd be like this, which is why I didn't say anything until now. So here it is. I got into school in Denver. I'm going to start in January. Tim is going to get a job down there and we're going to live together. There. I said it."

Dare kept running the words through his head over and over as if to make some sense of them. It sounded like Sophie was leaving and moving in with that little prick Tim Wallace.

"Can you say that again?"

Sophie took a big breath and let it out noisily. "I'm moving to Denver for school. Tim is going with me."

"You can't—"

"Stop there," Sophie interrupted, her voice firmer than he'd ever heard it before. "The decision has been made. I'm of age and I'm going. Girls all over this great nation of ours go off to school when they're eighteen and the world keeps on spinning. I want this, big brother, and you will not stop me."

"But—"

"No. The decision has been made," she repeated in a no nonsense tone, although her lower lip trembled slightly. "You can either make the rest of my time here in Valley Station pleasant or you can be a dick. Those are your two choices. That's it."

Dare wrestled with emotions he wasn't used to dealing with and avoided as often as possible. Fear. Love. The pain of separation. Mostly fear, though. Sophie was a young girl and she had no idea what evil there was in this world. He'd seen it, been up close, and the visions still haunted him at night. If she wasn't close by he couldn't protect her. She'd be out there alone.

The worst thing was she didn't see how vulnerable she was.

"I don't think you should go."

Her blue eyes, so like his own, filled with tears. "You want me to stay? And do what, Dare? Get a minimum wage dead end job that leads nowhere? Because that's what we're talking about if I stay here. My life will basically be over before it's started. And the worst thing is that you know that. It's why you left when you were my age. You know this and you're holding me back for some selfish reason that I cannot even begin to comprehend. Do you not want me to make something of my life?"

It wasn't that simple. Either-or. This or that. It was far more complex and he wasn't sure he had the words to explain it.

"Of course I do. You deserve everything in the world. But leaving town with Tim Wallace isn't the way to accomplish it. You have to be patient."

Her mouth fell open and then she laughed, but she didn't sound amused. "What am I waiting for? Prince Charming? I think this little podunk town is fresh out of those. If I want to do something in my life, I can't wait around for someone to rescue me. I have to do it myself and that means taking chances. Something that you excel at and yet you don't want anyone else to do it."

Dare flushed as Sophie reminded him of his past. He may have done some foolhardy things in his youth but now he acted like a damn adult.

Except the other night when he'd danced in the rain with a sexy little tattoo artist. That had been out of character for the adult Dare. Obviously he hadn't been thinking straight, or at all for that matter. His libido had been doing the talking. Rayne had looked gorgeous, wet from the storm, her smile wide and her eyes lit from within, a joy she seemed to radiate. He'd wanted to get closer and be a part of it.

"Earth to Dare." Sophie waved her hand in front of his eyes, pulling him back to reality. "You're not listening again. Should we table this and try again another time? Not that it matters. I'm going and there's nothing you can do to stop me."

Christ on a pogo stick, he was in deep today. Half of his brain was still thinking about Rayne and the other half was desperately trying to keep his little sister from making a horrible mistake. If he'd had any brain cells left he would have been concentrating on bringing a killer to justice, but the women in his life had him twisted sideways and upside down.

"You're right. Short of physically restraining you, I can't stop you. But I can keep telling you that Tim Wallace isn't the wonderful boyfriend that you think he is. I've seen his type before and it always ends the same. As for moving, I don't want you to go. There are closer schools, Sophie. You could even go to school online. You don't have to leave Montana to get an education."

"I don't have to. I want to."

Anger and frustration had given way to sadness and Sophie was blinking back tears, leaving Dare to feel like the worst big brother on the planet. He loved his sister and only wanted to protect her but he didn't want to hurt her either. That wasn't what this was about.

Dare took in a controlled breath, letting it out slowly. "Let's table this for a few days. That will give both of is time to think about it. I'm a little blindsided and if we keep talking about this I'm going to say something I can't take back."

Sophie nodded. "Fine. But I won't change my mind."

"You've said that already."

"You haven't been listening very well today so I thought I'd say it again. I want to be sure you've heard me."

He'd heard her all right, and hadn't liked anything she'd said.

"I understand how you feel. Let's just get the check, okay? I need to get back to the office."

He signaled the waitress and pushed his plate away, his appetite gone. This was easily the worst lunch he'd had in months and it had nothing to do with the food.

"And Dare?" Sophie leaned forward, a smile playing on her lips. "I'm getting that tattoo as well. You can't stop that either."

Duke Wallace – older brother of Tim – squirmed in his chair as Dare leaned across the interrogation table, his palms flat on the smooth surface. Deputy Billy had picked up Duke at the local watering hole and brought him to the station. Dare had seen Duke's beat-up truck in some of the security footage from a Harper eatery that had been visited by Patrick Moulson at the exact same day and time.

Dare pushed the folder closer to Duke, pictures of a deceased Moulson front and center.

"Do you recognize him? Take your time. This is important. It's a man's life."

"I don't need to take my time. I don't know him. Never seen him before."

There was a tinny note of desperation in Duke's voice that was music to Dare's ears. Duke was hiding something. It might not have anything to do with Moulson, but he was lying. Dare had questioned too many suspects not to know when one wasn't telling the whole truth.

"Listen, I'm not busting your balls about anything you've done. Not this time. I'm only hoping you noticed this guy when you were there that day. Frankly, I'm having trouble believing you when you say you didn't see him. Your body language is telling a different story. You're sweating. Your hands are trembling, and shit, you can't sit still. You're awful nervous for someone who is as pure as the driven snow." Dare tapped the photo with his index finger. "Let's try this again. Do you recognize him?"

Somewhere Duke must have found his balls – or at least wanted Dare to believe he wasn't nervous – because he sneered and leaned back in the chair, propping his foot on the table. "No. Shit. Leave me alone. You're only harassing me because you don't like my brother giving the high hard one to your baby sister."

Dare was dying to wipe that fucking smirk off of Duke's face with his fist but this was business not pleasure. Deep down, Dare had known his sister wasn't a virgin but hearing this little puke talk about it didn't set well. Keeping a tight lid on his emotions was second nature though, and nothing Duke said or did was going to rattle his demeanor. He had to keep control of this discussion.

But first he needed to make a point.

Dare reached over and knocked Duke's foot off the table before leaning down and caging the man in with his arms, their faces inches apart. "I wouldn't mention Sophie if I were you."

He kept his voice soft, menacing, and icy as hell. Duke seemed to get the message, swallowing hard but saying nothing.

"Now you were at the barbecue joint at the same time as this man. If you don't know him, did you see him? If he was with people did you see them?"

Duke shook his head, twisting in his chair. "No, I've never seen him. Tim, Sophie, and I were there meeting an old friend of mine from high school. We sat down, had a few beers and some nachos, but Sophie didn't drink or anything. She had a root beer. Then we came back to Valley Station. That's it. I didn't talk to anyone else and I didn't notice this guy. I swear, Sheriff."

Dare stiffened at the mention of his sister's name. "Sophie was there?"

"Yeah, it was the three of us and we didn't stay more than an hour. I dropped Tim and Sophie off at your house and then picked up my girlfriend. We went to see a movie. There were witnesses."

Dare's fingers curled into fists and he had to consciously relax them one at a time. "If you remember anything I want you to call me."

Duke pasted on a fake smile. The animosity was mutual. "You'll be the first person I tell."

Dare didn't believe him for a minute.

Now he needed to talk to his own sister about a killer. This day was going downhill fast.

CHAPTER EIGHTEEN

Rayne settled Sophie in a comfortable chair, her boyfriend Tim close by holding her hand. The entire situation was messed up and Rayne would certainly hear about this from Dare, but the fact was…he wasn't the boss of her.

Running this business was her livelihood and turning away a paying customer wasn't a smart idea. That customer might be the sheriff's sister, but she was old enough to consent to this and Rayne had given her a lecture that would have scared off most other people. Sophie wanted this and Rayne wanted to make sure that she didn't get it from someone who had little idea as to what they were doing.

"Your brother is going to kill me. Heck, he may kill you too. Then me again just for fun. Either way, he's going to be mighty unhappy. You've thought this through, right?"

"I have. I know he's going to have a kitten or a cow but he doesn't get to run my life. It's going to be a hard lesson for him to learn but I'm determined he will learn it."

Rayne had a sinking feeling this tat was simply the opening shot in an ongoing battle for control of Sophie's young life. Dare wouldn't give up without a fight.

"Just relax then. I need to run into the back room for a few supplies. I'll be right back."

The shop was empty this late in the evening and Rayne had turned her door sign to *Closed* to give Sophie more privacy. The back room was still cluttered from the break-in, supplies in stacks instead of put away neatly. Rayne needed an uninterrupted afternoon to organize everything but she never seemed to have the time.

She had everything balanced perfectly in her arms and was turning off the light switch with her elbow when she heard them.

Raised voices.

Dammit, it was Dare. Did he have some sort of radar as to the whereabouts of Sophie? She wouldn't put it past him to have implanted a chip in the back of her neck so he could keep tabs on her all hours of the day.

Striding into the front of the shop, she dumped her armload on the table and turned to face the man that hadn't called her since their date.

"Good evening, Sheriff," she said loudly enough to be heard over the argument brewing between brother and sister. "Can we keep it civil tonight?"

Whatever she expected him to say or do, she sure as hell didn't think he'd clamp his large hands on her shoulders and propel her backwards until they were in the storeroom. He slammed the door behind them and bent his head so they were eye to eye.

Rayne was trembling inside. She wasn't a stupid woman and Dare looked livid, but images of Dare dancing in the rain with her kept coming to the forefront of her mind and keeping her from turning around and running. Ultimately she didn't believe he'd hurt her.

He'd yell. Probably a bunch. He's stomp around and growl as if this was the end of the world and only her acquiescence could save it. But this man wasn't going inflict any damage on her person.

"I thought we talked about this." His voice came out as a deep rasp, clearly unhappy but then that was nothing new. "I told you not to ink Sophie."

Straightening her spine, she placed her hands on Dare's arms and gave them a push. "Unhand me, Dare. I don't enjoy being manhandled."

His hold loosened and his arms fell back to his sides as he took a step back. "Fine. I apologize."

"Thank you. Now if you're going to make a scene please leave my place of business. I won't have that kind of drama here."

"Then don't ink Sophie," he retorted. "I told you not to."

Rayne rolled her eyes at his high-handed attitude. Boy, he was barking up the wrong tree trying to order her around. This might work with his airheaded blonde girlfriends but it wouldn't work with her.

"And your point is? You don't get to decide who my customers are, Dare. This is my business. I don't tell you how to run yours or place citizen's arrests when people speed down Main Street. I can't afford to let a third party's capricious nature mess with this shop. If you and Sophie have issues you need to deal with them and stop putting me in the middle. I tried to scare her off, believe me, but she's determined. If she's going to do this I'd rather do it myself and not send her to some fly by night shop that will do God knows what. I know you're trying to protect her, but so am I."

Like a fish out of water, Dare's mouth gaped open, closed, and then opened again. Rarely at a loss for words, he appeared to be completely flummoxed.

"Cat got your tongue?"

Dare's head fell back and he stared at the ceiling for several heartbeats before facing her again.

"Fuck."

Rayne couldn't help but laugh. "That's the eloquent curmudgeon we all know and love. Care to elaborate?"

"I hate it when other people are right," he sighed, resignation in his tone.

"So do I. Luckily it doesn't happen to me often."

He rubbed the back of his neck, and she noticed the dark circles under his eyes indicating he hadn't had much sleep lately.

"I need to talk to Sophie and Tim. It turns out they and Tim's brother were in the same restaurant at exactly the same time as our victim. I want to know if they saw him or anyone he may have been with."

That was interesting news. "So you were looking for your sister to ask her questions and you found out she was here. Cue the general anger and frustration. Have I guessed correctly?"

Dare glared but she wasn't too scared. "You're right again."

She was on a roll so why not go for broke. "In addition, you're freaked out that Sophie was in the same room with possible bank robbers and killers. Also correct?" He gave her a curt nod. "So you stomped in here treating her like a naughty toddler, so she'll have no choice but to leave for Denver sooner and you won't be able to protect her there even though you can't really do it here either. You just can't admit that."

Dare sat heavily into a chair and leaned his elbows on his knees. "Damn, woman, you're annoying. Anyone ever tell you that?"

Rayne inwardly snickered. He didn't know the half of it. "Tons. Loads. You're not even close to the first."

"I'm not surprised but I am sorry I barged in here like that. Sometimes my brain doesn't engage correctly when it comes to someone I care about."

She liked a man who could apologize and didn't make it sound passive-aggressive.

"Thank you and I appreciate that. I can understand it too. My family can make me crazy as well, although I'm sure I do it to them too. So are you going to talk to Sophie and Tim?"

"What about the tattoo?"

"Now you're just giving me a hard time. You don't want her to have it and you have a perfect excuse for why she can't get it today. You need to talk to her about a murder. It doesn't get much more important than that."

She could swear she saw a smile ghost across his lips. "You are fun to tease."

"But not fun enough to call for a second date?"

Dammit. She hadn't meant to say that. She hadn't meant to say anything at all about it.

His cheekbones were streaked with red. "About that...I meant to call but work kind of got crazy."

"Sure. I get that." Rayne shrugged her shoulders as if it didn't matter. It didn't really. The kiss had been awesome and they'd had fun, but that didn't mean she was disappointed. "Just so you know I've been busy too."

Dare scratched his head and stood, grabbing one of her hands in his. "I truly meant to call and I'm sorry I didn't. The fact is I'm not very good at balancing work and a personal life. I tend to get wrapped up in the job. If I ask nicely, will you go out with me again?"

Rayne rolled her eyes even as her heart tumbled in her chest. "I'd love to. I won't even make you run around in the rain this time. Maybe we can just have a nice meal or something, completely warm and dry."

His expression went blank at that and he dropped her hand.

"What about that guy?"

Rayne looked around the room. They were the only two people in it. "What guy?"

"The guy you were having lunch with the other day."

Rayne had only gone out to lunch one day that week...Oh hell! He was talking about James. The handsome sheriff was jealous. This was too delicious and a part of her wanted to see how jealous he could get but she wasn't that cruel. She wouldn't want him to do that to her.

"That was James and he's just a friend."

Dare crossed his arms over his broad chest, a dubious expression on his face. "He paid the check and he put his hand on your back when you walked out. It looked closer than friends."

He was jealous and she shouldn't enjoy it, but she did. Butterflies fluttered in her stomach at the thought of this gorgeous man not wanting her to be with anyone else.

"I'm not sure how it looked but I can assure you he's just a friend. We ran into each other and he joined me for lunch. I don't know if I'll even see him again. I doubt I will. He's a veterinarian over in Springwood and a friend of Jared's."

Dare stared down at the toe of his well-worn boots. "I don't want you to feel like you have to go out with me if you'd rather..."

She'd had enough. Playing games weren't her style. She smacked his chest with her palms, pressing them against his warm and solid frame. "Shut up, Sheriff. God help us both, it looks like we like each other. I don't want to date James, okay? I want to date you. How's that for getting things out into the open?"

When he raised his head, she almost staggered back in shock. Dare was smiling.

Smiling. A blinding, beautiful smile that took her breath away and sent electric tingles to some very intimate places.

The asshole was all even white teeth and fucking dimples. He was sexy and gorgeous and it was all she could do not to jump his bones right then and there with his sister and her boyfriend not fifteen feet away on the other side of the wall.

"God help us is a good way to put it, honey, because you and I are going to be the death of one another," he drawled, that grin still on his face. "So what do you say? Want to get something to eat after I talk to Sophie and Tim?"

Praying that "get something to eat" was a euphemism for something a hell of a lot more personal she nodded her head, not able to get a word out before his lips came down on hers. The kiss was all-consuming and finished much too quickly, leaving her weak-kneed and dizzy.

He pressed a quick kiss to the tip of her nose. "Let me get this over with and then you and I can have some time alone."

Trailing after him as he reentered the front of her shop, Rayne had to admit she was curious as to what Tim and Sophie saw that day. This might be the break they'd been waiting and hoping for.

CHAPTER NINETEEN

"How about these seats?" Rayne pointed to the back row of the movie theatre. They'd driven all the way to Bozeman to see this movie so they didn't have to sneak around. But out of sheer habit they were still doing it. Not wanting to argue, he nodded and they slid into the chairs, settling their popcorn and sodas in the armrest slots.

Dare was tired of sneaking around. For the past two weeks, he and Rayne had been meeting in out of the way places to keep their relationship private. At first it had seemed like the prudent thing to do. The gossip in Valley Station traveled faster than light and a tidbit about the sheriff dating the sexy tattooed newcomer was sure to be tasty. The more salacious the better.

But now it was starting to feel sleazy the way they skulked around as if they were ashamed of one another. The fact was Dare was proud as punch to have Rayne on his arm. He'd learned a thing or two about the fierce little lady since they'd begun dating, and most of it he liked.

Sure, she was outspoken and a trifle loud about her opinions but it came from a place of passion. When she spoke about abused children and animals or the environment, her eyes would light up and she'd get this fierce expression that made his dick painfully hard and his heart flip flop against his ribs.

She hugged hard and kissed harder. She didn't pick at her food like so many women and she could play video games as well as he could. She smelled like vanilla and rain and her skin felt like the softest satin under his fingertips. Unfortunately, he hadn't explored every inch of her flesh yet but he lived in hope. They'd been taking it slow and he was at the end of his proverbial rope. He needed her, wanted her, ached to bury himself deep inside her. She was on his mind constantly when he should be working or sleeping. He had it bad and the only cure was to get the little lady in the sack. Once he'd sated his hunger things would go back to normal.

"Popcorn?" Rayne held out the oversized tub and he grabbed a handful, bending his head to drop a kiss on her cheek in the dark theatre. The lights had dimmed and the previews had started. Grinning happily, she settled back into her chair and rested her head on his shoulder. She'd told him the previews were her favorite part, which cracked him up. She could watch those on her laptop for free but she said it wasn't the same as on a big screen. It was cute that something that simple made her so happy.

The romantic comedy wasn't his kind of film and he ended up spending most of it watching her watch the movie. In the flickering light, her expressions would go from happy to sad in an instant before turning to angry. When the lights finally came up she was dabbing a tissue at her eyes.

"That was so good. Didn't you love it?"

He was a lousy liar, especially with this woman. She could see right through him without breaking a sweat. "Um…I think it was a chick flick, babe. But I'm glad you liked it."

She pushed against his shoulder and giggled. "Too mushy for you, big guy? All that lovey-dovey stuff too icky with girl cooties?"

Girl cooties? This girl was seriously adorable. He was becoming quite fond of those purple streaks in her hair and the half dozen ear piercings.

"I like a man's movie," he boasted with a grin. "Car chases. Maimed bad guys. And explosions. Lots of explosions."

She slapped her forehead and laughed loudly, causing a few heads to swivel but they only displayed indulgent smiles.

"I'm sorry this movie was too touchy-feely, but how about I make it up to you and buy you some ice cream? Any flavor."

Dare pretended to ponder the offer. "Hot fudge and whipped cream?"

"Deal," Rayne instantly agreed. "But there's no cherry in this scenario. That's long gone."

Choking on his laughter, he led them out of the theatre and to the truck. He hadn't had this much fun in years.

Rayne sighed contentedly as she ate the last bite of her hot fudge sundae made with mint chocolate chip ice cream. Dropping the plastic spoon into the paper cup, she sat back in her chair and patted her full stomach.

"That was delicious. Are you enjoying yours?"

While Rayne had ordered a medium-sized sundae, Dare had teasingly ordered a jumbo since she was paying. Of course she wasn't surprised that he'd managed to put a major dent in the sweet confection; his appetite was legendary and she'd seen him put away massive quantities of food.

"I am. So much so that it's almost gone." He pushed the paper cup across the table, closer to her. "Want a bite?"

Rayne wrinkled her nose. "I'm not a big butter pecan fan, especially when you've mixed it with hot fudge. I would have gone with caramel."

"It was a toss-up, but fudge usually beats everything else. This marshmallow cream is pretty good too."

He had strange taste in ice cream, but he was so enthusiastic about it she thought it was sweet.

"Is there anything else you wanted to do while we're here in town?"

"No, do you? I guess it is getting late." Dare checked his watch while a spoonful of hot fudge dripped back into the cup. "It's a long drive back so we should get on the road."

"That sounds good." Rayne slid her purse strap onto her shoulder. "I'm just going to run to the ladies' room before we leave. I'll be right back."

"No problem. I'll check messages."

Dare pulled out his phone and scrolled through his texts and Rayne couldn't help but wonder what the human race had done to look busy before cell phones. Talked to each other, probably.

The bathroom was located down the end of a long hallway and she ducked into the ladies' room and quickly took care of business before touching up her lip gloss. With one last look in the dingy mirror she headed back to the table. A man wearing jeans and a dark hoodie heading in the other direction brushed against her and she stepped to the side, only to have his arm wrap around her middle like a steel band, her breath lodging in her throat.

Before she could react he'd latched onto her purse, tugging it toward himself in an attempt to steal it but she wasn't a pushover. Adrenaline surging with a fight or flight response, she remembered a few things from her self-defense class in college, yelling "fire" and trying to knee him in the groin or elbow him in the solar plexus. She wouldn't give up her handbag without a fight although her palms, slick with sweat, made it difficult to hold onto the soft leather.

The massive size and strength difference put her at a huge disadvantage and her heart accelerated in her chest as she ineffectually wrestled for dominance, his large hands bruising her arms. In seconds, she found herself slammed down on the cold, unforgiving tile, her shoulder and hip taking the brunt of the fall. Wind knocked out of her, she struggled to take a breath as the thief sprinted away and out of the side door, hopping into a truck that had pulled around the building and speeding into the night.

"Christ, are you okay?"

Dare was leaning over her, pulling her to a sitting position, and she winced when his fingers ran across her shoulder. She was going to have a hell of a mark there from this special little interlude.

"I'm...okay. But he got my purse." It took effort to even speak and she sucked in oxygen to hopefully keep the room from spinning. "He got away."

Growling something under his breath, he ran his hands down her arms and legs. "We'll call the police but I'm more worried about you right now. It doesn't look like anything's broken but you might need to go to the hospital. Did you hit your head?"

Rayne raised her gaze from the gray tile and almost passed out again at the sheer rage in Dare's expression. It was probably just as well that the slimy thief had managed to get away because the man before her looked capable of ripping a body from limb to limb.

"No. I'm just banged up. Can you help me to my feet?"

They'd attracted quite the crowd in this tiny hallway and she was feeling claustrophobic. Dizzy, hurting, and still fearful, she needed fresh air and some space. Instead of giving her a hand,

Dare simply scooped her up into his arms, bridal style, and carried her over to a booth in a quiet corner of the shop. The manager was fluttering around them, apologizing in one breath and bitching about her job in another. Apparently she'd wanted to be a dancer.

"The cops are on their way. Can you tell me what happened, babe?"

"Some guy grabbed my purse and made a run for it. I tried to fight him off but he was too strong. He must have had a friend to help him because he jumped into a truck and they peeled out of here."

Dare was scowling again, the smiles and laughter left behind. "A little thing like you probably didn't have much of a chance. I'm just glad you're okay. I've done a shit job of taking care of you tonight."

Rayne ran her fingers over the wrinkles in his forehead. "It isn't your job to take care of me. Besides, I'm fine. But I may need your help when we get back to town. I don't suppose you know how to break into a house? My keys were in my purse and I don't cherish the thought of sleeping on the porch until the locksmith can get there."

His gaze dropped to the floor, and if anything his expression turned darker. There was a hell of a lot more going on here. He smoothed her hair back and tucked a few strands behind her ear.

"I was on the phone when you were attacked, which is why I didn't get to you immediately after you yelled." He sighed heavily and stood, sliding into the booth next to Rayne, his arm around her shoulders. "I was talking to Deputy Billy, hon. Someone broke into your house tonight. Coupled with what happened here? I don't think this purse snatching was an accident. Somebody wants something you have or they think you have."

Fuck me. This seriously can't be happening.

CHAPTER TWENTY

Rayne's home looked like a tornado had run through it. Cushions on the floor, drawers pulled open and the contents tossed, and every item in her closet thrown on the floor. They'd even stripped her bed and cut into her mattress, pulling out the innards.

What in the hell were they looking for?

There was no doubt now that the person in her shop had been searching for something in particular. Something they thought she had and they wanted enough to kill another human being for it. But she had no idea what it could be.

Thankfully the burglar hadn't hurt Spartacus, who she found crouching under the bed. It had taken both her and Dare to coax – make that drag – him out. The feline had added a few scratches to her bruised body, but he was now nibbling on some cat food and allowing one of the deputies to pet him.

She hadn't even realized tears were running down her face until Dare was dabbing at them with a big white handkerchief. "Easy there, babe. It's going to be okay. I promise you."

"Liar," she whispered, shoulders shaking as powerful emotions welled up and came out in the form of sobs. "This is about as awful as it gets. They've fucked up my house, shop, and they've stolen my purse. I'm pissed off. They don't get to do this to me."

She cried when she was angry, so it looked like she was sad when in actuality she wanted to punch someone in the dick. It didn't help that every step she took was pure agony after the body slam she'd been subjected to in the ice cream parlor. Her left side hurt like a bitch. She was going to sport a lovely mixture of purple, blue, and black tomorrow.

"You need to sit down and I still think you need to see a doctor. You can barely move, woman."

He was growling again but she didn't argue as he led her to a chair in the kitchen. Her sofa and recliner were destroyed, long cuts in the fabric and the stuffing thrown everywhere. Her gut clenched painfully at the thought of some stranger pawing through her belongings, including her lingerie.

Assholes. Perverts.

There was a special place in hell for whoever did this.

Rayne cupped Dare's jaw and turned his face so she could look into his icy blue eyes, almost silver-gray in this light. "I want you to find who did this and kick their ass."

"I promise. But you can't stay here tonight. The forensic team is really just getting started and your bed is destroyed anyway. I can take you to my place or I can call your sister."

Camy would have kittens if she saw Rayne beat up like this, but staying at Dare's seemed so…intimate. She was already panting after him and sleeping under the same roof wouldn't make things any better. "I can stay at a motel."

"You cannot stay at a fucking motel." Dare's brows were pulled down and his forehead wrinkled. "You need someone to keep an eye on you. If you don't want to worry your sister then you're staying with me."

Rayne didn't have the energy to argue and she simply nodded, gathering her sweater around her more closely, suddenly feeling cold and vulnerable. She didn't know what these people wanted, and if they didn't find it she didn't know what they'd do. Tonight they'd only knocked her down but later she might not be so lucky.

"Why don't you pack a bag? You might be at my place for a few days. It may take awhile to get this all cleaned up."

That was an understatement. It would be easier to bulldoze the place down and start again.

Carefully she stood, putting most of her weight on her right leg before slowly walking back to her bedroom. One glance at the utter devastation and her stomach lurched dangerously, sending her directly to the bathroom to hurl her hot fudge sundae, buttered popcorn, and bacon cheeseburger into the toilet. Sliding down to the floor with her back propped against the bathroom vanity, she grabbed a towel and wiped her mouth, groaning at the acrid taste on her tongue.

Gross. She hated throwing up and avoided it all costs.

"Jesus, I'm taking you to the doctor right now. No arguments."

Tears leaked down her cheeks and it was hard to breathe with the feeling of helplessness weighing down on her chest like a lead balloon. The fight had leaked right out of her and all she wanted to do was curl up in a ball on her bed and sleep for a week.

Except her bed was demolished. Shit, she didn't even have a place to be depressed. How sad-sack was that? Right now she was a big old loser.

Dare scooped her up again just as he had at the ice cream parlor and carried her back into the bedroom, setting her on the torn-up mattress. This was becoming a habit and she kind of liked it. He was so much bigger and stronger than she was he

143

could literally pick her up and put her anywhere he wanted to and she hadn't given him a whisper of protest either time. She had a feeling it was something that was going to happen quite a bit.

"I'm fine. Whenever I'm upset it goes straight to my stomach. What I need to do is brush my teeth."

Standing in the center of the room, Dare's gaze darted to each corner of the devastation and then back to her.

"I can pack for you if you like. What do you want to take?"

Rayne reached out her hand and he placed his in hers, their fingers tangling together. His hand was big and warm and just the thing to make her feel slightly sane in the midst of all this chaos. She was glad she was going home with him. It was truly the only place she'd feel safe.

"That...person who was here touched everything. That's what made me boot my dinner and snacks. I can't wear clothes that he's fondled. I have a gym bag in the trunk of my car with a change of clothes and some toiletries in it. I'll just take that. Tomorrow I'll buy new clothes."

The way she felt at the moment there wasn't enough detergent in the world to get her clothes clean enough to wear again. They were tainted and held bad memories. As far as she knew there wasn't a stain remover strong enough for bad karma.

"It's going to be okay." Dare knelt down in front of her, his hands resting on her knees. "I know you're freaked out right now but I'm not going to let anything happen to you."

Scraping her hands down her face, she sniffled at the tears she was trying to hold at bay. "What in the hell do they want? What are they looking for?"

"We're going to find out." He swept a few stray tears away from her cheek. "I'm going to ask something of you, Rayne, and

I know it's going to be hard but I want you to try. I need you to trust me. Can you do that? Can you trust that I'm going to keep you safe and find out who did this?"

Experience with men in the past told her that ultimately she couldn't depend on anyone but herself to take care of things when the shit went down. Hadn't her mother constantly harped on the fact that a woman had to stand up and take care of herself? It had been ingrained from an early age.

But her heart was telling a different story. It wanted to extend that trust Dare was asking for and believe when he said he would protect her. As an adult woman, it wasn't often she needed to ask for safety but this was an exceptional moment. She couldn't do this on her own and even if she could, it wouldn't be easy.

"I trust you. I do. It's just not my normal behavior to hide behind someone like a scared little girl."

"It might not be normal but, honey, it's smart. You're being targeted and we don't know why. Until we do, I'm going to have a guard on you every moment of the day. You're going to get good and sick of my company."

"Not before you get sick of mine. I'm used to living alone and I probably have some anti-social habits."

For one, she snored. She also liked to eat right out of the refrigerator and she was bad about cleaning up after herself. She also liked to fall asleep watching cheesy television. None of these behaviors would endear her to a roommate.

"Me too," he agreed. "As I said, you're going to run screaming from the house within twenty-four hours. Just wait. Sophie says I'm like a bear with a sore paw in the morning."

"How about we agree to not speak to each other until our second cup of coffee?"

"Sounds like a good plan. Now let's get you back to my place. You can soak in a hot bath and have a drink. A big one."

It was the best offer she'd had all night, and that included the ice cream and popcorn.

CHAPTER TWENTY-ONE

Rayne wrapped the terry cloth robe around her still damp body, covering up the black and blue bruises that had already formed on her hip, thigh, and shoulder. The hot bath had helped the initial soreness but she was going to be hurting for a few days at least. She needed to ask Sophie or Dare if they had any ibuprofen. Or a rubber mallet to smack herself in the forehead so she'd sleep. Either one would work fine.

There was a small knock on the door and Rayne tightened the belt on the borrowed robe. By the sheer size it had to be Dare's, as it swamped her smaller figure but she didn't have much in the way of clothes in that gym bag. A pair of panties, socks, jeans, bra, and a sweater were the only items she had to put on and she needed them for the morning. The robe would have to do for what was left of the evening.

Rayne cracked open the door cautiously. "Yes?"

Sophie held out a handful of clothes – yellow with daisies. "Dare thought you might like something to wear to bed so I brought you one of my pajama sets. It should probably fit you okay."

Opening the door wider, Rayne gave the younger woman a big smile. Sophie had been more than welcoming when Dare had informed her that Rayne was spending the night and perhaps longer. In fact, Rayne would even call Sophie's reaction excited, exclaiming that the balance of estrogen and testosterone in the house had shifted. Rayne had giggled along with Sophie and Dare had glowered.

He'd worn that same expression when he'd questioned Tim and Sophie about the day they'd been in the same restaurant as the murder victim. Sadly neither one of them remembered the man or had any information that would help the case.

"Thank you so much. I know I'm being a pain dropping in here unexpectedly like this. I'm really very grateful."

"Are you kidding? It's awesome having company and I love your cat. He's found a spot on my windowsill that he seems to really like. I hope that's okay. I just feel bad about what happened to you tonight. That really sucks. How long do you think it will take to clean up? I can help you if you like."

Since Misty was in Seattle Rayne might take her up on that offer. "I'm not sure. I'll need to order a new bed and furniture but I can't touch anything until the insurance adjuster comes by and takes pictures. Hopefully he'll come tomorrow, but the big thing I need to do is go buy a new wardrobe. It gives me the willies thinking about wearing clothes that this guy touched."

Rayne shuddered and Sophie made a sympathetic face. "If you're looking for a buddy to go shopping with I'm your gal. I'd love to go. If I can't buy new clothes I can at least enjoy helping you."

"You don't need any more clothes, young lady. Your closet is overflowing as it is." Dare's booming voice traveled from down the hall. "Give Rayne the pajamas and ask her to join me in the living room. I have her drink."

Alcohol. That sounded perfect.

Sophie rolled her eyes with such an expression of disdain

that it instantly brought back all of Rayne's teenage years in one fell swoop. "Yes, O brother dear. Hold your horses, will you? She just got out of the bathtub."

"I'll be out in a few minutes. I just need to brush my hair."

Rayne accepted the nightclothes from Sophie, who giggled and pointed down the hallway to where her brother had stood seconds before. "Take your time. Dare's always barking about something but he doesn't bite. Although he might if you ask him to. He's single, you know."

Before Rayne could reply Sophie sped off down the hall and down the stairs, leaving Rayne to quickly change into the pajama shorts and tank top, the latter quite snug. She had larger breasts than Sophie and the material was pulled tight across her nipples. In a modicum of modesty, Rayne shrugged the robe back on before heading down to the living room, a cocktail calling her name.

"Are you feeling any better?" Dare asked, holding out the highball glass of amber liquid. She'd assured him she could drink whiskey with the boys and he'd clearly listened. He hadn't skimped on the amount, the glass half full. She couldn't wait to feel the burn down her throat and then the inevitable mellow haze that would follow. With any luck, she'd sleep soundly tonight and not lie awake thinking about events she couldn't control.

"Yes, thank you. The bath was just what I needed." She accepted the glass and took a large gulp, closing her eyes to savor the flavor on her tongue. "I'm going to be a glorious rainbow of purple and blue tomorrow, though. I hope that jerk gets a bad case of hemorrhoids."

Lips quirking slightly, Dare took a long drink of his beer before waving his hand toward the sofa. "Why don't you sit down and relax? I can put in a movie if you like. Sophie has all the latest, I believe."

"No, thanks." Rayne eased down on the couch, her body protesting every movement. "What I'd really like to hear is if you found anything. You said your sheriff friend was going to join you at the house."

After Dare had dropped her at his home with Sophie, he'd posted a deputy at the door and then returned to her place. The entire situation should have reminded her of jail but instead the guard made her feel safe.

"Tanner did join me. Unfortunately, we didn't find anything that would help us figure out who did this. The forensic crew might come up with something though. At least that's my hope. In the meantime you'll be protected at all times. I won't have them coming back and hurting you."

She was scared; she couldn't deny that, but was she truly in danger? "They left me alone tonight. If they want something that means they don't care about me, right? I mean, it's not like they want me dead or anything."

There was a great deal of hope in her voice, and by the look on Dare's face it shouldn't be there. "Honey, they knew where you were tonight. They knew you were at the ice cream parlor and that your house was empty. Think about that for a moment."

Frowning, she mulled his words over in her mind. Nothing seemed out of place. Of course criminals would prefer to come when she wasn't there. It would make their job much easier. She was about to ask him what he was talking about when it hit her like a two by four across the back of the head.

"Damn. They were following us. Following me. They've been watching me. Oh God, that is so creepy."

A frisson of fear ran down her spine and she pulled her knees to her chest, wrapping her arms around her legs. The violation of being watched, followed, stripped every sense of comfort from her and her body trembled, raw fear bubbling in her already nauseous abdomen. She couldn't imagine what she'd done to deserve this and she wanted it to stop. Immediately, if not sooner. She was a private person who liked to keep to herself, always had been. This invasion of her life was not something she could tolerate.

"Probably waiting for the perfect moment." Dare came to sit beside her and pulled her onto his lap, stroking her spine soothingly. "I'm actually surprised they didn't try to break into your home during the day, but I think we can thank your erratic daily appointment schedule for that. They never knew when you would be home or away. Until tonight, of course, when I took you out of town. Then they had plenty of time to look through your home, plus send someone to steal your purse, thinking that it would look like a simple mugging. But after tonight we have learned a few things. I know it's not much of a consolation prize, though, after all you've been through these last few weeks."

For once, Rayne allowed herself to draw strength from Dare, snuggling into his arms and laying her head on his shoulder. "If anything good came from this I would like to know about it. What did you learn?"

"We learned that there has to be more than one man. Someone was at your home at the same time you were mugged. That's at least two, if not more. I'm thinking three or four based on the general destruction they wreaked on your home." His fingers languidly stroked her cheek and her eyelids fluttered shut in response, her breathing growing ragged. "The second thing we learned is they want what they think you have more than they want you. That's damn good news. The bad news is if they get desperate and don't want to keep looking."

"Then they'll torture it out of me," Rayne finished for him, her eyes snapping open. "That's something to look forward to. Being beaten for the location of something that I don't even know exists. Lucky me."

She didn't mean the words to come out so bitterly, but the whole evening was so screwed up. She wanted her life to go back to when her worst problem was keeping Camy from criticizing Rayne's hair color and tattoos.

Or as she would call them from now on…the good old days.

Dare gently turned her face so she was gazing directly into his eyes. "No one—let me repeat that—no one is going to be beating anything out of you, missy. I'm going to make sure that you are absolutely safe until we get these guys and put them behind bars. I just wish we could figure out what they're looking for. I was thinking that perhaps our victim hid the bank robbery money in your shop and then came back for it. Did you ever leave him alone?"

"No. He never even left the front counter area of the shop. We talked and then he left with the promise to be back the next day. I never saw him again, at least not until that night."

Rubbing the back of his neck, Dare sighed in frustration. "We'll figure it out. Maybe Moulson was distracting you in the front of the shop while one of his cronies was hiding the money in the back. It would be the last place anyone would look for stolen cash. Do you keep that door locked at all times?"

"Sometimes it's open for deliveries." She shifted uncomfortably on the cushion. "After what happened with the fire in my last shop I tend to keep the doors unlocked. I have an irrational fear of being trapped when it's ablaze. I know it's silly but I can't help it. And please don't bother asking which it was that day because I honestly couldn't tell you. But I will say that when I do get deliveries I can hear them from the front where I'm working."

"If someone deliberately didn't want you to hear it might be different."

Rayne sipped at her whiskey. "But we didn't find any money. Do you think Moulson got it and hid it before he was shot? Is it outside somewhere?"

Dare's hold tightened on her and he pressed a tender kiss to her temple. Helpless against this sweet side to the sheriff, Rayne allowed herself to be petted and comforted. "I'll check again tomorrow. In the meantime, you look exhausted. Do you want me to show you to your room so you can get some sleep?"

The whiskey was doing its work and she was pleasantly drowsy. "I think I am ready for some shut eye. Lead the way."

Rayne allowed Dare to help her to her feet before heading upstairs, his touch gentle on her bruised body. Hopefully things would look much brighter after a good night's sleep because she had a buttload of crappy things to deal with in the morning. Thank heavens Dare had given her a strong shoulder to lean on. Tonight he'd shown her the tenderness and care he was capable of. All the growling and scowling in the world didn't cover up the fact that he was a good, kind man.

The kind of man she could fall for. Big.

CHAPTER TWENTY-TWO

"She's pretty," Sophie remarked when Dare came back downstairs to grab a snack from the kitchen. He hoped Rayne could get some sleep after all she'd been through tonight and all the unanswered questions. "You should totally ask her on a date. I think she's into you."

With everything that had happened, he'd completely forgotten his relationship with Rayne was a secret. So it was amusing to hear his sister urge him to ask their houseguest on a date.

Popping some cubed cheddar cheese into his mouth, he chewed and swallowed before answering. "What makes you think she's into me?"

"The way she looks at you. You know, like she doesn't care that you're a big old grouch who is never happy. So are you going to ask her out? Did you kiss her goodnight?"

He hadn't and that had been a major disappointment. As he'd walked her to the guest room, he'd been able to smell the clean scent of her skin and his body reacted predictably. A sweet scented woman and a bed were a recipe for only one thing.

A raging hard-on.

His cock didn't understand that simply because there was a comfortable horizontal surface nearby didn't mean Rayne was willing or even able to assuage his lust. She'd been covered in bruises, after all, and limping badly because of her hip. He'd have been a real asshole to try and make a move on an injured, frightened woman.

"You're nosy," Dare finally shot back at his little sister. "I'm not one of your BFFs that you can giggle with and talk about boys while practicing kissing on a pillow. Rayne is a classy lady and doesn't deserve to have anyone gossip about her."

Sophie's brow wrinkled in confusion. "Kissing a pillow? Who does that? Did you do that when you were a teenager?"

"Focus, Sophie," Dare growled in a warning tone.

"That's right. You were never a teenager. Or even a child. You popped out of the womb a grown adult with the temperament to match. What a party pooper."

With that, his sister flounced up the stairs but at least had the good sense not to slam her bedroom door and wake Rayne. With a shake of his head he finished his snack and headed to bed, knowing tomorrow would be a long day. He'd have to put a search team in the woods behind Rayne's shop – again – and hope the second time would be more productive than the first.

Stripping out of his clothes, he quickly brushed his teeth and crawled, exhausted, between the covers. He'd barely closed his eyes when he heard a woman's scream that sounded a lot like Rayne, jolting him from sleep. Heart in his throat, he glanced at the bedside clock and saw that he'd actually been asleep for a little over four hours. Jumping out of bed, he ran down the hall to the guest room and didn't bother to knock, throwing open the door.

Rayne was sitting up, her breathing labored and her body curled into a ball. He could hear her sobs and see her shoulders shaking with emotion. As much as he himself was uncomfortable displaying his softer or more joyous feelings, he didn't hesitate to sit next to her on the bed and wrap his arms around her shaking figure.

"Shhh, babe. It's okay. You're fine. I'm here and I'm not going to let anything hurt you ever again, do you understand?"

He kept his voice low and soothing, crooning praise in her ear as she tried to gather some semblance of control. Hiccuping, she took a long shuddering breath and scrubbed at the tears on her face. At this moment, she looked more like a lost child than a grown woman but the body that was pressed close to his was definitely mature. He could feel the tips of her breasts through the thin material of their t-shirts and feel the petal-like softness of her skin brushing against his as she scooted to find a more comfortable position.

"I had a bad dream."

Running his fingers through her tangled tresses, he rocked her in his arms as her breathing and heart rate returned to normal. Her fingers gripped his lower back, the fingers splayed and her cheek was pressed to his chest as he spoke quietly, telling her over and over that everything was fine and nothing would happen to her while he was there.

"Dare?" He heard Sophie's voice in the hallway. "Is everything okay? Does Rayne need anything?"

Rayne stiffened in his arms but didn't pull away, which he took to be a good sign. "Yes, go downstairs into the kitchen and pour her a glass of ginger ale. She's probably thirsty."

Sophie's footsteps echoed down the hallway and stairs as Dare cupped Rayne's chin and lifted her face until their gaze met in the dark room, the only light coming from the hallway. "Do you want something to eat or anything? I can have Sophie make you some eggs or toast."

"No." Rayne gave a small headshake, sniffling back the tears. It broke his heart to see her this scared when she was normally so brave and confident. It was a testament to her strength that she hadn't succumbed to tears a long time ago. "I couldn't eat. But the ginger ale does sound good."

Dare had thought it might, especially if her nightmare had upset her already nauseous stomach. "It might help to talk about it."

Another shudder ran through her and she pulled away slightly as if she needed more breathing room. Dare loosened his hold but didn't let go, knowing she needed the emotional support whether she realized it or not.

"I dreamt someone came in the bedroom window." She pointed to the window along the wall that overlooked the back yard. "They tried to grab me and I struggled with them. They kept asking me 'where is it?' and I tried to tell them I didn't know but they wouldn't listen."

Fresh tears began to fall as Sophie returned from fetching a cool drink and Dare held the straw to Rayne's trembling lips. "Drink, honey. It will make you feel better."

With both hands to keep the glass steady, Rayne greedily drank until it was gone. "Easy there, honey. Do you want some more?"

"No, I'm fine." Rayne fell back against the pillows with a groan. "Dammit, I hate being like this."

Dare placed the empty glass on the nightstand and picked up her hand, stroking the palm. "Like what? Human? You've been through some unusual events and they're going to affect you. If you don't deal with it now I guarantee you it only gets worse."

Half sitting up, Rayne wrinkled her nose. "Do you speak from experience? Is this a story I haven't heard?"

"Baby, I was in combat, so yes, I speak from experience, and no, you're not going to hear any stories. I don't talk about those days at all. They're best left in the past. But I did have to deal with them, so don't even think about denying that you're upset and scared. The first step is to acknowledge your emotions."

Damn, he sounded like the shrink he'd seen when he came back from the Middle East, but all that therapy had helped him. He was in a hell of a lot better shape now than those first few years.

Sophie was still standing next to the dresser, and if Rayne needed to talk more in depth she might feel strange in front of the younger woman. He needed to shoo Sophie back into her own room.

"Don't you have to get up early, Sophie? You should check on the cat too."

Sophie was employed at the local bakery while she worked at her painting and drawing. She was incredibly talented and Dare was proud of his sister and how hard she worked on her craft. She talked about going into graphic design or perhaps even textile design. Whatever she did, he knew she'd work hard and succeed.

Without Tim Wallace.

Sophie must have been half-asleep on her feet because she snapped to attention at his words. "Spartacus is asleep. But yeah, I need to be at the bakery by four but I'll be off work by noon. Maybe we can go shopping in the afternoon, Rayne."

"I'd like that," Rayne replied softly. "I'm sorry I woke you up, especially as you have such an early wake up call. Thank you for taking care of Spartacus."

"It's no big deal. He's a good kitty. I don't need much sleep." Sophie bumped her shoulder before turning to leave. "Call me if you need anything. I'm just down the hall."

Once they were alone again, Dare lifted her hand and brushed the knuckles with his lips. It was frightening how quickly she'd crawled under his skin and burrowed into a hole in his heart he hadn't even known was empty. He wasn't in love with her or anything. It was way too soon to be talking about that kind of emotion. But he did care about her. She was like a tiny kitten, ferocious one minute and heartbreakingly vulnerable and sweet the next. It had been a long damn time since he'd dated a woman he cared about this much.

"Do you want to talk some more about it, honey? This house is really safe. No one is going to come through that window. Not only is it locked, but I have extra self-installed locks as well, plus we're on the second floor and they'd have to be Spiderman to climb the outside of the house."

Sitting up, Rayne's gaze fell to the floor and then returned as she nervously licked her lips.

"Will you stay with me? Just until I fall asleep?"

His arousal reared its ugly head and he had to remind himself she asked that question in the most innocent way possible. She wanted to feel protected and cared for, and ramming her from behind with his hard dick wasn't the way to do that. Instead he lifted the covers and slid in beside her, the sheets cool against his overheated flesh.

He could do this. He could be there for her without his libido getting in the way. But that didn't mean it would be easy.

"I'll stay with you as long as you need me to. Just scoot over a little, okay?"

She did as he bade but not nearly enough for his comfort and peace of mind. He stretched out on the bed with her curled next to him, her head on his chest and her leg thrown over both of his, sending his pulse rate through the roof. He had to focus not to roll over and trap her body under his.

Wrapping an arm around her slight frame, he dropped a kiss on the top of her head, her hair silky under his lips. Their position was both heaven and hell, pleasure and pain. The feeling of intimacy as he held her was sublime but the throbbing demand of a certain portion of his anatomy was making it *hard* to sleep.

Pun completely intended.

It was going to be a long night.

CHAPTER TWENTY-THREE

Rayne was warm. Quite warm, bordering on stifling hot. It was like she was lying in bed next to a blast furnace that only had one setting – surface of the sun. She wasn't the happiest of morning people and she'd slept like hell last night until Dare had come in to soothe her after a nasty nightmare.

Dare.

Not bothering to open her sleepy eyes, she wriggled against the heat source and was poked by something long and hard for her trouble. Her lids flew open and she realized she had just rubbed herself against a very aroused male animal with an unknown appetite. Did he wake up like a pussycat and toddle off to make breakfast or was he a voracious panther that wanted to devour his bedmate?

Having sex with Dare hadn't been forefront in her mind last night when she'd been so frightened but it was now, crowding out any other rational thoughts. His body was pressed up against the back of hers, and she could feel not only the heat emanating from his skin but the dip and planes of his muscles. Her fingers itched to trace them, following some unseen map and exploring heretofore undiscovered territory.

Just lying next to him, smelling his masculine scent, was

ratcheting up her arousal and sending messages of lust and desire to her brain. She didn't want to think about the mess of her house or her stolen purse or her ransacked shop. She really didn't want to think about that man that had been shot behind her building. If only for a little while, she wanted to pretend none of that happened and she was simply enjoying an early morning with a gorgeous, sweet man.

As if he could read her thoughts, Dare's hand slid from her shoulder to her hip, his fingers tightening on the rounded flesh while his other hand came around the back of her head, turning her lips toward his own. His impressive cock was trapped between their bodies and she could feel it pulse with each beat of his heart.

"Good morning," she breathed mere seconds before he captured her lips with his own. Reaching around, she slid her arm around his neck and ran her fingers through his silky brown hair, delighting in the shudder of his body at her ministrations. Dare wouldn't be her first man but she'd had a hot and cold sex life. Few men truly understood what she liked and craved and she could only hope Dare would be one of them. "You stayed with me."

"I said I would be here as long as you needed me." Dare's voice rumbled in his chest, sexy and growly in the morning. "Do you want me to leave, Rayne?"

He was asking more than that and she gave him her answer by pushing her ass back against his hard erection nestled between her cheeks. Groaning his approval, he kissed a wet trail from her lips, over her jaw, and down to where her pulse beat frantically at the base of her neck before sucking on the delicate flesh. Her nails dug into his bicep at the zip of pain even while he soothed the hurt with his tongue.

A flood of moisture soaked her sleep shorts and she pressed

her thighs together to ease the building ache deep inside. His tongue traced an intricate pattern on the sensitive flesh of her shoulder before blowing gently on the artwork – a pale pink rosebud – and sending shivers of pleasure straight to her clit.

His rough hands cupped her breasts, the thumbs brushing back and forth over the tips and driving her slowly out of her mind. He'd barely touched her really, but already she was on fire for him, flames licking at her skin and the heat making her gasp and moan with absolute sinful pleasure.

"What do you need? Tell me and I'll make sure you get it."

His urgent tone only served to amp up her arousal even higher. Turning in his arms, she dropped kisses onto the hard planes of his chest and abdomen, letting her tongue dip into his belly button. Reaching out, she tugged at his boxer shorts, wanting to rid him of anything that kept her from her goal. He chuckled and helped her slide them down his muscular thighs, tossing them aside without a second thought.

His cock, thick and long, sprung free and she sucked in a breath at the thought of him deep inside of her, fucking her fast and hard. That was her favorite and what she craved, although she'd found that men seemed to be reluctant to use her as roughly as she wanted them to. It was as if she was made of fine china and they thought she might break. Consequently, she was often left wanting and frustrated when the sex was done and the guy rolled over to fall asleep. She didn't want that to happen with Dare. If this relationship had any future, she needed him to understand. She'd do anything for him as well as long as it didn't involve a goat or an underage cheerleader.

"Give it to me rough, hard, and fast. That's what I need."

Pulling back, Dare gazed at her with worry in his blue eyes, now dark with passion. A sweeping glance down her body told her he was concerned about her size compared to his and he needn't. He'd never hurt her, of that she was quite sure.

"I won't break." She wrapped her fingers around his cock, hot and pulsing under her palm, and slowly began an up and down motion from root to tip. He closed his eyes and sighed as he thrust into her hand a few times before drawing back with a moan.

"I won't break either, baby. I'm a big man and can handle some roughhousing. I like my sex raw and dirty so I'm in sync with you there. If you're sure, that is. I can give you what you want but you need to be sure you understand what that means."

A rush of pure unadulterated desire welled up inside of her, creating a tight coil of arousal in her abdomen that almost stole her very breath away.

"I'm sure," she panted, scooting down until the head of his cock was level with her eager mouth. She couldn't wait to taste him and feel him slide over her tongue. "I'm tougher than I look."

"You said you liked fast, and this first time probably will be because I'm already too far gone to hold back much. But after that I'm going to take my time fucking you. I may like it down and dirty but I don't like to be rushed. I want to savor all the naughty things I'm going to do to your delectable little body."

Rayne didn't bother to reply with words, instead engulfing the head of his cock with her mouth and sliding down his length until he bumped the back of her throat. Dare let out a ragged groan as she tightened her lips to create the tightest, wettest pussy she could before pulling back up to the tip and then pushing back down. She wanted to give him the most authentic feeling of fucking her mouth and he clearly thought she was doing something right. His hands tangled in her hair, guiding her head up and down as his dick conquered her mouth.

"Fuck, that's so good," he grunted. "Never been so hot and

tight before."

Her fingers fondled his balls already pulled high against his body. He was close and she couldn't help but feel a surge of pride that she'd sent him this far this fast. So she was shocked when he tucked his hands under her arms and lifted her off of him, her lips sliding off with a loud pop. Giggling, she allowed him to quickly shuck off her tank top and sleep shorts, lying back to let him look his fill. She'd never been ashamed of her body although it wasn't near perfect. Her boobs and hips were too generous and her legs too short, but her waist was tiny and her thighs strong so it wasn't all bad. Men seemed to like what they saw just fine.

His fingers reached out to trace the butterfly tattoo on her ribcage, the touches light but effective, sending sparks of electricity straight to her clit. She writhed under his close regard but he clearly wouldn't be rushed. All of this would happen at his pace.

Dare was licking his lips as if she was a sweet dessert on a buffet and he hadn't eaten in week. Wait, make that a month. His eyes almost glowed with devilment and she decided to let him take the lead and see what he came up with. She'd asked for rough and hard and she dearly hoped he could give it to her.

"You want it rough? Hang on then. But if it's too much all you have to do is tell me to stop and I will in a split second. If you're not enjoying something just let me know."

His head dipped and he caught a beaded nipple between his teeth, biting down until she yipped with pain but her body responded as if he'd lavished the most luxurious pleasure on her. Her pussy clenched with need and her clit swelled in anticipation of what he might have in store for it. She tried to rub her thighs together but Dare was having none of that.

He chuckled and placed his big body in between her legs so

they were spread wide. "No, ma'am. You don't get to relieve the pressure. You wanted it like this and I'm going to give it to you. I'm going to make all your fantasies come true."

She'd had so many raunchy dreams they'd be here all week. Not that it was a bad thing if they were. It wasn't. But they both had to make a living, not to mention catch a few bad guys.

"What are your fantasies?" she asked as he suckled on the rosy tip of her breast, pulling it to the roof of his mouth as she wriggled and squirmed under his questing fingers. One hand plucked and pinched at the other nipple while the other traveled down her torso and over her hip until it sat at the entrance of her drenched pussy.

He didn't press those digits inside of her, but instead drew out the pleasure by tracing her folds everywhere but the spot she needed it most, coating his hand in her honey. She thrashed underneath him but his size and strength easily held her under his control. She'd asked for this and he was giving her what she wanted, and then some.

"Baby, you're my fantasy. A woman who is comfortable enough to know what she likes and isn't afraid to ask for it. But be warned, my treasure." That smile that never ceased to knock her over was in full force, wicked and gleeful. "Before this is over, you won't be asking. You'll be begging. You see, that's what I like. I can't wait for the pleas to let you come fall from those pretty full lips."

For a man who didn't say much or hardly smile, he had his dirty talk down pat.

"I don't beg so I can't see me doing it now."

She glanced pointedly down at his reddish-purple cock glistening with precum at the tip. She'd never found a man that could hold back longer than she could and as much as Dare had impressed her so far, she doubted she had now. He'd give in far earlier than she would.

"I'm completely in control. Can you say the same?"

Before she could even begin to answer he thrust two thick fingers into her wet pussy, making her cry out with pleasure and pain. Any discomfort quickly dissolved as he found and stroked that sweet spot inside of her while his lips, tongue, and teeth tortured her nipples until they were delightfully sensitive and sore. White hot heat swept through her veins and the coil of arousal tightened in her belly until she could barely breathe. Her clit begged for attention and she reached down to touch it, but he slapped her hands away with an evil grin.

"Uh uh, naughty girl. No touching yourself. That's my job now and I take it very seriously. You'll wait until I say and not a second before."

Why had she ever wanted him to smile? Now that he was, he looked more than a little dangerous but definitely exciting. His emotional unpredictability was part of his allure.

"Alpha bastard," she whispered accusingly but moved her hand back to her side, clutching the sheets between white-knuckled fingers.

His head bent, he gave her slit a long lick from opening to clit, his tongue tracing the same trail his fingers had blazed only moments earlier. Changing up the rhythm, he never lingered long in one area and deliberately avoided the swollen button that would send her straight to paradise. Rayne's entire being was shaking with arousal, white-hot and powerful. She lost herself to the maelstrom and allowed herself to be pulled down into the dancing flames. Her lids fluttered closed and her world became this moment with this man. Nothing else existed. No demands. No problems. Just pure ecstasy delivered courtesy of Dare Turner.

"Please." Rayne barely recognized her own voice, but damn

if she hadn't begged. Despite the pain he must be in he'd held back until she barely knew her own name. Need and want were her overriding emotions and he played on them like a virtuoso.

"Yes, baby. I want you to come for me now. Come all over my fingers."

Sucking her clit into his mouth, he lightly scraped the sides with his teeth, sending her into orbit. Like a freight train crashing into a wall going a hundred miles an hour, her orgasm slammed into her, making her scream out Dare's name, her voice hoarse and needy. Her fingers curled into his hair as she rode his lips and tongue through her climax. It left her shaky and disoriented but he didn't give her a minute to recover.

Rayne found herself flipped gently over onto her belly, his hands on her hips pulling her back onto her knees so her ass was high in the air, being extra careful of the bruises on her left hipbone. His palm caressed a buttcheek as he pressed wet kisses along her spine and shoulders.

"Are you sure about this? I'll give you the ride of your life but I need to hear it from your lips. Tell me you want it."

Dear God in heaven, Rayne wanted it so badly she could taste the sweet and spicy pleasure already. He was afraid of hurting her but she knew deep down he could never do her permanent damage. A few bruises and sore muscles seemed like a small price to pay for the sin he was about to lavish upon them both.

"Give it to me," she hissed. "Hard. Fast. Rough. Do it."

His cock traced her wet pussy and rubbed against her clit until she keened with pleasure and frustration. She tried to push back against him but he simply chuckled and held her easily.

Leaning down close to her ear, she felt him whisper, his breath warm on her neck. "Do I need a condom? I'm clean and haven't been with anyone since my last physical."

Rayne had to give him props that he was still thinking clearly. Protection hadn't even drifted into her pleasure-addled brain.

Panting with excitement and anticipation, she shot an impatient but grateful look over her shoulder. "I have an IUD. You're good to go. Fuck me."

"Hold on."

Digging her elbows into the mattress, Rayne braced herself and slid her knees farther apart into a more comfortable position. She needn't have bothered though as Dare simply held her by her hips and lifted her off the bed so her bent legs rested on his powerful thighs. His cock nudged at her entrance and he gently pushed the head into her welcoming pussy, the broad tip stretching muscles she hadn't used in way too long.

Desperate to be filled, Rayne wriggled her hips in invitation but Dare's fingers only tightened on her waist in response. This fucking was on his timetable only.

Before she could catch her breath, he'd thrust his cock in to the hilt so he was balls deep inside of her, the walls of her pussy struggling to accommodate his large girth. With one stroke he'd pushed all the oxygen from her lungs and she struggled to inhale as he set up a punishing, brutal pace that had her pressing her cheek against the bed and clawing at the bedspread for purchase.

The room was filled with the sound of skin slapping on skin and tortured groans and pleas, most of them from her own lips. The heavy musk of sex, sweat, and pheromones hung in the air, teasing her nostrils and amping up her arousal. Dare's fingers tangled roughly in her hair, pulling back until she was looking over her left shoulder. His hold just tight enough that he was giving her what she wanted but not so violent that it was painful.

"Watch me fuck you. Don't close your eyes or I won't let you come."

It all became a blur. His hips snapping over and over again, driving his cock deeper than she'd ever had before. At one point he changed the angle of his thrusts to hit her g-spot and with every stroke he sent her higher and higher until she was hanging on the precipice waiting and hoping to fall over the edge.

So fucking good. She'd be sore later but she didn't care. He rode her hard and mercilessly and it was everything she'd ever hoped for and more. This was what she'd craved for so long but had been denied.

Dare was battering her pussy so hard she'd scooted up on the mattress, her fingers fisting the pillows as if it was her last hold onto sanity and the real world. But the real world was wildly overrated.

"Dare...please...now..."

Her verbal skills had long abandoned her as flames licked up and down her limbs and settled low in her belly. Pressure built in her abdomen, coiled so tightly she was almost fearful of its detonation and whether she could survive.

Afraid he'd keep his promise and not let her orgasm, her gaze had never left Dare. His skin glistened with a fine sheen of sweat and the cords on his neck stood out in stark relief as he pounded her hard and fast. His jaw had clicked shut and his blue eyes were almost black with passion and he looked beautifully masculine and – for now, at least – all hers.

"It's time."

Those were his only words but not his only action. He reached around and placed two fingers on her clit, pressing and rubbing the swollen button. Rayne's entire body froze, every muscle contracting in excruciating pain, but then the pleasure washed through her bones all the way to her fingers and toes. Wave after wave shook her world and she let it all pour over her in a psychedelic rainbow of sensation until it slowly ebbed away, leaving her worn out and limp.

At some point Dare had also reached his peak, growling as he so often did, but this one was far more feral and wild and it sent a pleasant shiver up her spine as they collapsed together, landing in a heap of arms and legs. Their breathing ragged, they gulped in air to their starved lungs as the sweat cooled on their skin. Dare eventually rolled onto his back, his arm still around her waist so she was tucked up next to him. Lying in his arms, she allowed herself the luxury to feel safe, warm, and cared for if only for a few more minutes. The real world would intrude soon enough.

She was half asleep when a loud *meow* startled her and she sat up in bed, the chilly air puckering her nipples. Spartacus sat on the nightstand wearing a look of total disgust on his whiskered face.

Dare scowled at the furry intruder, apparently not enjoying the idea of a feline critic of his technique. "Shit, how long has that cat been in the bedroom? I bet Sophie put him in here when she left for work this morning. Do you think he watched us?"

Laughter bubbled up at the absurdity of the situation. She'd gotten laid for the first time in forever and her cat had witnessed the whole thing. Spartacus might be getting revenge for having him fixed. Or maybe he was a furry little perv. Either thought wasn't very comforting.

The situation was kind of funny if you didn't think about it too hard.

"I think he did and I don't think he was too impressed. He looks like he wants to give us a manual or show us a porno."

"He can eat kitty litter, dammit. I don't need a fucking cat telling me how..." Dare's eyes widened as if he was seeing the cat for the first time. "What the...has anyone told you your cat looks like Kirk Douglas?"

CHAPTER TWENTY-FOUR

S pending the day in bed with Rayne had sounded good but he had a mountain of work on his desk and a veritable crime spree in his little town to investigate. He'd left Rayne tucked up into bed and put a deputy on the front door. Now he was leading his men in searching the area around Rayne's shop for any place that Moulson or his friends might have hidden a load of cash. Tanner was helping out by loaning him some of his own deputies since Dare had already lost one guarding Rayne.

"Do you think they'll find anything?" Dare asked Tanner as they walked a gridline into the trees behind the shop. It was a chilly but sunny day and they couldn't ask for better weather to be conducting a search. "We've been over this once before."

"It's worth a try, but I also think we should search around Miss Dunn's home as well since they so lovingly tossed it last night. How is she doing, by the way? She's got to be pretty shaken up about all this."

Rayne was shaken up but had a spine of solid steel. She might have shed some tears and let her fear give her a nightmare but when he'd left this morning she'd looked brave and even defiant. She wouldn't let this situation get her down.

"She's fine. She had a rough night but this morning she was

better. She's tough."

Tanner's eyebrow lifted and a smile played around his mouth. "She spent the night with you. That's…interesting."

To anyone who didn't know the carnal pleasures Dare had shared with Rayne, it shouldn't be interesting at all.

"She needed protecting and the easiest way to do it is to have her close." Dare shrugged as if it was no big deal. Because it wasn't. Having Rayne at the house didn't have anything to do with his feelings. "It was the most efficient choice."

"Sure, that's why you did it," Tanner smirked. "It wouldn't have anything to do with the fact that she's kind of hot? That wouldn't have factored into it would it?"

"It did not," Dare growled, already tired of this conversation. "She might be in some danger and I'm protecting her. That's it."

Clearing his throat, Tanner nodded sagely. "If she'd been ugly you would have done the same, I'm sure. But let me tell you, my friend, it's easy to see that you have feelings for her. It's written all over your grumpy-ass face, so get over it. You actually look happy for once in your miserable life."

The ribbing from Tanner was harmless enough but Dare didn't like the idea that his short association with Rayne had changed him. Or at least the appearance of change. Deep down he was the same guy whether he smiled more or not. He wasn't the type to be able to make a woman happy for the long term because he couldn't be happy. Not truly. He danced around the edges but ultimately he wasn't a man who took joy in life. He'd long ago come to terms with it.

"Rayne is a nice girl but that's it. I'm not looking for a rela-tionship or anything."

A woman like Rayne would eventually get tired of Dare's bullshit issues so there was no sense in getting serious. He wasn't the type to make a woman happy, at least not long-term.

"The love of a good woman is a rare thing. If one offers it to you, you'd be a fool to turn it down. It's the best thing in life, my friend."

"We're not in love," Dare denied, the muscles in his shoulders and back stiffening. This whole thing was getting out of hand. If Tanner could see how much Rayne was beginning to mean then she probably could as well. That wasn't good. He didn't need her feeling sorry for him.

Damn, was this morning just a pity fuck? Feeling sorry for the asshole sheriff who was never happy so she'd thrown some pussy his way?

"I didn't say you were, but I remembering meeting her at Jared and Misty's wedding and I liked her. She seems like a good person with a good heart. You know she didn't let Jared give her any money to help rebuild her business. She kept saying it wasn't his fault."

Dare hadn't known that but it sounded like Rayne, always putting others before herself. Last night she'd actually suggested she stay in a motel as if he'd let her be alone when she was hurt and scared. All because she didn't want to be a bother.

"Rayne and I are just friends. I seriously doubt I'm her type."

He vividly remembered dancing in the rain with her. The way she laughed and smiled. Her face upturned along with her hands lifted towards the heavens. Raindrops had slid down her smooth cheeks and shoulders and she'd spun around and around, giggling like a little girl. It had felt like his heart stopped beating for the longest time and then it suddenly felt too big for his chest. He'd never seen a more beautiful woman than she was at that moment. And she had no idea that she was. She thought she needed purple stripes and ink to make herself stand out.

"What do you think is her type?"

Dare stopped in his tracks at the question, the answering

burning a hole in his gut. He'd known he wasn't the man for Rayne, but to say it out loud made it feel so real. And final.

"A man that will put her happiness first. The kind of guy who likes going out and having fun, maybe dancing or seeing a movie. A guy who comes home every night for dinner and doesn't work strange hours with stranger people. The kind that smiles and laughs at her jokes and her friends think is a catch. That's the kind of guy Rayne should be with."

Tanner pursed his lips, seeming to ponder Dare's description. "What about a man who would protect her? Put his life on the line? What about a guy who would never look at another woman and tell her she was beautiful every day? Those things are important too. A woman doesn't need a court jester, Dare. And you wouldn't believe the hours she'll put up with as long as you show her she's the most important thing in the world to you. You're selling yourself short."

Dare couldn't take this personal crap any longer. This wasn't the kind of conversation that he relished and he wanted to put a stop to it sooner rather than later.

"I'm fucked up, Tanner," he growled, exasperation in his tone that he couldn't hide and frankly didn't want to. "Let me repeat that. Fucked up. Hell, my issues have problems. I'm no good for anyone and that's the God's honest truth. If Rayne Dunn had a lick of self-preservation she'd run from me faster than the roadrunner from the coyote. I don't even know how to be happy, for fuck's sake."

"You're right," Tanner smiled easily. "You're a mess. Not like me when I met Maddie. My life was completely smooth and totally under control. So was I, for that matter. In fact, I'm practically James Bond."

Everyone knew how fucked up Tanner's life had been so he was obviously pulling Dare's leg. It didn't change things though.

There were degrees of fucked up and Dare was off the charts.

"I get it. You had problems. I have problems. It's not the same thing."

Tanner gave him one of those Yoda looks that all the guys talked about but never wanted to be on the wrong side of. Serious philosophy was about to spout from the man's lips and Dare's only choice was to stand there and take it like a man.

"I don't know why you're afraid to let yourself be happy, Dare, but I'm sure there's a story there. Probably one that has to do with a painful childhood and terrible memories. You think you're not good enough to be loved and so on. Well, whatever. Here's the thing and listen very closely, okay? You're not a child anymore. You're a grown ass man. Whatever happened to you isn't a valid excuse anymore. If it bugs you, get some help. If it doesn't then put it in the past where it belongs. But don't let it be a reason to take the easy way out. Relationships and love are hard. They're work. It's easier to be alone and feel sorry for yourself. Think about that next time you make some lame-ass excuse. Now let's get back to work because all this personal bullshit is uncomfortable between two men, goddammit."

Dare sure as hell wasn't ready to bare his soul. Not even to Tanner. Instead he scowled and began to walk the grid again.

"Uncomfortable is an understatement, Tanner. Let's decide to never discuss anything but football and beer ever again."

But not talking about it didn't change a thing. Dare wasn't the right kind of man for Rayne and he was only setting himself – and her – up for heartache later on. It would be far kinder to end things now before she ended up hating him. He couldn't stand for her to feel that way.

✧ ✧ ✧ ✧

Tossing her gym bag on the bed in Dare's spare room, Rayne

grabbed her change of clothes and inspected what she had to work with this morning. A pair of white cotton panties, white cotton bra, blue socks, blue jeans, and a beige cable knit sweater with a boat-neck. It wasn't high fashion but they were clean and presentable. At this point she couldn't ask for much more. She was long overdue for a wardrobe makeover so she'd go shopping this afternoon. Buying clothes wasn't her favorite activity so she tended to wear them until they were almost rags.

Folding her discarded clothes from last night, she shoved them back into the bag along with her travel toiletries, her fingers rubbing a scrap of paper at the bottom. Sighing at her habit of keeping receipts far past their useful life, she pulled it out intending to throw it in the small trash can next to the bed, but quickly realized this wasn't a receipt. It was a drawing from the shop.

It wasn't a complicated design although it was visually interesting. It looked like a shield with a line drawn down the middle. The right side was a drawing of an overflowing pot of gold while the left looked a little like a dartboard. But it was whom it belonged to that had her hand shaking and her heart racing.

This was the design she and the murder victim Patrick Moulson had discussed.

She'd thought he'd taken it with him when he left but somehow he must have slipped it inside her gym bag, which had been placed on the counter. She'd been hoping to make it to the gym but the shop had become too busy. Instead she'd thrown it in her trunk...and well, out of sight was out of mind. She hadn't made it to a workout since.

Her stomach twisted in her gut but she knew deep down that this is what they'd been looking for. It had to be. There was nothing else he'd given her.

Now what did it mean?

Rayne tucked the drawing in her pocket with the intent to take it straight to Dare but her phone chimed instead.

Misty.

"Hey listen, I need to get to Dare. I found something that might help the case."

Rayne continued stuffing her belongings in the gym bag and zipping it shut.

"What did you find?" Misty asked excitedly. "I was actually calling because I heard about last night. Are you okay?"

"Good news travels fast. I'm fine but my house isn't. It's a wreck and I need to meet the insurance adjustor there later this morning, but first I need to take this drawing to Dare. It's the design for the shooting victim. It was stuffed in my gym bag and I didn't find it until this morning."

"Holy shit. Do you think that's what they were looking for?"

"It has to be. What else is there? But it's just a design for a tattoo. Why would anyone care about that? It isn't worth any money or anything. It's nothing to kill or die for."

Misty giggled on the other end of the line. "You do make a good point. So send me a picture of the design. I want to see it."

Perhaps Misty could make heads or tails of it. "Hold on. Let me take the photo and send it to you. Let me know when you've got it."

Quickly, Rayne snapped the picture and attached it to an email. She waited without saying anything while it flew through cyberspace.

"Got it. Let me open it up and take a look." More silence. "Hmmmm…kind of cryptic. It looks like a coat of arms actually from my history class in high school."

"I'll try and look up these symbols online. See if I can find anything on them."

The cry of a baby pierced the air and Misty sighed. "I have to go. Lizzie has a cold and she'd been fussy the last few days, which means it's only a matter of time before we get it too. I just wanted to make sure you were okay. Call me when you know something."

"Will do. Give her a big kiss from her Auntie Rayne."

Hanging up, Rayne patted her pocket and grabbed the gym bag, heading downstairs. She needed to see Dare as soon as possible. Maybe he could tell her what was so important about a stupid drawing.

CHAPTER TWENTY-FIVE

After wrangling with the insurance adjustor for way too long, Rayne marched into the sheriff's station. Impatient to see Dare, she'd been annoyed as hell when the adjustor had called as she was leaving Dare's home. Apparently, the adjustor was outside her house but she wasn't there, which made him cranky. Pointing out that he was two hours early didn't seem to make any difference so she'd turned her car around and headed back to her place. Her meeting with Dare would have to wait. The drawing wasn't going anywhere but the adjustor had made it clear he wouldn't wait forever.

Now it was lunchtime but Dare was nowhere to be found. Instead, Sophie and her boyfriend Tim were hanging out in his office and drinking fancy coffees from the shop a block over. Rayne had a feeling that if Dare knew that Tim was sitting in his chair with his feet on the desk he'd have a coronary right before ripping the younger man a new asshole.

"Are you looking for Dare too?" Sophie asked with a smile. "He was supposed to meet me for lunch but I think he blew me off."

Rayne also doubted Dare had invited Tim along but she could be wrong.

Probably not.

"I am looking for Dare. Do you know where he is? I sent him a text but I haven't heard anything back."

Draping her jacket on the back of the chair, Rayne gratefully lowered herself onto the seat with a sigh. The adjustor had her prowling around the attic with him – for what reason she had no idea – and she'd wrenched her back. Another reason not to like the little weasel. He'd given her a song and dance about processes and protocols that meant she wasn't getting her check for a while, although now she could start on cleaning.

"He was out searching around your shop this morning. I thought you'd be there."

"No, I had to meet with the insurance demon. Oops, I mean the adjustor. I cancelled my appointments today and tomorrow. I may close all week. The cleanup on the house will take forever. Plus I spent an hour on the phone canceling credit cards and making plans to get my driver's license replaced. Thank goodness I had a spare car key at home."

Her cell phone vibrated in her pocket and she checked the caller, hoping it was Dare.

Camy. Hell no.

Grimacing, she declined the call and stuffed it back into her pocket. Her sister must have heard what happened and was probably frantic, something that Camy excelled at. But Rayne needed to have a talk with Dare about the drawing before facing her sister.

"Do you still want to go shopping?" Sophie asked, draining her latte and reaching for Tim's empty cup as well. "Let me find a trash can to toss these and if you still want to go we can make a plan of attack."

Sophie disappeared around the corner and Tim pushed up the brim of his cowboy hat and grinned. "You and the sheriff make a nice couple, Miss Dunn. How long have you two been dating?"

"Not long," she admitted but didn't feel comfortable discussing her relationship with Dare. It still felt too personal. "How long have you and Sophie been going out?"

"A few months. She's a sweet girl."

He did seem to truly have feelings for Sophie, although whether they were as strong was a question. Only time would answer it.

"She is. I'm glad you realize that."

Tim didn't take offense. "I do. It's nice that she has people that care about her. I only have my brother Duke."

"Are you close?"

"Hell, yes. We fight like cats and dogs, but when the chips are down there isn't anything we wouldn't do for one another. There isn't anything he wouldn't do for me and vice versa. We're all we've got and we don't forget it."

Sophie rejoined them but Tim was already pulling on his jacket. "I've got to get back to work, babe. I'll call you later. Have fun shopping." Tim nodded to Rayne. "It was nice seeing you again."

"You too."

Tim dropped a kiss on Sophie's lips and made a hasty exit, leaving the two women alone. Sophie checked her phone and then refreshed her kiss-smeared lipstick.

"So are you up for some shopping? I could use a new pair of boots for this winter."

Rayne thought about the drawing in her front pocket and shook her head. "I need to talk to your brother first. It's about the case."

Perching on top of Dare's desk, Sophie crisscrossed her legs, elbows on her knees. "I don't know how you can stand to talk to my brother about work. If you let him, he'll go on and on about it until you want to stuff cotton in your ears."

"Actually, I think he's a pretty interesting guy and I'm fascinated by how they're working my case. On television they make it look so easy but clearly it's anything but."

"Most of what he does is routine so when he gets a real case like this he gets excited about it. Not that anyone would know. He only has one expression and that's pissed off."

Rayne knew that wasn't true but she wasn't about to tell Dare's little sister what made him smile. But she couldn't stop herself from asking the question that had been bugging her since the day she'd met him...

"Has he always been like this? Grouchy and growly?"

Her chin resting in her palm, Sophie rolled her eyes. "God, yes. For as long as I can remember anyway, but then he's ancient compared to me. I can count on one hand the number of times I've seen him smile. He's just unhappy all the time."

Sophie didn't see what Rayne did. Dare wasn't an unhappy or depressed man. If anything he seemed...scared of being happy.

"I know you both lost your father not long ago. It takes time to get over the death of a loved one."

"Dad was much older than my mom—it seems like he was sick for a long time so his death wasn't a shock. He and Dare didn't get along very well either. They argued a lot and Dare spent as much time away as he could, first in the military and then in another town as a deputy. He'd volunteer for every holiday shift so he didn't have to spend them with us."

This wasn't a surprising revelation but it made her sad to think that he avoided situations that might bring him joy or comfort.

It was none of her damn business but she'd already asked

personal questions and she really wanted to know what made Dare tick. She wasn't ashamed to admit he fascinated her.

"Why didn't they get along?"

Sophie stretched out her legs, wincing at her stiff muscles, and stared at her shoes for a moment before answering. "From what I could pick up from their arguments it had to do with Dare's mother. I don't think she was a very nice person. In fact, I think she was downright awful."

Rayne's heart dropped to her knees. "Did she hurt Dare?"

"I don't know. From the way they talked, I don't think she was a warm, loving mother but that doesn't mean she hit him or anything. I do know that Dare was angry with Dad because he never intervened. It caused a great deal of strain in their relationship."

Having studied enough psychology in college, Rayne was aware that a disturbance in the parent-child bond could screw someone up good. Her mind was already racing, putting together possible scenarios of why he acted the way he did. They were all probably wrong, but she couldn't help the wave of sympathy that came over her when she thought about him as a child with an unfeeling mother and indifferent father.

"Thank you for telling me, Sophie. It helps to understand why he acts so gruff most of the time."

"Do not tell him I told you." The young woman's eyes were wide and she covered them as if in fear. "He would not appreciate me revealing anything about his personal life. He hates any appearance of weakness."

"I won't say a word," Rayne promised. "If he mentions it I'll pretend I have no idea."

"He won't mention it." Sophie hopped down from the desk as the front doors of the station burst open and Dare strode in. "He acts like he never had a childhood. Hey, big brother."

Dare came to a stop next to Sophie with his usual grumpy demeanor. It didn't mean anything, of course; he could have caught the murderer and found the money and he'd still look the same.

His tense gaze flickered to Rayne before returning to Sophie, his expression immediately softening. "How was work today?"

"I'm rolling in dough, Dare." Sophie waited for her brother to laugh at the lame joke but he only sighed and crossed his arms over his chest. She shoved at his shoulders with a giggle and a toss of her hair. "Get it? I work in a bakery and I'm rolling in dough. Jeez, you need to lighten up. You'll die early of a heart attack and pasty white is not your color."

"Hilarious," Dare bit out. "I was trying to make small talk."

"Don't hurt yourself." Another giggle from Sophie as she swung the strap of her purse over her shoulder and turned to Rayne. "I'll head down to the coffee shop and get another latte. Why don't you meet me there after you talk to this sour puss?"

Rayne agreed and Sophie bounced out of the sheriff's station, a smile on her lips. Brother and sister couldn't have been more different.

Digging in her pocket for the drawing, Rayne turned to Dare. "You'll never guess—"

"We need to talk," he said flatly, his eyes almost an icy gray. Rayne shoved the design back into her jean pocket and settled into her chair, dread building in her gut. Something was off and not the usual gloom and doom. Dare was pacing back and forth, his gaze darting all around the room. Whatever they needed to talk about wasn't a pleasant subject. Had something else happened? Was there another dead body?

He marched over to his office doors and shut them with a click, closing them off from everyone. No, this wasn't good at all. His hands were still on the doorknobs, his wide back to her.

"What's going on? Did you find something out? Because I have–"

"I don't think we should see each other anymore."

Rayne's hands tightened into fists. "Could you repeat that?"

He still didn't turn around which pissed her off. If he was going to dump her ass, the least he could do was look her in the eye when he did it.

"Listen, I don't think things are working out. I think we should call it off while we're still friends. Of course, you'll still be protected until we catch these guys. That goes without saying."

But who was going to protect Dare from her?

CHAPTER TWENTY-SIX

"End it?" Rayne echoed as she sat down, crossing one leg over the other casually if she heard these words every day; meanwhile she could feel anger churning in her abdomen and trying to claw its way out. "Can you turn around, look me in the eye and say that or are you too chicken shit?"

His shoulders stiffened and he slowly turned to look at her, his cheeks stained red with embarrassment and probably some anger too.

Good. She wasn't feeling all happy go lucky either.

"I know you're upset—"

"Fuck you," Rayne interrupted, barely able to keep her rising anger in check, and she jumped to her feet unable to keep still, despite the fact that she'd just sat down. Her neck had grown hot with fury and her palms were sweating with the heat, but no way was she going to be mollified like a hysterical woman at a crime scene. "Oh wait, I did that and look where it got me. Dumped like yesterday's trash. Is this how you usually work, Sheriff? String them along until you get some pussy and then give them the 'it's not you, it's me' speech? Well, fuck you."

She'd actually thought the bastard was a nice guy. She'd fallen for the grouchy, emotional cripple bullshit and now look where she was. Hurting because she'd actually allowed herself to start to care for the jerk. It wasn't her usual modus operandi. Wise for her years, she rarely fell for a guy and ended up with a broken heart. Not since she turned thirty, anyway. But he'd been so sneaky and unassuming. Smug asshole probably planned this all along.

But something funny happened when she cursed at him. His entire demeanor shifted into something she'd never seen on him before. His shoulders slumped, his lips turned down, and she could swear his hands shook when he shoved them in his pockets. For a guy who had hit and run, he didn't look nearly as jubilant about it as he should. He looked incredibly miserable.

More than usual.

"I never meant to hurt you and please don't consider this as me dumping you. You're a wonderful woman and any man would be lucky to have you."

"Except you," Rayne shot back, still hurting although much less. He wasn't swaggering around like a conquering hero, which made the entire situation much more bearable. "And let me tell you it sure feels like I'm being dumped. What would you call it?"

Looking down at his boots for the longest time, she heard him take a deep breath before answering. "I think we both know this wasn't going to end with us pledging undying love to one another and then driving off into the sunset to live happily ever after. All I'm doing is moving the logical conclusion forward."

"The logical conclusion? Fucking and running was the logical conclusion? If it was so logical why am I questioning it?"

They'd had this great night together and now he was bailing. It didn't make any sense. Except…that perhaps the night hadn't been that great for Dare. Had he been pretending to enjoy the sex?

Hell, he was a guy so of course he enjoyed it, but maybe he

was put off by her request for it rough and dirty. Maybe he thought she was slutty and unladylike.

Dammit, this was why she didn't date. Relationships sucked and love hurt.

Love? No! It was lust. Plain old lust. Infatuation. Love this quickly was out of the question.

"Rayne, I'm not exactly the kind of guy women fantasize about spending their lives with. Do you honestly think I could make you happy?"

This might be his way of saying he didn't want to fulfill her sexual proclivities. He must think she was a big ho-bag, and that pissed her off again. If a guy liked it rough everyone thought that was okay, but if a female did? There must be something wrong with her.

Damned if she would beg any man. She had more than her share of pride and she would be fine with or without the sexy lawman. There would be a lot less orgasms but life wasn't perfect.

"I haven't been unhappy, Dare, but I can see you've made up your mind. If you think this isn't working then obviously it's not. So let's just wave a wand over whatever it was between us and call it quits. No hard feelings."

She'd try. Eventually she wouldn't want to knee him in the balls, she was almost sure of it. But he should probably keep his distance for awhile. A week or two. She didn't hold a grudge long.

His brows pulled down and his lips twisted in something that resembled a grimace. "I still want to be your friend, Rayne."

She had to blink back the tears that sprang to her eyes upon hearing those words. They were the kiss of death and her chest squeezed tightly as she pondered the implications, none of them happy.

"We were never friends. Now we're not friends again. It's okay, though. I know that you'll do your duty as a police officer, which is actually why I'm here today." She dug the design out of her pocket and slapped it down on his desk, the sharp pain that ran up her arm easing the matching one in her heart. "This is a design Patrick Moulson brought into the shop. I found it in my gym bag so I assume he slipped it in there for whatever reason. This could be what they're looking for."

Dare picked up the drawing, studying it although he wasn't sure what he was looking for. It was hard to concentrate on the case when he couldn't get the conversation with Rayne out of his head. He'd assumed she wouldn't be all that upset.

He sure as hell didn't want her to think he'd simply been using her, as it was the furthest thing from the truth. He liked her. Too much, really. But they were heading for a crash if they stayed together. He didn't know how to be in a relationship and make a woman happy other than between the sheets.

He rounded the desk and sat down in his chair to give the design his full attention but one question in his head wouldn't leave him alone.

"How did you find this?"

"It was stuffed in my gym bag which was stuffed in my trunk. I've been...bad about going to the gym lately. Sue me."

"And you don't remember him putting this into your bag? That's a big thing to forget. It's been there this whole time while we've been wandering around in the dark."

"I did remember my dealings with him. I remembered he brought in the sketch. I remembered he was going to come back for a quote. I do not remember him stuffing the drawing into my gym bag when I wasn't looking, so needless to say I didn't know to look for it."

This case was going to be the death of him. He didn't want to yell but it was difficult to control the frustration he felt. "So you left him alone long enough to hide it in your gym bag. This is news, Rayne. Where the hell was your gym bag? You said he never left the front of the shop."

Rayne leaned forward, her hands planted on the desk and her jaw tight. "He didn't. I was getting ready for my next appointment and he came in. My gym bag was sitting on the counter. The only time I turned my back was for about thirty seconds when the phone rang and I needed the appointment book. It must have been then that he put it there. He never moved from where he was standing. Not once. Believe me, no one is more surprised than I am that he managed to do this."

Scraping his fingers through his hair, Dare sighed in resignation. "I'm sorry, I'm just frustrated. This whole case has been a clusterfuck from the beginning and I wish we would have had this a long time ago."

Turning on her heel, Rayne walked over to the window, her back to Dare. "And you think I don't? If I'd known it was there my house might not have been trashed and I might not have been mugged. This hasn't exactly been a picnic with rainbows and unicorns for me either, Sheriff, so fuck you and the horse you rode in on. I've about had it with you today and honestly, I think it would be best if I left. See you later."

Grabbing her jacket from the chair, Rayne marched toward his office door but he couldn't let her leave like this. He'd been a jerk – more than once in the last fifteen minutes – and he needed to fix this fast. "Rayne, wait. Please. Stay." She halted but didn't turn around. "I understand you being mad at me but what do you have against my horse?"

Reluctantly she looked up at him, a smile tugging at her lips.

"You don't have a horse."

"That didn't stop you from telling him to go fuck himself. And I did have a horse when I was a kid. His name was Galahad and he was the best horse ever and not worthy of your anger."

She walked away from the doors and leaned against the edge of the desk, her posture still defensive. "You're pissed at me and I didn't do shit. I won't be your punching bag."

"You're right and I'm sorry. I jumped down your throat and made this about you when I should be thanking you for finding it at all. Most people never go to the gym."

It was his second lame attempt at a joke and she was slowly softening toward him.

"God, you're such an asshole."

"I am," he quickly agreed, noting that she didn't look all that upset with him anymore. "Have been all my life. No one could put up with me for long and this is proof."

"Is that why you did it? To prove that dumping me was for my own good? You really are a bastard."

She was tensing up again and he didn't want that. They had work to do on this drawing and he needed her relaxed and receptive. He needed her to remember every word that Patrick Moulson had said about this design. Obviously there was something important about it, although what it was wasn't as clear.

"Acting like an asshole just comes naturally to me. I don't have to try or plan it. It's a superpower sort of thing. And I apparently need to say it again. You weren't dumped. A man like me would never dump a woman like you. That would be crazy."

Tilting her head, Rayne's gaze ran him up and down, appraising him like a prize bull. His cock twitched in his pants and he had to remind himself that he'd ended things minutes earlier. There would be no naked fun between the two of them no matter how much he wished it were different.

"Does insanity run in your family?"

"Sadly we're sober as judges. And no fun. Isn't that what everyone says about me? That I'm no fun?"

Dare had long since grown accustomed to his reputation in town as a surly son of a bitch…as long as he was a bastard who got things done.

"Actually they whisper outlandish stories about how you got the nickname Dare. I heard you were a daredevil that likes to live on the edge. They say you had a death wish when you were younger."

"You shouldn't listen to the town busybodies. They embellish every little thing until it's unrecognizable."

She'd never know about his past and that's the way it would stay.

Rayne pointed to the drawing. "So now what do we do?"

Dare had been thinking about that and he had an idea. "This drawing has two symbols, and I know a guy who used to work for the government who might know what they mean. This could be some kind of code."

CHAPTER TWENTY-SEVEN

Camy slapped a bottle of wine between Rayne and herself, placing two glasses next to it as they sat at the kitchen table. Camy's husband and baby had gone to bed and it was just the two of them in the quiet house. Pouring two generous glasses, she handed one to Rayne, giving her an encouraging smile.

"So tell me everything. No detail is too small. Spill."

It was difficult at first. The story came in fits and starts but as the wine began to take effect, Rayne found the words flowing as easily as the libation.

"So he dumped me," Rayne sighed, taking another gulp of her drink. "Needless to say I couldn't stay at his place anymore so here I am. We had a one-night stand—or one-morning stand is more accurate after dating for a few weeks, then he pulls the plug. I must have disgusted him or something. Maybe I'm too fat or I'm not blonde. Whatever it was, he couldn't wait to end it. Now he's meeting up with some ex-government guy to talk about the drawing while I fight with insurance companies and the DMV."

Camy frowned, her brow wrinkled. "Why are you fighting with the DMV? What do they have to do with this?"

Rayne rolled her eyes and groaned at all the work there was still left to be done. Being the victim of a crime sucked in more ways than one. "My purse was stolen so I need a new license. Dealing with the credit card companies wasn't too bad but the DMV has been a real pain in the ass."

"I'm so sorry all of this happened to you." Camy leaned forward, wagging her finger in front of Rayne's nose. "But you should have called me, sis. I've been worried sick since I heard about the break-in at your house. Then I find out all of the other things that have been happening in your life. Maybe you should have stayed in San Francisco. Valley Station hasn't been all that kind to you and it's all my fault. Are you mad at me?"

Rayne wasn't angry; she was exhausted. She wanted to crawl away and sleep for a week, forgetting about all the crap going on in her life.

"No, I am not mad at you. And I'm sorry I didn't talk to you earlier today. Honestly, I could only handle one thing at a time. I knew you'd be upset and I was already upset enough for both of us."

Camy refilled their glasses but didn't put the bottle down, instead shifting her gaze to the front door. "Should we take some of this to Deputy Billy? I hate to think of him sitting out there all night in the cold. Did he piss off the sheriff to get this assignment?"

Rayne plucked the bottle from her sister's fingers and set it down on the table. "I don't think he's allowed to drink on duty. As for sitting out in the cold, he's in his cruiser and it has heat. We invited him in and he said he was supposed to stay out there. Dare also said that another deputy would be coming by at midnight so he won't be alone the whole time."

"So what happens now?"

The wine wasn't helping Rayne's mood. If anything, she was

feeling even more sorry for herself and the tears welling up in her eyes couldn't be stopped. A few even rolled down her cheeks, and she scrubbed at them with the back of her hand while Camy patted her arm and told her everything was going to be okay.

She was probably right but at the moment things sucked. This morning her world had looked much brighter and now it felt like the world would never be right again.

This was what happened when she drank too much wine and wallowed in her bad luck. Getting back to work was the best medicine for this melancholy but even that brought back memories of Dare.

"I clean up the house and buy new furniture. I get a new driver's license and credit cards. I open the shop back up. It's simple, really."

"And Dare? What about him?"

"What about him? It's over. Done. It's in the past. He doesn't want me and that's fine. It's his loss."

"It is his loss," Camy agreed readily with a grim smile. "He couldn't do any better than you and he ought to know that. He's such a mean-faced, grouchy asshole. The more I think about it the more I think you're better off without him. The man can't even smile."

Rayne couldn't suppress her own smile at the pleasant memories she had of this morning.

"He can smile, and it's glorious when he does."

Camy snorted. "I bet I know what makes him smile. It's what makes most men smile. Then they roll over and start snoring or ask you to fix them a sandwich."

"Dare didn't do either of those things."

Camy smacked the table, her expression militant. "Don't you defend him. He's a jerk and we need to find you another guy. A better guy. Someone that will make Dare Turner look like the big loser that he is."

Draining her wine glass, Rayne slumped forward on the table. Her head spun from the alcohol and her eyelids felt heavy with fatigue. She needed sleep more than a new boyfriend.

"I don't think another man is the answer. It might even be more of the same problems. Maybe I just wasn't meant to be coupled up like other people. I'm better off on my own."

Spartacus hopped down onto the table, seemingly from out of nowhere. He'd been hiding since the trip from Dare's home to Camy's; clearly the crying baby jangled the feline's nerves but it felt good to have her closest friend by her side. The cat head-butted her and meowed loudly as if to tell her to get off her ass and stop feeling sorry for herself.

"You're right, Spartacus. What I need is a good night's sleep. Things will look better in the morning."

"They always do." Camy scratched Spartacus behind the ears. "We can talk again in the morning. I'll help you clean up your house tomorrow."

Rayne stood and scooped up the furball, dropping a kiss on the top of his head, much to the cat's disgust. Overt displays of affection were not his cup of tea. Quiet dignity was more his style.

She bid her sister goodnight and slowly climbed the stairs to the guest room. She didn't really know if tomorrow would be a better day than today but she did know one thing…

It was time to move on from Dare Turner.

✧ ✧ ✧ ✧

Dare hadn't felt this miserable in a long time. Maybe years, which was why he and friend Sheriff Evan Davis, ex-US Marshal were sitting at his kitchen table pounding whiskey and discussing the drawing. Evan hadn't seen anything in the two symbols that he recognized but he'd scanned it in and sent it off to an old colleague in the FBI.

With business out of the way, they were discussing women in general and Rayne in particular and getting messy drunk in the process.

Evan refilled their glasses with the Irish whiskey. "You either like her or you don't. That's the only question that matters."

Scraping his hand down his face, Dare shook his head at his friend's oversimplification. It wasn't about Rayne. It never had been. This was about Dare and everything that was wrong with him.

"Of course I like her. She's amazing. And sexy." He had to concentrate to keep from slurring his words. "But that doesn't mean I can keep her happy. Shit, I don't even know how to be happy. And it's not the same for you, Davis. You know how to be happy, dammit."

Evan chuckled and took a gulp of his liquor. "Let her show you how if you don't know. Hell, the only reason you're a grouchy little prick is because you're such a tight ass. Relax and let yourself be happy. I've never seen anyone wound as tightly as you are. You're like a human, walking, talking Eeyore, and I don't mean that as a compliment. And might I remind you that Eeyore didn't have a girlfriend. Ever. It's not an attractive quality in a mate—all that feeling sorry for yourself is a turnoff."

"I have issues," Dare blurted, the alcohol loosening his tongue. "If she finds out she'll probably dump me."

"So you did it for her? Smart. That way you won't get hurt." Evan slid the bottle across the table to Dare. "Wait, you are hurting so that shit didn't work. Time for Plan B."

"I don't have a Plan B. I'm not sure if Rayne and I should be together, to be honest."

Except that his heart felt like he'd ripped it out of his chest and stomped on it a few times. He missed her and it had only been a few hours since he'd last seen her. He wanted her here…in his house…in his bed.

In his arms.

Where he could keep her safe. Right now Deputy Billy was watching over her but Dare wanted to do it himself. She was too precious and he wouldn't allow anything to happen to her.

Evan knocked back his whiskey and grinned. "Then sit here and drink with me. Get lousy drunk. It might make you forget, but probably not. When a woman gets under your skin, it's hard to shake them loose."

Dare didn't know much about Evan's private life. Hadn't really thought much about it, to tell the truth, but then it had always been business between them. Sure, they both liked to drink beer, shoot darts, and watch sports but they'd kept it superficial, friendly but nothing deeper. Pretty much how Dare dealt with everyone in his life.

"Are you speaking from experience? Do you want to talk about it?"

Evan's eyes widened and then he threw back his head, laughing his ass off which only served to make Dare squirm in his chair. He was trying to be helpful, goddammit, and this was his reward.

"Fuck no, Turner. I do not want to talk about it. But yes, I have some experience with women. I've broken a few hearts and had my heart broken too. This is what happens to human beings. Pain and joy are just two sides of the same coin. You can't have one without the other. To be honest, I don't know shit about women and I probably never will. But I do know that a good one doesn't come along very often."

"You sound like Tanner," Dare groused. "Since he married

Madison he's all happy and in love and wants everyone else to be the same. Maybe it isn't in the cards for all of us."

Evan's smile died and his expression turned a little sad. "We should all be as happy as that bastard. He has everything in the world."

"He's lucky."

Shaking his head, Evan poured another whiskey for them both. "Correction, he's scared. Scared because when you have it all, it can be taken away from you like that." Evan snapped his fingers in front of Dare's face. "You can lose everything in a second. Life changes that fast."

His stomach queasy with acid, Dare didn't even want to imagine something bad happening to Tanner and Madison. They were two of the best people he knew. They'd earned their happiness.

"How does he do it then?" Dare marveled. "How can he take that chance every day? He put his heart on the line and life can smack him down at any moment, but he just keeps going like it won't happen. He just keeps living and loving. It's like he's in some crazy denial."

"You don't know a fucking thing about life, do you?" Evan was looking at him like he was insane, and maybe he was. At the very least he was drunker than he'd been in a long time. "All of life is a chance. There are no guarantees. If you're looking for one you're out of luck, my friend. I just never realized what a pussy you were, afraid of your own shadow. That part is a surprise."

Dare slammed his fist down on the table but Evan only chuckled. "I'm not a pussy and I don't need a guarantee."

"Don't you? You ended things pretty fast with that girl when you thought she might do the same. Those don't seem like the actions of a fearless man. But hey, what do I know? Want another drink?"

Dare wanted several more.

And a second chance.

CHAPTER TWENTY-EIGHT

R ayne was having the most wonderful dream. She was lying on a beach with azure waters and crystal clear skies. She could smell the lingering aroma of coconut and hibiscus mixed with the salty air as a pair of warm, masculine hands massaged sunscreen onto her shoulders. A smiling Tom Hiddleston sat behind her doing the honors and giving her that sexy grin she loved so much.

She sighed and let herself relax under his sensual ministrations. "Tom, this is exactly what I've been needing. That feels so good."

He opened his mouth to say something to her, but whatever he said was drowned out by a pounding noise in the distance, shattering the peace and quiet. She turned and ran her hands up his arms and around his neck to tangle in the curls at his nape. He leaned forward, his lips so close to hers, and said...

"Open the goddamn door, woman. I need to talk to you."

Her eyes flying open, Rayne sat straight up in the bed, her gaze darting all around as she tried to remember where she was and what was happening. Her pleasant dream was shot all to hell, that one thing was for sure. There was no beach. No suntan oil. No Tom Hiddleston.

Damn.

There was yelling and pounding though, and she dragged her arm across her face trying desperately to wake up. Still groggy, she realized the sound was coming from downstairs and the voice was a very loud Dare Turner who must be standing on the front lawn with a bullhorn. Or maybe that was simply his naturally bellowing voice.

What in the hell?

Throwing off the covers, she jumped out of bed, wavering slightly on her feet as her entire body had yet to wake up fully. Shrugging on her old ratty robe, she stumbled down the stairs to find that Camy and her husband were a few steps ahead of her. Mike had jerked open the front door and was doing some yelling of his own at the bellicose sheriff on the front lawn.

"Rayne! I need to talk to you, baby. Will you come talk to me?"

Incredibly, the words sounded slurred and it occurred to her that Sheriff Dare Turner might not be completely sober.

That explained a great deal.

Camy snorted and pulled her robe more closely around her body. "If he wakes up the baby, I'll geld him with a Swiss Army knife. Don't think I won't do it, either. She's teething and getting her to sleep has been a nightmare."

"He's leaving," Rayne retorted, the anger she'd felt earlier rearing its ugly head once again. He'd dumped her and now shown up drunk on her front step. What was this? High school? She was no prom queen and he sure wasn't a prince. She'd go outside, slap some sense into him, and send him on his way. "Just give me a minute."

Mike was on the front porch whispering loudly but Dare didn't lower his voice in the least, apparently too inebriated to quiet down. "I need to talk to Rayne. I won't leave until I do."

Cinching the belt on her robe, Rayne stepped into a pair of boots next to the door. They were huge on her tiny feet and they probably belonged to Mike but she didn't care. With bedhead and sheet-creased cheeks, she wasn't going to wow Dare with her beauty anyway.

She placed her hand on Mike's shoulder. "Let me handle this. You and Camy go on back upstairs. I'll get rid of him."

"I need to talk to you, baby. I made a mistake."

Deputy Billy was hovering in the background, obviously not sure what to do with his drunk boss. Rayne waved him back into his vehicle before grabbing Dare by the ear and dragging him into the house.

"You've made more than one mistake, Sheriff. Now shut the hell up. If you wake the baby, I can't promise you'll get out of this alive. Do you understand? How did you even get here? I hope you didn't drive."

"Ow. Shit. Ow. Dammit, woman, that hurts. Let go of my ear. Fuck."

Rayne didn't let go until she'd pulled him through the living room, kitchen, and onto the back porch, kicking off the oversized boots on the way. Fury burned in her abdomen and she could even feel it heat her skin. Dare Turner was a gigantic pain in the ass.

"I said shut up. You need to keep it down. It's the middle of the damn night and people – normal people, anyway – are sleeping. Now answer my question. Did you drive here? Because that would be stupid."

Now free from her hold, Dare straightened and took a step back. "I took a taxi. I may be drunk but I am the sheriff around here. I haven't completely lost my mind."

"Really?" she breathed, poking her finger into his broad chest. "Do you think standing on my sister's front lawn is the action of a sane man? Because I don't think it is. I think you've stepped over the edge, Sheriff. What in the hell are you thinking?"

His hand captured her fingers, bringing them up to his lips. "I'm thinking that I fucked things up between us and I wanted to talk to you."

One sweet gesture wasn't going to put out the head of steam she had going. He'd dumped her and she'd do well to remember that.

"I don't see that we have anything to talk about. We fucked. You ended things. End of story. As far as I can see the only person who fucked up was me. I actually believed you were a human being instead of a huge sphincter."

"I'm not a sphincter," Dare hissed, a drop of spittle at the corner of his mouth. "Shit, you're a ball buster."

She didn't need this hassle in her life. It might not have been glamorous or exciting, but her life hadn't been all that bad before he came into it. "Then aren't you lucky you called time out on our relationship? I'm relieved, too. I need a man with some backbone who doesn't run at the first sign of intimacy, you big pussy."

That last crack might have been too far. Even in the dim porch light, she could see the red creep up Dare's neck and a muscle ticking in his jaw.

Lesson learned. Don't call Dare a pussy.

"I'm not a..." To her surprise, his voice trailed off and he jogged down the porch steps into the middle of the yard where he stood staring at the sky for the longest time. Rayne didn't say a word, somehow realizing he needed this moment of silence to gather his thoughts and round up his emotions. She sunk down into the porch glider and watched as his shoulders rose and fell with each hard breath he took. Several minutes later he turned and stomped up the steps and knelt down in front of her, grabbing her hands with his big, callused paws; his gaze skittered all over the porch and then locked with hers. He looked like he was suffering from some horrible pain and she had to push down the softer feelings he evoked. She was still furious.

"I am a pussy. A big, scared pussy. You got close and I ran. It's just I didn't think someone as happy as you are would be content with a man like me. I don't know how to be that way, Rayne. I want to be but I just don't know how. I figure eventually you'll get tired of it…me. That's why I did it. It was stupid and I regret it but that's why. I'm sorry you got hurt by my cowardice."

Her anger drained away as if a plug had been pulled at the bottom of a sink. It took a real man to admit he was scared and Dare was doing it on his knees. He had this apology thing down to a science and she couldn't muster any more hate as he looked into her eyes and waited for her reply. She didn't censor the first words that came into her head.

"You are such an asshole."

He jerked back but then must have noticed her smile, because he was starting to smile too. As usual, it took her breath away. There ought to be a law about it and she would discuss that very subject with him. Soon. But first…

"I know," he nodded. "A real sphincter. You could do a hell of a lot better than me, sweetheart."

She was starting to think that wasn't the case. It sounded kind of pathetic but the men in her life previously would never in a million years have come over here to apologize. They only showed up drunk in the middle of the night for a booty call.

"Maybe, but I kind of like you, even when you act like an ass. I was all set to be pissed off at you and then you had to go apologizing and being humble. Which, by the way, doesn't take away from your alpha vibe at all, much to my dismay. I'm not sure how you pulled it off, frankly, but I'm impressed."

He was kissing the tips of her fingers, still smiling, and a thousand butterflies began to beat at her ribs. Damn, she had it bad for this guy. She'd planned to kick him out on his rear and now he was practically seducing her with his puppy-dog eyes.

"I'm still a little drunk," Dare admitted, pressing his lips to the palm of her hand. "But I do know how to say I'm sorry. And I am sorry, baby. Your sister must think I'm a real loser showing up like this. I'll send her flowers or something to make it up."

"If anyone gets flowers in this scenario, Sheriff, it's going to be me. Now get up off your knees and let's go in the kitchen. I'll make you some coffee so you can sober up. Then if you want to continue this relationship with me you can tell me why you think you can't be happy."

His face fell but she wasn't going to let him wriggle his way out of this one. She deserved to know what his problem was and he was damn well going to spill it. Preferably over coffee and chocolate cake in her sister's kitchen.

CHAPTER TWENTY-NINE

D are had known it wasn't going to be that easy. Apologize. Agree that he was an ass and a jerk. Rayne would fall all over him in gratitude and they would pick up where they left off.

Sort of.

She'd thrown down the gauntlet in her own inimitable style that he adored so much. She didn't take any of his bullshit and he admired her for it. She had more grit and backbone than any ten women he knew and here she was open to the idea of forgiving him for being a shit.

All he had to do was come clean.

So of course he delayed for as long as possible, drinking his coffee and putting away a huge slab of chocolate cake. Rayne nibbled on hers, her gaze rarely straying from his face as she waited semi-patiently. After three cups of coffee, he couldn't put it off any longer. Fuck it. She wanted to hear it, he'd tell her. Minus any fancy wrapping or pretty bows. Just the bare truth in all its ugly glory.

"My mother hated me."

He paused, mostly for effect and it worked. Rayne's eyes widened but to her credit she didn't take the bait, instead sitting back in her chair with a patient expression.

"My childhood wasn't what you would call happy. Or care-free. Or any of those other adjectives that make being a kid sound fun. I was nervous and scared pretty much all of the time. You see, my mother was a walking time bomb and I never knew when she would go off. I only knew what set her off."

Licking her lips, Rayne placed her hand over his. "And what was that?"

"Me." Dare scraped a hand down his face at the memories he'd worked hard to bury all these years. Most of the time, he didn't even think about his mother; she'd been gone for a long time, after all. His behavior was more learned than anything. It was a habit he'd adopted to try and keep his home peaceful. "I set her off. Specifically, me being a typical kid and having fun such as playing or laughing. Some days she'd be fine with it and others she'd lose her mind, screaming and yelling. I'd usually get hit with the belt and I'd promise to be quiet from then on and I would be. Until the next time I forgot and acted like a kid again. It was a cycle we repeated over and over again for years until I eventually figured out that she was just a miserable woman who wanted everyone around her to be the same way."

"What about your father?"

Dare snorted at the mention of his dad. "He was no help. When Mom would get like that, Dad would do anything to make her calm down, including blaming me for getting her riled up. Everything was always my fault. According to her, I was a bad seed."

He watched as Rayne swallowed hard, her eyes dark with pain. He hadn't meant to dump this on her and would have taken it to his grave if she hadn't pushed him tonight. Now she was feeling sorry for him when he was the one would should be apologizing. He'd let *that woman* color his world view yet again.

She'd told him he wasn't good enough and he'd believed her

for too long. He knew deep down she wasn't right. She'd treated him and everyone around him like shit until her dying day and he'd vowed to get out from that oppression. But some habits die hard and occasionally he could still hear her voice in the back of his mind. Each word like a slap to the face of his younger self.

You're a failure. You're an evil little boy. You'll never amount to anything. You can't listen to the simplest instructions. You're just stupid. You can't be my son.

"A bad seed? What does that even mean? She sounds like a real bitch, and your father doesn't sound like a prize either. They messed you up good."

His sweet Rayne had a mouth on her and she'd summed up this situation quite well. His parents had done a number on him and he was still feeling the effects, although just having this woman on his side made things much better.

"I'm what is known as damaged goods, sweetheart. That's why I said you could do better than me, and that's why I ended things this morning. I'm not sure I can make you happy and I don't want to fail you. You deserve better than that."

Rayne buried her face in her hands for a minute then looked back up at him, her eyes bright with unshed tears. He didn't need her sympathy – had never needed anyone's – but he wouldn't turn it down. His chest was tight with emotion and it wasn't about his fucked up past. It was about…Rayne…and the way she made him feel. Whether he wanted to or not. Because if he had a choice he'd choose not to but that simply wasn't an option any more. She'd burrowed deep into his heart and now he had to figure out what to do next.

"Everyone is damaged in some way, Dare," Rayne said gently, reaching to cup his jaw, his dark stubble tickling the flesh of her palm. "Some more than others but no one is perfect. I'm sure not and we could list all my faults, but let's not. As for making me happy, Dare Turner, that's not your job. Being happy is *my* job. I make that decision every single day. Sure, you can affect my mood but ultimately I am responsible for my happiness and you are responsible for yours. I can't make you happy or love you happy. You have to want to be that way just because it's a nicer way to live and not because you think that's how I want you to be. You don't have to change for me and I mean that. I care about you just the way you are. You can be yourself and I'll be me.

Despite him being a jerk, Rayne was making this easy for him. He didn't deserve it and honestly was more than a little suspicious. There had to be a catch.

"Just be myself? That doesn't sound right."

Apparently he'd said something hilarious because she laughed, albeit softly so as not to wake her family. Her eyes twinkled with mirth and she seemed genuinely amused by his confusion.

"I know, right?" Rayne giggled. "But it doesn't have to be complicated. I like you, Dare Turner. You don't have to try so hard."

Flummoxed, Dare shook his head, not sure what to say or do. He'd never experienced this level of acceptance and it threw him off his game. Could he trust this new emotion unfurling between the two of them? It felt good, but so many things did that ended up being bad for a person.

Like the whiskey he'd imbibed earlier tonight that was rapidly wearing off.

"Don't you want to change me?" he finally asked. "Don't you have a list of complaints with my grouchy demeanor being the first on the list?"

Rayne stood and walked over to the sink to rinse her coffee cup. "Seems like a complete waste of time, if you ask me. I've never known a man to change unless it was for the worse. Do you even want to? I don't think my opinion should be all that important. I'm sure you have some things you wish I would change but I doubt you'd write them down and submit them as a request."

No, he wouldn't do that. He'd always thought Rayne was a little too brash and loud, but now he could see that she was simply straightforward and honest. She didn't tolerate much bullshit, which was just fine with him since he didn't either. She didn't pull her punches and he always knew where he stood with her, which was a first. He'd had too many relationships where females liked to play mind games with him.

"Maybe I should change. As I said, my behavior is really habit. I'm not that pissed off at the world every day but frowning feels more natural than smiling."

Finished clearing up the cups, she came to perch on his knee, dropping a kiss on his forehead as if he were a good boy who had eaten his vegetables. "I'd rather you have an honest scowl than a fake smile. If you're happy then you should smile all you want. But don't try to be something you're not just because you think that's what I want you to be. You have a crappy job, Sheriff, so I can imagine there are days that aren't puppies and rainbows, and that's okay."

He had one more thing to confess and his conscience would be clear. Gathering up his courage, he set aside his dignity. "I've talked to a therapist about this after I came back from the Middle East. I guess the government was worried about me."

Instead of the look of disdain or disappointment he'd expected, Rayne actually looked happier. What the hell? She was happy he needed the shrink. That was a first.

"That's wonderful that you did that. What did the therapist say?"

"That I wasn't a danger to society or myself."

Rayne blinked a few times. "That's...good. I'd never think you were but I'm glad that the US government agrees. Did he or she say anything else?"

That pain in the ass talked all the time, asking him how he felt about everything. Some things he didn't feel anything about and that wasn't going to change for a shrink. Certain events and people in the world didn't deserve to have others wasting energy on them.

"That I was angry at my father because he didn't intervene."

A major understatement if there ever was one.

"Did you and your father make peace before he died?"

"No," Dare answered shortly. "He made a lot of excuses but never owned his part in all of this. He knuckled under to my witch of a mother because he wanted to keep the peace. Except our house was never peaceful. It was only after she died that there was any happiness. And then he married and started a new family because his first one was broken. So no, Rayne, we didn't make peace."

She wanted everything tied up with a bow like an after school special but that wasn't how life worked. Not his, anyway. He'd tried to forgive his father, he truly had, but the old man had blamed Dare with his last breath.

"That's too bad," she said in a small, sad voice that clearly felt badly for him, which was a waste. He was damaged but not angry or bitter. Life happened and he'd played the cards he was dealt as best he could. "You don't blame Sophie, do you?"

Just the thought of his cute little sister made his lips quirk up. "Of course not. I love her and she loves me. We're family and that's why I came back to Valley Station. It's also why I don't want her to leave, especially with that slime Tim Wallace. I've got a bad feeling about him that I can't shake."

Dare's intuition was rarely wrong and it was only a matter of time before he figured out what the issue was with Wallace.

"I feel kind of guilty. My childhood was pretty uneventful compared to yours. My parents are kind of hippies, but other than that we were a normal family."

Lifting an eyebrow, Dare ran a finger along her hip where he knew a tattoo lay under the layer of cotton. "Maybe too normal? You like to stand out, sweetheart."

She leaned down and pressed her lips to his, running her tongue along his lower lip and making him shudder with need. As usual, his inked princess had him hard in less than ten seconds.

"I think you like it too. I think you want to shine and dance. You need to strut, my love. You have so much good in you but you've been hiding it for too long. Let it out and I promise you it will all be fine. You won't get hurt."

He wasn't a child any longer where the world could easily pierce his armor. Few people in this world had that kind of power over him.

She was one of them.

"I'll dance, but only with you, Rayne. Will you dance with me? Right now and right here?"

There was no music but it didn't make any difference. He needed to hold her in his arms like he needed his next breath.

"I'd be honored, Sheriff Turner."

The honor was all his.

CHAPTER THIRTY

Perhaps Rayne should have held onto her anger longer but that simply wasn't her style. She didn't like to hold a grudge or make someone pay for an action they regretted. If Dare was truly sorry, and he certainly seemed to be, it wouldn't be right to not extend some forgiveness his way. From his story he'd been treated cruelly enough, although he seemed fairly healthy after what he'd been through.

He was smart and successful and had trouble letting go of his emotions. It wasn't all that uncommon, especially in a man. If she could help him unwind even a little bit she'd think it a win over his past. He deserved far better than what he'd been given.

So now she was in his arms, dancing in her sister's kitchen, her bare feet on the cold ceramic tile but the rest of her body warming up nicely as he pressed her closer, her cheek resting on his chest. She could hear the steady thump of his heart, and her own pulse sped up in response as her fingers tightened on the hard muscles of his back.

There was no music so Rayne found herself humming a favorite song from her teenage years and Dare didn't seem to mind. His large hand was splayed on her hip while the other cupped the nape of her neck so that her chin was tipped up and their gazes locked. His normally icy blue eyes were dark with passion under the fluorescent lights of the kitchen and their bodies brushed each other softly with each movement, sending lightning sparks of pleasure through her veins.

A warm flush ran down her flesh from forehead to toes and her knees would have given out if he hadn't been holding her so snugly against him, his hard cock pressing into the softness of her belly.

Strong arousal began to build and her mind whirled as she tried to think of a way to have him – right here and now – without waking up the entire neighborhood or at the very least the household. She was already fantasizing about his magic mouth and that devil penis along with those mad-skilled hands. It wasn't fair that he could turn her into a puddle of goo, but then it was so incredibly damn good that it didn't really matter. She was greedy and she didn't care if he knew. She wanted him, all of him, deep inside of her as soon as possible.

Her gaze landed on the pantry door and suddenly she had Dare by the arm and was dragging him across the floor and shoving him into the smaller room off the kitchen, closing the door behind them. She wrapped her arms around his neck and leaped into his arms, her legs winding around his lean middle. Dare was laughing so hard he almost dropped her but caught her as her ass was about six inches from the hard tile.

"Shit, don't drop me. I'm trying to be romantic here and initiate makeup sex."

His face was tucked into the curve of her neck but she could feel his chuckle tickling her skin. "Romantic? You shove me into a closet to fuck and that's romantic? Not that I'm much better. Hell, I'm starting to think we deserve each other."

"So I'm romantically challenged," she admitted as she began to work on the buttons of his shirt. "But you are getting laid out of this, Sheriff. Do you want me to stop so we can wait for a fancy hotel suite and champagne?"

"Fuck no. Do you?"

"Fuck no. I say we go for it. Quietly. My sister, brother-in-law, and niece are sleeping upstairs and if we wake up the baby Camy will murder us without a twinge of regret."

His shirt fell to the floor and she let her palms run all over his warm skin, the muscles firm under her fingers. He closed his eyes and submitted to her exploration and she felt a surge of empowerment run through her. She wanted to touch and taste every inch of him and she wouldn't be denied.

Starting at his hairline she pressed kisses across his forehead, down his jaw, and around to his ear where she nipped at the lobe. She must have been doing something right because he quickly took the two steps required to brace her against the closed door, molding his body to hers, his hard cock digging into her hip.

Her fingers lightly traced a path from his neck to his flat male nipples, and she ran her nails over them, delighting as he sucked in a breath and his head fell back against the hard wood with a thud. Bending her head, she lapped at one brown disc and then the other until his hold on her hips became almost painful and his breathing was ragged. Hot and hard, he was pressed against the seam of her cotton pajama pants, her robe having somehow fallen off in the last few minutes. She rubbed her pussy against him, drawing moans from both of them and sending a fresh burst of honey down her thighs.

Her legs sliding to the floor, she let her tongue wander down his abs, listening to the hiss of his breath as she dipped into his belly button before painting a wet line around the waistband of his jeans. He seemed to shudder under her ministrations so it was a shock when she was suddenly lifted off her feet and her mouth captured with his.

The kiss was hot, wet, and definitely from a man intent on reasserting his dominance. His tongue swept her mouth boldly and she trembled in his arms as he finally let her toes touch the ground.

"You're not in charge here, baby girl."

Rayne bit her lip and looked up at him from under her lashes. "Well, I was until just a minute ago. But I think you kind of liked it if you're honest, big guy. Or is this—" she bumped her hip against his hard cock, "just a figment of my imagination? I have been known to hallucinate when I don't eat regularly."

His smile was pure sin and her heart lurched in her chest as his hands gently pressed down on her shoulders.

"Then we should put something in that sassy mouth of yours, shouldn't we? Take every bit like a good girl and maybe I'll give you a reward."

Dropping to her knees, Rayne reached for the button-fly of Dare's jeans. If this reward was anything like the last ones, she'd be very good indeed.

CHAPTER THIRTY-ONE

Dare was floating on a cloud of pure pleasure, Rayne's mouth wrapped snugly around his cock all warm and wet. Her fingers flexed on his hips as he thrust carefully, not wanting her to choke but needing desperately to feel her lips and tongue sending him straight to heaven. Pressure built at the base of his spine and he closed his eyes to savor the coming explosion.

His knees turned to water and he fell heavily back against the pantry shelves, his shoulders knocking the shelf contents askew and pulling him out of his aroused haze. His lids flew open just in time to see a sack of flour along with two boxes of microwave popcorn drop directly on Rayne, his reflexes too dulled to stop the disaster.

Flour flew everywhere and Rayne yelped and then cursed, her arms flying to cross over the top of her head protectively but it was too late. They were both covered in white powder and it even hung in the air like falling snow, tickling his nose and making Dare sneeze. Rayne rubbed her head where the two boxes had beaned her and she fell back onto her bottom, obviously dazed by the collision.

His near-climax forgotten, he fell to his knees and caressed her hair, pressing a kiss to the crown of her head. "Are you okay, baby? Talk to me."

"I'm okay. More surprised than hurt. What the hell happened? One second I was, you know…and the next…bam."

Her voice was fainter than usual but not pained, which was a good sign. He tried to clean the flour off of them but it was a losing battle and only made things worse as he smeared the white powder onto their damp skin.

"I got cockblocked by some dry goods, mainly ten pounds of flour and some Orville Redenbacher. My main concern is your head. Do you know your name? What year is it?"

Dare's heart screeched to a halt in his chest as Rayne's shoulders began to shake and she buried her face in her palms. He tugged at her arms trying to see what she was hiding, sure she must have some sort of terrible gash on her forehead or perhaps a concussion causing a seizure. He was about to grab his phone and call 911 when she fell back onto the floor, holding her stomach.

Rayne was laughing. Hysterically. Giggling like he'd tickle-tortured her, she was rolling from side to side, her face red and tears falling from her eyes, mixing with the flour and making some sort of paste on her cheeks.

Despite the painful hard-on he was sporting, Dare couldn't help but join in. The ridiculousness of the situation simply could not be ignored. They'd been getting busy in a kitchen pantry and it came back to bite them. They shouldn't be all that surprised.

"Seriously," Dare said between laughs, his face hurting from smiling so wide. "Are you hurt or anything?"

Rayne scrubbed at her tears and cleared her throat, trying to straighten up. "No, I'm fine. It really was my dignity that was hurt. The bag of flour hit my shoulder and not my head, so I got lucky there and the boxes were pretty light. What about you?"

Glancing down at his still erect cock, Dare gave a mock

grimace. "It's been a...hard...evening."

Rayne started giggling again, slapping at his shoulder. "No jokes, funny man. When I laugh, I get the hiccups. And when I get the hiccups, we can't finish this because all I can think about is getting rid of them."

That's my girl. Play through the pain.

"You still want to finish?"

He shouldn't be this turned on, covered in flour from head to toe, but dammit, she made him laugh. She made him deliriously happy and he simply couldn't resist a woman that held that kind of power over him. He was helpless, mesmerized, under a spell and he couldn't be more thrilled about it. He never wanted to be free.

"Do you?" She was peeking at him from under her ridiculously long and dark lashes and giving him that coquettish smile he loved so much. "I'm game if you are."

Dare had turned down sex a time or two in his life for very good reasons but he sure as hell wasn't going to do it now. If Rayne was still in the mood, he was all in.

Not yet, exactly, but he intended to be very soon.

Reaching for the waistband of her pajama pants, he tugged them down to her ankles before throwing them onto the floor, white dust puffing up and billowing in the air. He ran his hands over her knees and up her thighs, pushing them wide so he could get his shoulders in between. He was overwhelmed with the urge to make Rayne come. Hard.

"Brace yourself, and try not to make too much noise."

Brows pulled together, Rayne propped herself up on her elbows to see what he was doing.

"What exactly do you think—"

She never finished her sentence as Dare leaned forward and ran his tongue from her opening to her clit and then back down again. He traced her folds slowly, savoring her taste, taking his time with only one goal. Driving his woman out of her mind with pleasure.

He needed for her to be awash in more pleasure than she'd ever experienced. He wanted tonight to be something special for both of them, and that began by giving to this tiny person that seemed to have an endless capacity to give to him.

She was moving restlessly under him, her fingers tugging at his hair trying to get him exactly where she wanted him. Instead of following her direction, he sent his tongue on the path less taken and ran it along the seam where hip met thigh, breathing in her heady scent a mixture of vanilla and the musk of her arousal. His cock pulsed with need but he ignored its plea for satisfaction as he turned all his attention to the woman now writhing beneath him.

"Dare, please."

The words came out as a husky groan and he moved his lips to her already swollen clit, ready to put her out of her misery and send her into orbit. He closed his mouth over the nub and sucked as her legs shook and her body bowed. Pressing her lips together, she muffled her cries of ecstasy as honey dripped down onto his fingers. Rayne moaned and began to relax, her orgasm receding. He didn't waste any time, sitting up and bracing his back against the shelves before lifting her from the floor so she was straddling his thighs.

"Ride me?"

Rayne's lips widened into a smile of delight and she reached down to grasp his cock, velvet over steel, running her hand up and down the shaft until he was groaning and lifting his hips in some sort of rhythm. The pressure in his lower back was beginning to build again and he pressed a kiss to Rayne's neck while his hands spanned the soft skin of her back, silky soft under his rough palms.

Lowering herself into him, she swiveled her hips and the walls of her pussy hugged him tightly. She sighed when he was in to the hilt and she closed her eyes and let her head fall back, hopefully luxuriating in the delicious sensation of being so incredibly full of his cock. It felt damn good on this end as well. Too good. He was ready to blow his load right the hell now.

His fingers gripped her hips but he waited patiently for her to move, letting her set the pace. Leaning forward, she braced her hands on his wide chest, their gazes colliding and then locking even in the dim light. To someone else she might look a mess, covered in sweat and flour, her hair in disarray, but to Dare no woman had ever looked this sexy in the history of the planet Earth. It aroused and humbled him at the same time that she'd chosen him to give this gift to. He didn't know what he'd done to deserve it but he would just count himself as one lucky bastard.

Taking her own sweet time, she began to sway her hips from the right to the left and then back again, over and over as she lifted up and then lowered herself back down. The hard ridges of his cock rubbed her clit from the inside as his thumb brushed the outside. Slowly. Deliberately. He smiled as she moaned her approval, speeding up her movements and being rewarded with a firmer touch on the sensitive button of flesh. He wanted her to scream his name when she came undone.

"Fuck, baby. You are so damn beautiful," Dare ground out, his teeth snapping together and a film of sweat covering his flesh. "So hot and tight. I can't take much more. I'm close."

He felt her pussy clench as her movements becoming almost frenzied in her haste to tumble over the edge. His hips snapped up again and again, thrusting into her welcoming flesh and hitting all the right places to send her over. Her legs began to shake and his world tilted on its axis before spinning out of control.

He pressed on her clit with his thumb and her pussy clamped down on his cock just as her climax hit, triggering his own fall. He groaned as searing heat traveled from the base of his spine, through his balls, and shot out of his cock. Calling her name through gritted teeth, he rode out his orgasm until it left him shaky and exhausted. Rayne had slumped on his chest and he ran his hand up and down her spine while he whispered silly words he'd never admit to in the light of day.

They lay there for a long while, reveling in the feeling of closeness and the wonder of what their bodies could do to one another. Unfortunately, reality was close on its heels reminding him of the cold, hard, and unforgiving tile under his back and the ten pounds of flour they'd managed to spill in their haste to fuck.

"Sweetheart," he began, hating to burst the bubble they'd created, but if he lay on the floor much longer he might be in the chiropractor office the next morning. As it was he was going to have a nasty hangover. "I think I might be lying on a spatula. Or maybe a box of pasta. Not sure, but it's digging into my ass crack."

Laughter bubbled from Rayne's lips and she lifted up off of him, untangling their arms and legs. The spatula turned out to be the emptied flour bag and he helped Rayne to her feet, surveying the absolute mess they'd made of the tiny room.

"I don't even know where to begin to clean this up." Dare brushed at Rayne's bare skin but the white dust clung as if the flesh was a lifeboat. This wasn't going to be easy. "Maybe we should hose each other down with the kitchen sprayer. Note to self – don't have sex in pantry."

Rayne had clapped a hand over her mouth to muffle the

giggling but she grabbed his hand and pulled him out into the kitchen.

Buck naked.

"Baby, where–"

Rayne pressed a finger over his lips. "Shhh…there's a laundry room that has one of those industrial size sinks. We can get clean there and in the morning I'll vacuum up the pantry. If I do it now I'll wake up the whole house."

"What will your sister and brother-in-law think?"

Dare was pretty sure they'd think he was one horny bastard who couldn't keep it in his pants and disrespected their sister in their own home. Way to make a good impression on her family. If he wanted a future with this woman, he'd need to win over her loved ones and this was no way to go about it.

"I'll just tell them I had the overwhelming urge to bake a cake and that I dropped the flour. I've been known to do stupid things so they might even believe it. In their efforts to never think of me having sex, they might even believe that you never showed up here drunk tonight."

Completely sober now, Dare blushed to the roots of his hair. He'd never hear the end of this from Rayne, Evan, Deputy Billy, or her family. And rightly so. He'd acted like an ass and he knew better.

"You must have found it kind of charming because you didn't kick my drunk ass all the way out to Main Street."

Rayne pulled a large cloth from a cabinet over the washer and dryer and wet it in the oversized sink on the other side before beckoning to him to come closer. She ran the warm, wet cloth over his face and neck, rivulets of water running down his bare chest. "You have a certain charm, Sheriff, but if I were you I wouldn't pull this little stunt again. You might not get lucky next time. I might not be so forgiving."

But she'd forgiven him this time.

He wouldn't mess up his second chance because he was falling hard for Rayne Dunn.

CHAPTER THIRTY-TWO

Rayne emptied the handheld vacuum one last time while trying to avoid the smirking countenance of her sister Camy, who was currently enjoying a piece of bacon and pretending to read the paper.

"I think that's about it. All cleaned up," Rayne sighed, tucking the vac back on the kitchen shelf. If she'd known it existed last night, she would have gone ahead and cleaned up the ten pounds of flour. "Did you leave me any bacon?"

"I most certainly did," Camy retorted. "Although I shouldn't have since I know you're lying to me. A big fat lie, too. There is no way you were baking a cake last night unless that's a euphemism for getting naked and doing the nasty."

Washing her hands, Rayne's eyes widened and she hissed in warning. "Keep your voice down. Mike might overhear."

Camy's brows shot up and she giggled so hard a delicate snort came out of her nose. "Are you kidding? My hubby might look like an all-American guy but he's a freak. Last night wasn't the first time that pantry has seen some action."

Rayne groaned and held up a dish towel over her face as if to hide from her sister. "Ugh. I do not want the details. I don't want to know anything at all about your sex life nor do I want you to know about mine."

"For someone who is supposed to be so free-spirited you're a prude." Camy shook a piece of bacon at her sister while Rayne poured herself a cup of long overdue coffee. "So was he any good? He seemed pretty drunk when he got here."

Choking on the hot brew, Rayne carefully set the cup on the table and plucked a strip of bacon from the tray. "I'm not going to answer that question since it's none of your business. I'm sticking to my story so drop it."

Sitting back in her chair, Camy surveyed Rayne from head to toe, smiling the entire time. "You looked pretty happy and content, so I'm thinking he was good and maybe even very good. He looks hot with that scowl he wears all the time. Like he might think I was a bad girl and needed a spanking."

"Camy!" Rayne exploded, slapping her bacon down on her plate. "You're a mother, for heaven's sake."

Camy giggled, her bare feet dancing on the tile floor. "But I'm not dead. And he is hot you have to admit. I bet he gives a good spanking." She sighed dramatically and waggled her eyebrows. "I just might have to tell Mike what a naughty wife I've been."

Rayne didn't want to hear this. She didn't want to have those pictures in her head but it appeared as if she was going to have to find a way to live with them, because her sister looked like she was just getting started. Dammit, if Rayne had known Camy was going to get all frisky from this she would have suggested they have sex in the garage.

"I hate it," Rayne said through gritted teeth. "Please – I beg of you – change the subject. I'll talk about anything else. Religion. Politics. Uncle Henry's toupee. Pick something."

The smile was wiped from Camy's expression. "You know the family doesn't talk about Uncle Henry's toupee. Ever."

"The let's make our sex life another topic that doesn't get discussed ever. It's too personal."

For some reason Rayne didn't want to talk about Dare and what he meant. She'd never been a shrinking violet when it came to sex and she'd had plenty of late night, alcohol-fueled discussions with her friends about the men in their lives but…this was different. It felt different. More intense and infinitely more real.

"My, my, my, you're awfully prissy these days. This little town is having quite the effect on you. Next thing I'll find out you've given up swearing."

"Screw that," Rayne laughed. "Not going to happen. I have the vocabulary of a well-educated sailor. It took me years to learn all these colorful words."

"I know you don't think so but I know a few myself. I'm not as uptight as you think I am, sis. I'm still me."

Rayne sipped her coffee, not sure where Camy was going with this. Her sister had changed since marrying and moving to Fairfield. There was no arguing with that fact but Rayne had never seen any regret from Camy.

"Of course you're still you," Rayne agreed readily. "But you have to admit that you're not exactly the same person that you were when you moved here. You're all grown up, married, with a kid now. You go to church and crochet blankets. You bake cookies and don't just eat all the dough from the bowl and make yourself sick. You're…an adult."

Camy sighed and pulled her knees to her chest, wrapping her arms around her legs, a pensive expression on her face. "It sucks being an adult. Don't get me wrong though. I love being a wife and mom but sometimes I just want to kick up my heels and have some fun. You still have fun."

Rayne's mouth hung open in shock. Her sister didn't have a

clue, but then Rayne hadn't taken much time lately to help her understand. If anything, she'd been avoiding spending time with Camy and it was clear that needed to stop. They couldn't possibly hope to understand each other's lives if they weren't an integral part of them.

"Fun? You think I'm having a lot of fun?" Rayne shook her head wondering if she should laugh or cry. "Okay, I did have some fun last night. I'll admit to that without giving any details. But most of the time I work ten to twelve hour days six days a week, and on the seventh day I spend most of it cooking, cleaning, or doing laundry. There are no big parties in my life, no wild nights of drinking and dancing. In fact, right now I have a babysitter out in the police cruiser in our driveway. I can't even go to Starbucks without a chaperone. The party animal I was in the past has given way to a woman that likes hot baths and bedtime before ten."

Camy wrinkled her nose. "Jeez, you're an adult too. I can't even live my wildest fantasies vicariously through you anymore. When did this happen? We're officially no fun."

"Speak for yourself. I can be a laugh a minute as long as I get enough sleep." Rayne reached across the table and patted her sister's knee. "How about when this is all over and I don't have a babysitter, you and me have a wild and woolly girls-only weekend? We can go into Bozeman and go dancing, eat chocolate, and maybe some shopping too. We'll act like we have no responsibilities for forty-eight hours. What do you think?"

Camy's smile lit up and she hopped out of her chair and headed straight for her laptop perched on the kitchen counter. "It sounds like a plan. I'll start checking hotels and restaurants. Maybe we can even invite Evie and Sarah from Denver to meet us there. Hey, maybe we could just go to Denver."

I've created a monster.

Camy was already tapping away at her keyboard and humming a happy tune. Rayne had a feeling by nightfall "Camy the Cruise Director" would have their weekend completely planned right down to the pillow fight before bedtime.

It felt good though to be finding a way back to the closeness she and Camy had once shared. Rayne wanted to make that connection again, especially when she thought about Dare and his father and mother. That had been a dysfunctional family and their estrangement was understandable. But the tension between Rayne and Camy came simply from not trying enough to understand each other.

Time to forgive the little digs and slights and put family – and love – first.

Dare tossed the empty paper cup into the trash and turned his attention back to the drawing. It was the only lead they had now and it had to mean something. There were people after this that were willing to do some serious damage to get it. It was important and he just had to figure out why. No small task apparently, because he'd been staring at it for the last hour and so far all he had to show for it was a headache.

After he'd snuck out of Rayne's home last night he'd had Deputy Billy drive him home where he'd managed to get a few hours' sleep, leaving Deputy Harris to protect Rayne. This morning he'd come in extra early and sucked down massive amounts of coffee along with two bear claws while he studied the design and looked up ideas on the Internet.

Nothing. The morning had been a gigantic bust and it hadn't put Dare in the best of moods. The deputies were giving him a wide berth and one had even closed the door to Dare's office without so much as a by your leave.

A knock sounded and then Deputy Jay stuck his head in. The lawman was in his early thirties but showed great promise if he could keep his dick in his pants. The young man was considered handsome by most of the ladies in town with his reddish-brown hair and goatee. He dated a different woman every weekend and seemed to be enjoying the hell out of his bachelor life to the point where he often came into work exhausted in the morning from screwing his brains out all night.

Lucky bastard.

Then Dare remembered what he'd been doing last night and had to clear his throat to keep from smiling. If one of his deputies saw him happy they might have a stroke, and Dare needed all the manpower he could get.

"Hey, Sheriff. I'm heading to lunch at the bowling alley. Did you want to come?"

Dare couldn't stare at this drawing one more second. He needed a break and some food.

"I'm coming with you." Dare held out the clear evidence bag that contained the drawing. "Have Margaret lock this back in the evidence locker and then meet me out front. I'll drive."

The bowling alley wasn't that far and within ten minutes Dare and Jay were tucked into a booth in the food area, the sounds of balls striking pins in the background.

"Thanks for inviting me. I needed the fresh air."

Jay gave his boss a lopsided smile. "Not sure the bowling alley qualifies as fresh air but I'm happy to have the company. If I came here alone, Susie would be trying to talk to me and get back together or something. That's never going to happen."

Dare peeked over his menu at the pretty brunette behind the shoe rental counter. She was a lovely girl but everyone in the area knew her reputation.

"Were you the only man who didn't know what she was

like?" Dare asked. "I've made sure to stay away from her since I came back to town."

Jay sighed and slumped in his seat. "She seemed really normal and nice whenever I talked to her. Real sweet, you know. Then I went out on one date with her and she's like a psychobunny. Talking about marriage and kids and meeting her family. Shit, I just wanted to get laid."

Dare hid his smile. Jay was learning a valuable lesson. "That's how it starts. Just wanting to get laid. She'll move on soon enough to some other poor bastard. In the meantime, why come here for lunch?"

Jay's eyes widened in surprise. "Because they have the best cheeseburger in three counties."

"That they do," Dare agreed, lowering his menu. Who was he kidding? He was getting the cheeseburger and an order of their special seasoned fries. "Just don't make eye contact with her. Look at the table or your shoes but not at her."

Jay's gaze immediately dropped to his hands wrapped around a water glass. "You know, I'm glad we came today even if Susie says something to me. I'm thinking that I'm getting tired of the local girls. I need to expand my horizons a little."

Just what Jay didn't need…to be known as a Lothario in more than this county.

"What did you have in mind? Checking out the girls in Springwood or Harper?"

The corners of Jay's lips turned up and his cheeks took on a reddish tone. "Actually I have a girl in mind. She's sexy as fuck too but smart. At least I assume she is. She'd have to be to run her own business and all."

Dare could only wonder about what Jay considered smart. If they could find their car keys and tie their shoes that would probably be enough for the young lawman.

"You should ask her out then."

Jay's smiled widened and he stood from the table, adjusting his gun belt and gazing at something or someone behind Dare. "Don't mind if I do, boss. I'll be right back."

Jay strode toward his target and Dare twisted in his chair to see what this sexy and smart woman looked liked, his heart dropping to his feet immediately.

She *was* sexy and smart. And sweet. And wonderful.

The woman Jay was going to ask out was Rayne who was sitting with her sister Camy and looking like they were going to order lunch.

The realization smacked Dare upside the head, making him rub his aching forehead. No one knew he and Rayne were dating. To the casual observer she was a free agent able to date or sleep with anyone she cared to.

Dare didn't like that at all but he couldn't think of one legitimate reason to stop Jay.

So he'd think up a bogus one.

CHAPTER THIRTY-THREE

"**D**id you know Dare would be eating lunch here?" Rayne hissed at her sister Camy as they sat down at a table in the restaurant area of the local bowling alley. They'd both had a craving for cheeseburgers and after dropping the baby off with her grandmother, they'd driven the ten miles to Valley Station for a quick bite since Fairfield lacked a place to find a great hamburger. "I don't like bothering him at work, sis."

Camy settled in her chair and picked up the menu. "As a matter of fact I did not know he'd be here, but you're hardly bothering him by sitting here and eating. Does he get pissy about little things like this? Because that might be a nasty red flag."

"He doesn't but I know he takes his job seriously." Rayne peered over her menu at Dare and the other deputy sitting across from him who appeared to be looking their way. "Who's with him? I haven't seen him before."

Camy smiled and waved at the young deputy, making Rayne bury her face in her menu. Her sister couldn't be cool if she tried.

"That's Deputy Jay Mallory. He's something of a Casanova but quite sweet."

Rayne groaned and gave her sister a small kick under the

table. "When I asked who he was I meant for you to sneak a look at him, not wave a flag. Don't you know how to be sly?"

"Why would I be sly?" Camy shrugged and snapped her menu shut. "He's clearly looking at you, so why are we pretending we don't see him? Oh look, he's standing up and coming over here. I can introduce you."

From the expression on the man's face, he wasn't going to be inquiring about the weather or the chances of the local team in the big game. Rayne had seen men who looked like that and invariably they asked her to dance or if they could buy her a drink. The whole situation was only made more awkward by the fact that her secret boyfriend-slash-lover was the young man's boss and sitting right there and watching the entire thing.

In comparison to the open happiness of Deputy Jay, Dare's face was a gray cloud of pissed off. He didn't look amused in the least and his ice blue eyes were currently gazing at Rayne with laser-like focus as if daring her to take up whatever the deputy offered.

The asshole was going to watch her squirm. Well, she had ways of getting even and every one of them was in the bedroom.

"Hey Camy, how are you doing? Long time no see."

The young deputy stood in front of their table with his thumbs hooked in his gun belt, a smile across his handsome face. Self-confidence oozed from every pore and Rayne knew she was going to have to take him down a peg or two whether she wanted to or not.

"Nice to see you too, Deputy," Camy said. "What have you been up to lately? Are you still planning to enter the fishing derby next month?"

Deputy Jay's face split into a grin. "Hell yes, I can't wait. It's my year and Duke Wallace knows it. I'll be taking home the trophy, just you wait and see."

The deputy's gaze drifted to Rayne and then back to Camy, his eyebrows raised in question. Camy picked up on the suggestion and waved a hand at her sister. "Have you met my sister Rayne? She owns the local tattoo shop and moved here to Montana from San Francisco. Rayne, this is Deputy Jay Mallory."

"Nice to meet you, Deputy," Rayne murmured, not wanting to encourage the young man in any way but it went against her friendly nature.

The deputy leaned in, placing his hands flat on the table so he was looking directly into her eyes. "How have we not run into each other all these months? Maybe we could have dinner one night and get to know each other a little. I could show you around to some of the local spots that you may not have discovered yet."

Rayne fiddled with her paper napkin, her gaze skittering around the bowling alley. "Right now I'm working so much I rarely have time to go out. But I do appreciate the offer—you're very sweet."

His smile became almost predatory as if he was a wolf and she was a juicy steak.

"You have no idea how sweet I can be. Maybe we could just go for coffee?"

Before she could answer a large and familiar hand came down on the deputy's shoulder.

"Our food just arrived at the table, Jay. You should eat before it gets cold. I'm sure these lovely ladies want to get along with their lunch as well."

Finally Dare had intervened. What he'd been waiting for she wasn't sure and she was a little annoyed about their secret relationship, although it had been just as much her idea as his. Perhaps she was just annoyed with him in general, but she ought to feel sorry for him. After his drunken binge last night he looked a little worse for wear with dark circles under his eyes and his hair askew as if he'd run his fingers through it too many times.

"Uh sure, Sheriff. I was just catching up with the ladies." Deputy Jay gave them a mock salute and headed back to the table. Dare nodded to them briefly, not addressing them directly before following the younger man, tension in the line of his shoulders. It was clear the two men were going to have an uncomfortable conversation and Rayne was distinctly glad she wasn't the deputy right about now.

Camy giggled as they watched the two lawmen dig into their cheeseburgers. "I think poor Deputy Jay is about to get his ass kicked and he won't even know why. Unless Dare spills the beans about your relationship of course. Do you think he will?"

"It's okay if he does." Rayne shrugged, quite fine with the idea of going public at this juncture. She and Dare had feelings for one another, although it was never going to be smooth sailing between them. They were both stubborn and opinionated like…mules falling in love.

Rayne and Camy ate their lunch in peace, chatting about the upcoming holidays and the cleanup at Rayne's home. Dare and Jay didn't come over again, although the young woman behind the counter in the main bowling alley sidled up to their table and appeared quite enamored with the handsome deputy. He seemed a little put off but Rayne couldn't help thinking they might make a nice couple.

"Are you ready to go?" Camy asked, popping the last French fry into her mouth with a sigh of bliss. "We need to head over to your place."

There was a chance Rayne's new bed would be delivered this afternoon along with the new linens she'd ordered.

"I just need to run to the ladies room. I'll be right back."

Rayne popped into the restroom, taking care of all that needed to be done, including a fresh coat of lipstick and a comb through her unruly locks. The early morning rain had turned her hair into a riot of waves and curls that simply wouldn't be tamed. The world would have to deal with her as she was. She exited the bathroom and ran right into a wall of muscle and bone. Dare, of course.

"How long have you been skulking outside the ladies room, Dare? That's creepy."

Her gorgeous lover simply rolled his eyes and crossed those muscular arms across his chest, pulling his shirt tight around his shoulders and sending increasingly dirty thoughts through her filthy mind. She could just grab him and pull him back into the restroom and one of the stalls… Bing, bang, boom, they could be back at the table in about five minutes. No one the wiser.

"I needed to talk to you." Dare snapped his fingers in front of her face. "Are you listening to me? You look like you're far away from here."

She was currently shagging his brains out in a dingy bowling alley bathroom. Hell, they weren't the most romantic couple in the world, especially after the interlude in the pantry last night. Would a quick hit in the ladies room be tacky?

Okay, yes, it would be tacky.

But would it be *too* tacky?

"I'm here," she said, pulling herself back to the present where they were standing a foot apart. Too far, if anyone asked her opinion. "What did you want to talk about?"

Dare pursed his lips and tapped his chin. He was nervous and it was extremely cute.

"I, uh, I'm sorry if my deputy put you on the spot like that. Once I had him back at the table I told him it wasn't professional to ask out a woman that our department is protecting."

Rayne quirked an eyebrow and had to press her lips together to keep from busting out in laughter. "You don't think that's a trifle hypocritical, Sheriff? After all, you're...fucking...the woman your department is protecting. He just wanted to take me to dinner."

Dare smirked—that's right, *smirked*—and it was the sexiest thing she'd ever seen. "Trust me, baby, he wanted more than dinner. He doesn't know it but he wishes he was me. I'm guessing he's not the only one."

"Did you tell him?"

"Fuck no. It's none of his business."

Rayne sighed and leaned against the wall. She was getting tired of acting like a double naught spy and hiding. "I had to tell Camy after you dumped me. Mike figured it out as well after you showed up drunk last night. He's not stupid."

"How'd they take it?"

Smiling, Rayne stepped closer to Dare so she had to crane her neck to look up at him. "Camy thinks it's hot and Mike wants to know what your intentions are. Prepare to be interrogated, handsome, because he's dying to act like a father or big brother."

"Camy would think it was hot," Dare chuckled, leaning down so he was nose to nose with Rayne but still not kissing her. "I can probably handle Mike, but just in case I'll take him out for a beer so we can talk man to man."

Rayne played with one of the buttons on Dare's shirt but kept her gaze on the floor. "Does Sophie know?"

"Not yet, but I can tell her if you like. What's all the questions about? You've never been afraid to speak your mind before."

That was true and playing the reticent card wasn't her style.

Better to just say it and deal with the fallout had always been her style. "I'm getting tired of all the cloak and dagger. It's exhausting. Can't we just go public?"

Dare placed his hand over hers and then lifted her fingers to his warm lips, just brushing the knuckles. The kiss sent tingles straight down her spine and all the way to her toes. "We can. I'm not against it and it will make me look like a huge hypocrite, but who gives a shit? I'm the boss. Jay will understand why I said what I said once he finds out we're a couple. Is that all that's bothering you?"

Everything was bugging her. She'd been mugged, robbed, and now had a permanent shadow in the shape of a cop.

"Having one of your men follow me is creepy," she admitted, nodding to the deputy trailing her today. He was sitting a few tables away from Camy and finishing his own cheeseburger. "I know why he's there but it doesn't make it any better. I'm not a rock star or actress. When someone follows me it feels strange."

"I have a stack of paperwork on my desk that I need to get done. You could hang out at the station with me. Then you'd be following me, not the other way around."

Leave it to Dare to come up with a solution that involved her orbiting his world. "I'm not sure that will solve the problem. Besides, I might get a furniture delivery this afternoon so I was headed over to the house, deputy in tow."

"How about coming over tonight for dinner? I can tell Sophie about us, we can watch some movies, then curl up for the night in my bed. I'll be there to protect you."

That sounded like a capital idea. Sex in a bed, for a change.

"Aren't you worried about what kind of example that might set for your baby sister? My spending the night, that is. She might want Tim to spend the night one of these days."

Dare growled low in his throat and yanked her closer so she was pressed against his hard body. Instead of fighting, she slid her hands around his neck. If they were coming out from undercover they might as well give the residents of Valley Station a good show.

"The hell he will. No way some guy is going to shack up with my little sister under my own roof. If she wants a man to spend the night she needs a marriage license."

He didn't know what he was asking for. "Don't say that too loud because she just might do it. Then you'd have Tim Wallace for a son-in-law and the Wallaces would be relatives."

"He's not spending the night." Leaning down, Dare pressed a sizzling kiss on her lips. "But you are. Pack an overnight bag and I'll pick you up after my shift about six, okay?"

"What about Spartacus?"

His brows shot up and he shook his head. "That damn cat can spend one night alone, can't he?"

Of course he could, he was a cat. But it was fun to tease Dare and see just how far he might let her push him.

"He might miss me."

"You're not bringing the cat, Rayne. Give it up now."

Giggling, she pressed a few butterfly kisses on the corners of his mouth. "Okay, tough guy. The cat will stay but on one condition."

"Name it."

Dare didn't look worried in the least and she didn't have a difficult hurdle anyway. This one was a piece of cake.

"Kiss me. Kiss me like you want to carry me to bed. I want everyone in this joint to know you belong to me."

He smiled and his lips hovered over hers so closely, she could feel his warm breath and smell the citrus of his body wash. "Do I belong to you?"

"Fuck yeah. Don't forget it, either. I'm not a forgiving woman."

His expression softened and those eyes darkened with desire. "Actually, you are. Not many women would have forgiven my bonehead move last night, let alone ended up on the pantry floor with me. You're one of a kind, Rayne Dunn."

Her cheeks flushed as images flooded her brain. Sexy, naked ones. But she didn't get a chance to respond as he slammed his mouth down on hers, kissing her until the room spun and she had to hold onto his shoulders for support.

She leaned against him, content to let him hold her upright while her fingers kneaded the tense muscles at the base of his skull. "That was hot, Sheriff. I can't wait for our slumber party tonight. Are we going to braid each other's hair?"

He was looking over her shoulder and this time it was him off in another world. She waved her hand in front of his face and he gave her his signature scowl as a reply.

"Earth to Dare. First it was me and now you. Are you thinking about tonight too?"

"No. I'm thinking about that old photo on the wall." He nodded toward a framed photo nestled in the alcove to the restrooms. "Have you seen it before?"

Rayne huffed and took a step back. "You're looking at photos and not fantasizing about tonight, huh? Boy, the romance fades fast, lover boy." She turned on her heel and moved closer to the photo. It was an old black and white of some men panning for gold. She'd heard there were gold strikes in Montana many years ago. "I've never seen it. Does it look familiar or something?"

Dare situated himself close to the framed photo, his face only a few inches from it before poking a finger at the glass. "Here. Look at this, Rayne. Right here."

She had to squint to see what he was pointing at, but when she did she almost stopped breathing for a second. Feeling light-headed, she grabbed onto Dare's arm to keep from falling to the floor. "The logo on the equipment is the same thing Patrick Moulson had designed into his tattoo. It's the same."

Her normally taciturn lover had a huge grin on his face. "Yes, it is. That mine has been closed and abandoned for years. Do you know what that means?"

It was the first lead real lead they'd had in weeks.

"Road trip."

CHAPTER THIRTY-FOUR

Dare turned right onto the dirt road and pointed to the north. "There isn't much left of the mine. Just an old building and some discarded equipment. It's about six miles from here."

Tanner tapped a message into his phone before slipping it into his pocket. "How long has it been abandoned? Who owned it? Maybe there's a connection."

"Since the late eighties, I think. Give or take a year or two. It was owned by the Cavendish family but they sold out to a big conglomerate who then stripped what they could before shutting it down. We can check but I doubt there will be anything to connect the two."

Tanner's gaze took in the desolate landscape. "Sure as shit is remote as hell. I guess this might be a good place to plan a bank robbery and then maybe hide the money."

The SUV bumped and rolled over the rutted and forgotten road, almost loosening Dare's teeth. "This location has to be important enough to make a man want to tattoo the logo permanently on his person. Whether they hid the money here is a question, but it means something."

Tanner grinned as Dare pulled the truck up to what looked

like an old shack. "Our job is to figure out what it means. We're professional lawmen. How hard could it be?"

Dare knew that Tanner was simply busting his balls so he chuckled in response and slid from the driver's seat, bringing along his cell phone. He walked behind the vehicle about twenty feet and pointed to a set of tire tracks that didn't belong to him.

"There's no reason to be on this road unless you're coming to this mine, but there's another set of tracks here. I'll get a few pictures and send them to the lab. Maybe we can get a make on the vehicle."

Tanner looked up at the clear blue sky. "When was the last rain? It's been about a week, hasn't it?"

Dare snapped the photos and quickly sent them off to Deputy Billy. "It was last Friday, I believe, so we know whomever was here visited in the last five to seven days. Now why would anyone be up here, that's the question."

Walking around the old building, Tanner tried to see in through the filthy windows but they were encrusted with dirt. "I doubt anyone would be up here for something lawful unless maybe some kids came up here to make out. But it isn't exactly conducive to romance. It looks more like a junkyard."

Broken and rusted shovels and picks were strewn across the clearing, framing the busted conveyor belt that led down into the hole in the ground. The opening had been covered up for safety by a large round wooden door with a padlock, and surprisingly it appeared to have not been breached by curious teenagers or would-be miners looking to make their fortune in a used up gold vein.

Dare tried the doorknob and of course it was locked. He looked over his shoulder at Tanner and gave him a smile. "Should I?"

"You are the law around here. Is there anyone that would

even protest?"

Not really, but Dare liked to do things by the rules if at all possible. That was the main reason Rayne's cute little ass was sitting at home right now. She'd begged to be able to come with him but he didn't want to have to worry about her safety when he was concerned about his own. Frankly, he didn't know what they were walking into. So far the trip had been uneventful, but things had a way of taking a turn for the worse when he least expected it.

"Step back," Dare warned, eyeing the flimsy lock. "We don't know if this is booby-trapped or something worse."

"Worse? What's worse than a bomb?"

Dare picked up a ratty shovel that was still in one piece. "Two bombs. A gunman. Easy listening radio."

Tanner snorted but did as he was asked. Grunting with effort, Dare swung the shovel, splintering the wood but the door didn't budge, much to his surprise. He'd thought it would disintegrate with any pressure whatsoever.

"Need any help there? Is it too much for you?" Tanner taunted with a laugh. "Should we tie the doorknob to the truck bumper and hit reverse?"

Dare looked up at the sky and squinted at the sun, keeping his frustration under control. He was glad it was only Tanner that had seen that and not his deputies. They'd never let him forget it.

"I don't think that will be necessary, Grandpa. I've got this."

Tanner took the ribbing in stride and stayed back while Dare wound up as if he were getting ready to hit a home run. The metal flat of the shovel made contact with the doorknob, which cracked and sailed over Dare's head while the lock broke under the impact, causing the door to fly back and hit the wall with a satisfying bang.

Tanner strode forward, his gun drawn, and peeked around the now wide open doorway. His stance was tense and alert so it was instantly noticeable when his posture sagged and relaxed. He held up his hand and waved Dare forward.

"Looks like we got here too late."

Dare holstered his own weapon with a sigh. Two dead bodies lay on the floor in a pool of dried blood. Three people were dead. And he was no closer to figuring out who was doing this. Something had to give and soon.

✧ ✧ ✧ ✧

Rayne slumped down onto Dare's living room couch, her bottom lip stuck out in a pout. "I can't believe I wasn't there. It wasn't dangerous at all and you're being overprotective."

Dare's brows shot up at her bold statement. "Overprotective? Baby, three people are dead...that we know of. There could be more. Money is a powerful motivator and if they think you know something they won't hesitate to come after you. From now on, I'm keeping you under close observation. You'll have me or a deputy on you at all times."

It sounded like one of Dante's circles of hell. Someone watching every little movement she made every second of the day and night. She adored Dare but that much togetherness was going overboard. She needed a little bit of privacy.

"If they killed those two men then they know what's on the tattoo," Rayne pointed out as he joined her on the couch. After a long day cleaning her house, he'd relieved the deputy watching her and brought her back to his place where he could keep an eye on her personally. Camy had protested at first but then been won over when Dare convinced her it was the safest place for Rayne. "They don't need me anymore. For all you know, the man has the money and is headed for Mexico or the Bahamas.

Wherever bank robbers go to retire these days when they no longer have to share the loot."

"The loot?" Dare laughed and propped his feet on the coffee table. "Who are you, Ma Barker?"

Rayne lifted her chin and shrugged, not letting his teasing deter her from the goal.

She didn't need protecting.

"I'm simply trying to get you to see sense, Dare. Whoever was looking for that drawing must know what it contains or they wouldn't have found the mine. It makes sense, don't you see?"

She put a little more pleading in her words than she normally would but she didn't like having a babysitter follow her around. Today the deputy had sat three tables away while she and Camy had eaten lunch. He'd just watched them. Eating. Then more watching. It was creepy and it gave her an unsettled feeling in her gut.

"Or the killer followed them there and that's how he found the location," Dare stated reasonably. "There are two parts to that design, babe, and they may still need the second half. I'm not taking any chances with your life."

"But you'll take chances with your own."

His arm came around her shoulders and pulled her closer so they were curled together, her head on his chest. "It's my job and I'm used to it. I'm not going to do anything stupid so don't worry about me."

Rayne poked him in the chest. "You're made of flesh and bone like everyone else. You need to be careful. Maybe I'll get you a bodyguard."

She could feel his chuckle under her cheek as he tugged at a stray strand of hair. It was hard to believe this content and smiling man was Dare Turner. "Tanner does a pretty good job of not letting me do anything dumb. When this is all over, I'd love for you to meet some of my friends like him, Seth, Reed, Griffin, and Evan. You'd get along with the wives really well, especially Presley. She's something else and keeps Seth on his toes."

Her throat tightening with emotion, she didn't reply but simply smiled and snuggled closer. She loved it when he talked about the future and now he was categorizing her with the "wives". She'd never had much of a yen for marriage and commitment but this man might be the one to change her mind. She could see herself spending evenings with him curled up on this sofa watching television or reading in bed.

"So stop trying to change the subject and tell me about the two men you found. What do you know?"

He'd already told her the men's names were Earnest Haines and Milo Yardley, both in their late twenties.

"Not much," Dare admitted, running his fingers through her hair in a soothing motion. "The two men are local and have a history of petty crime. Mostly bar fights but one of them has burglary on their rap sheet. We'll cross reference any prints from your shop and home break-ins to them."

"Did you know them?"

"In passing. I was never the arresting officer although I knew of both of them. They weren't bad guys, just more like troublemakers when they were drunk. Both of them had trouble holding down a job and have worked at several of the local ranches before getting kicked to the curb. Honestly, I didn't even know they knew each other until today."

In a small town like Valley Station there weren't too many secrets, but there had to be some.

"We're a secret or we were," she pointed out to him. "So if they were friends or business partners they could probably keep that a secret too."

"For how long though? You and I haven't been dating long, and after today at the bowling alley I'm pretty sure the cat's out of the bag. You've got a hickey on your neck, babe, and people are going to notice."

Rayne slapped a hand over the red spot she'd seen in the mirror earlier. "Is it that bad? It didn't look like much of anything this afternoon."

Dare waggled his eyebrows and grinned. "It's turning a love-ly shade of purple. I like marking my territory so be warned."

Slapping him ineffectually on the chest, she rubbed the sore flesh and gave him a dirty look. "I'm not territory, you male chauvinist pig. If you mark me, you can be damn sure I'll mark you."

"Be my guest, baby." Dare held his arms wide in invitation. "Make my body your canvas. Wait, you've already done that, although no one can see it."

"I'm serious, Dare."

"So am I. You want to give me some love bites or hickeys, you go right ahead. I'll wear them proudly."

"You are a sick, sick man." Rayne lifted up and threw her leg over both of his so she was straddling him. She wanted to be able to look directly into his eyes. "I worry about your mental health."

"I am a sad specimen, but I'm all yours."

She brought her hands up to cup his jaw. "You did it again, dammit."

Dare gave her a long suffering sigh. "What did I do this time, baby girl?"

"You got us off the subject again. I want to know about the murders. Talk and don't change the subject until you're done."

"I only have preliminary information to go on until the au-topsy, but it appears that Haines was shot in the chest at point blank range, maybe a .38. That blood spatter is near the middle of the room from what I observed, but Yardley's was closer to the door. His entry wound appears to be in the back so I'm guessing he was running away possibly after seeing Haines shot."

"They trusted each other," Rayne murmured, trying to picture the scene in her head despite not being there today. "It doesn't sound like Haines was afraid."

"If they were partners and money was involved, they should have been. There's little honor among thieves as I told you before. Clearly, someone wanted to keep it all for themselves."

"But this is it, right? Tanner saw four bank robbers and now three of them are dead. That leaves one."

His lips twisted as he ran his warm hands down her spine to rest on her bottom. "Theoretically, yes. But they could have other partners who weren't with them at the bank. I can't say for sure that the bloodshed is over."

"So what happens now?"

"I investigate Haines and Yardley. Their friends, family, enemies, business dealings. Anything and everything. I want to know their favorite food and what fabric softener they used. Somehow I need to find the connection to the fourth man. When I do, I'll find him and the money."

Dare sounded exhausted, his eyes bloodshot and not from drinking too much last night. This case was wearing on him and Rayne wasn't sure how to make him feel better. She only knew she wanted to fix everything for him. She'd never had that urge before, and to be honest it scared her. He had become that important in her life.

If that wasn't love she didn't know what was.

"You will." She ghosted her lips across his, bringing a smile to his face. "It's only a matter of time."

His hands slid up under her t-shirt while the other palmed

the globe of her ass and his mouth began to explore the curve of her jaw. It was quite a compromising position to be found in and that was exactly where Sophie saw them when she burst into Dare's house, calling for her brother.

Rayne froze, her eyes wide as Sophie stood in the middle of the living room taking in the lascivious scene, her own mouth hanging open in shock.

"Um, is there something you want to tell me, big brother? Are there going to be little Dares and Raynes running around soon?"

Christ on a crutch, Rayne wasn't ready for that. Being in love was a big enough adjustment.

Dare's fingers crept into the neutral territory of her middle back, and he seemed to swallow hard before answering his sister.

"I can explain. I mean, we can explain. It's not what you think."

That was news. "It's not?" Rayne asked. "I thought it was."

He shifted uncomfortably, a dull red suffusing his cheeks. "Well…it is…but it isn't. What I'm saying is…it's not just physical."

He was cute when he was embarrassed and she simply couldn't keep her mouth shut. He'd probably kill her later but she only lived once and perhaps the deputy would protect her.

"Really? I'm just here for the hot sex. You're a big stud, Dare Turner."

From the growl he emitted, she'd poked the bear.

Again.

CHAPTER THIRTY-FIVE

Would this day ever end?

Dare was beginning to think that he was caught up in some never-ending loop and that he would be dealing with the women in his life over and over until he passed out from sheer mental and emotional overload.

Rayne had climbed off his lap and into the easy chair next to the couch while Dare stood to greet his little sister and try to repair whatever damage to her psyche had been inflicted by seeing her brother get to second base with his girlfriend.

But Sophie didn't look all that traumatized. She looked pissed off.

She shook her finger at him, a scowl that looked a heck of a lot like his on her face. Clearly she'd inherited the ability to convey displeasure with the lift of an eyebrow. "You kept it a secret from me and everyone else. That's not a respectful way to treat a woman."

Dare looked at Rayne, who had her hand clapped over her mouth trying not to laugh, and then back at his militant little sister. She didn't understand the situation but damned if he wanted to explain it. It was his life and he didn't owe anyone reasons for his actions.

"You're brother treats me just fine, Sophie. It was my idea too."

"See," he challenged his sister. "No complaints. I'm a perfect gentleman."

Rayne snorted loudly and he knew she was thinking of his drunken visit to her doorstep last night. "Perfect? That's a stretch."

"Maybe perfect wasn't the right word," he allowed. "How about we just say that I've treated you well?"

Rayne's smile was way too amused. "Was that before or after you dumped me? I just want to be sure we're both talking about the same thing."

A gasp from Sophie had Dare hanging his head in shame. Shit, a guy makes one mistake and no one ever forgets. "I apologized for that. It was a mistake. A big one."

"Dare Turner, did you hurt this poor woman's feelings?"

Rayne held up her hands, still giggling at Sophie's indignation. "It's okay. He explained and apologized."

"I would hope so. He's lucky to have someone like you in his life. Not like those airheads he's dated in the past."

"They weren't that bad." Dare wasn't sure why he was defending himself since he didn't disagree with Sophie, but he didn't like that his baby sister was the one pointing it out.

"Really?" Sophie sat down on the sofa, crossing her legs. "How about that Gloria? She was a brain trust. She thought Canada was part of the United States. Or we could talk about Sienna and her plan to become a life coach. Never mind that she was broke, living with her parents, and had never actually achieved anything. She thought it would be a job where she'd have a lot of free time."

Dare's cheeks were hot with embarrassment and he'd had about enough of this entire conversation. "I get it. My previous taste in women left something to be desired. But your taste in the opposite sex isn't much better, sis. Tim Wallace is a loser. He can barely hold down a job."

Sophie's brows pulled down and her countenance turned stormy. "He's not like that. He's just figuring out what he wants to do with his life, that's all."

"By the time I was his age people were shooting at me in a hot desert. I didn't have the luxury of just quitting and walking away when others were counting on me."

Crossing her arms, Sophie pressed her lips together. The universal sign that she was done listening. "You don't have to be an ass about it, Dare. The fact is you're not dating him so you don't have to like him. I'll be leaving here for Denver soon enough and then you never have to see him or me again."

Dammit, this conversation was going entirely the wrong way. He didn't want her to leave, he just wanted her to see Wallace for what he really was.

Not good enough for her.

"That reminds me that we need to have another talk about Denver. I understand if you want to go to school but I don't like the idea of you living with him. Maybe you could get a nice girl as a roommate."

"Like a nun? Isn't that what you mean? You don't want me to have sex but I bet you and Rayne do it all the time."

"Not all the time…" Rayne was trying to help but this might not be the moment. "I do have a job, although I haven't been doing much of it lately."

A banging on the door had Dare pivoting on his heels, thankful to be distracted by something – anything – else. Brothers and sisters were not meant to discuss their respective sex lives. It was wrong in about eight different ways.

He yanked open the front door and his relief died immediately. Tim Wallace stood on the other side of the threshold, a grin on his face that didn't falter when he saw Dare. If the young man had a lick of sense he'd be terrified, but he appeared blissfully unaware of Dare's animosity.

"Hey, Sheriff. I'm here to see Sophie."

Dare growled an incoherent response and stepped back for the boy to pass. He had to quell the urge to take out his service revolver and march Wallace back to his truck with the directive to never darken this door again.

Sophie hopped up from the sofa and threw her arms around her boyfriend. The young man had the audacity to kiss her, slipping her the tongue right in front of Dare. He was about to rip them apart when Rayne insinuated herself between him and the young lovers.

"Can we talk in the kitchen for a minute?" she whispered. "Let's leave them alone."

She led the way and he followed reluctantly, not sure it was the best idea to give Sophie and Tim any privacy. Dare's house had a pantry too.

She placed her hands on his shoulders and looked him right in the eye. "Dare, I'm going to give you some advice. If you don't lay off Tim, you're going to push your one and only sister away. It doesn't have to be like that but you have got to respect some boundaries. She's eighteen and I can tell you from experience that a first love is a powerful thing. If he's what you say he is, sadly, the only way she's going to figure that out is the hard way. I know you're trying to save her from a broken heart but it doesn't work like that. She has to find out for herself."

"She was giving me advice. She said I didn't treat you respectfully. But it's wrong to give my opinion on her relationship? That doesn't seem fair."

She sighed and slid onto one of the barstools at the kitchen island. "She said her opinion, you refuted it, and she dropped it. End of story. You said your opinion of Tim, she said you're wrong, now it's time for you to drop it."

Dare looked over his shoulder where Tim and Sophie were in the living room locked in an embrace. "Tell me you think that guy is good for her and I'll leave it alone and never say another word."

Propping her chin in her hands, her lips turned down. "I can't say that, Dare. He does seem to lack ambition but I'm not sure that's a totally fair evaluation as I don't know him very well. He is sweet to her and I haven't heard anyone say he cheats. I guess he does drink and play cards too much and that does worry me. But I don't get a vote, babe, and neither do you. It's up to Sophie."

Dare rubbed his temples to sooth the blooming headache that was beginning to pound beneath his fingers. "Fuck. This is so messed up. I'd make a lousy father."

"You'd make a wonderful father." She slid her hand around his waist and pulled him closer. "Because you really love her and want the best for her. You're going to be an amazing dad, Dare."

Images of Rayne and himself playing with their children in the park swamped his senses and he had to put out a trembling hand and grab onto the counter for support. He'd never thought of himself as a family man but the urge to build that with this woman was overwhelming. His stomach heaved and rolled and he wasn't completely sure he could keep down the protein bar he'd wolfed down in the truck.

"I didn't have much of a role model but thank you. I think you'd make a good mother too."

Looking up at him, she dug her tiny chin into the spot over his heart. "Aren't you a sweet talker? Be careful there, Sheriff, we might actually start talking about the future and all that icky stuff."

They were going to have that discussion but after the murder and bank robbery were solved and put to bed.

"We can't have that now, can we?" He let his hands explore the soft skin just under her t-shirt. "You know what? You make me happy."

He heard her sharp intake of breath and then unshed tears sparkled in her eyes. "You make me happy too, my big grouchy bear. Deliriously so."

It was more than he'd ever thought possible.

CHAPTER THIRTY-SIX

D are shoved his phone back into his pocket. They'd finished a late dinner after ordering pizza for the four of them plus Deputy Billy outside guarding the house. Rayne and Sophie were loading the plates into the dishwasher while Tim and Dare argued about who had the best team in the NFL. It had almost been friendly between the two men and Rayne was proud of Dare for trying to be nicer to the young man. Of course, the fragile peace was broken when Dare's cell interrupted reminding him that there was still a case unsolved.

"I have to get back to the office. They're talking about doing the two autopsies tonight. I'm sure I'll be late. Will you be okay here?"

Nodding, Rayne dropped a kiss on his lips. "We'll be fine. Deputy Billy is on duty and honestly, I'm in for the night. I'll watch some television and then go to bed."

Dare's attention turned to his sister and her beau. "About time for you to get going, isn't it, Tim?"

Sophie rolled her eyes and pressed closer to Tim's side. "Relax. Tim and I are going to watch a movie, and then he'll go home."

Muttering under his breath, Dare nodded and snagged his

keys from the counter where he'd tossed them earlier. "I'll call and check on you a little later. Don't hesitate to contact me if you need anything."

Rayne walked with him to the door and helped him on with his jacket. The temperature had fallen quite a bit after sundown. "We'll be fine but you be careful. I'll see you in the morning."

He gave her a smile that was just for her. "I'll try not to wake you when I get home."

It felt private and intimate, as if they were a couple that slept together every night. It was…nice. Her heart contracted in her chest and she let herself gaze into his blue eyes, getting lost in their depths until he reluctantly pulled his gaze away. "I better go. They'll get started without me."

He walked outside and stopped to say something to Billy before climbing into his truck and driving away. Sad that he was leaving but happy that she would still be here for his return, she headed back into the kitchen to finish the dishes.

Sophie closed the dishwasher with a flourish. "All done. You're really the guest here."

"I like to help. Standing around letting people wait on me would seem strange." She leaned her hip against the counter. "So what movie are you guys going to watch?"

"Anything you want. I don't have a preference."

"*Fast and Furious*," suggested Tim with a grin. "Damn, I love that movie."

Rayne was fine with it so they all three settled into the living room – Tim and Sophie on the couch and Rayne in the easy chair – and watched the film. About halfway through her mind began to wander and she went into the kitchen to grab a soda. Popping open the can, she dug into her purse on the counter and pulled out a copy of the tattoo drawing that had led Dare to the abandoned gold mine.

She pulled out a chair and settled at the kitchen table, studying the second half of the drawing, a circle that looked slightly like a dart board. If the first half of the design meant something, what did the second half mean?

"Are you okay?"

Sophie was standing in the doorway, her forehead wrinkled with concern. Rayne lifted up her soda can as if to make a toast. "I got thirsty. Don't you like the movie?"

Giggling, Sophie sat in the chair across from Rayne. "I love it. At least I did the first dozen times I saw it. It's Tim's favorite movie so we watch it a lot." She reached out her hand and turned the paper so she could see the design. "What's this? Did you draw it?"

"It was the tattoo design that Patrick Moulson wanted but never ended up getting. The first half here," Rayne pointed to the pot of gold, "turned out to be the logo of the mine company where the two bodies were found. But the second part is still unknown. It has to have some meaning but I don't know what."

"Um, ladies," Tim stood in the doorway, wearing his jacket and shifting from one foot to the other. "I was thinking maybe I should take a soda out to Billy. He's been sitting there all by himself and he must be thirsty."

Rayne blinked a few times, her brain trying to shift gears from studying the drawing to a seemingly everyday request. "Of course, that's a good idea. Just grab one from the refrigerator. It's a sweet thought and I'm sure he'll appreciate it."

"You're so thoughtful," Sophie cooed, reaching out to brush his hand as he walked by them. Tim quickly retrieved a can and shuffled out of the kitchen. Her smile turning to a frown, Sophie held the paper close and examined the design. She pointed to the quasi-dart board symbol. "Is this what you're questioning? This right here?"

"Yes, we don't know what it means."

Sophie looked up at Rayne, her eyes wide with shock. "I think I might know. I've seen it before."

Excitement raced through Rayne's veins and she grabbed Sophie's hands, squeezing them between her own. "Oh my God, I wish we'd shown you this before. Where have you seen it?"

"There's an old cave about twenty miles from here. You take the main road out of town for fifteen miles then turn right at the Carlson's old red barn and follow that dirt road for another five miles. It's a huge rock formation. You can't miss it. Honestly, the only reason I know it is because that's where some of the high school kids in this area go to drink beer and party. This symbol is painted on one of the rocks. If Dare knew I had been out there drinking he'd have a stroke."

A rush of euphoria had Rayne so light-headed she had to close her eyes for a moment. "We have to call your brother. He'll want to go out there right away."

She dug in her replacement purse while Tim rejoined them in the kitchen, his hands stuffed in the pockets of his jacket. "Listen, I couldn't help but overhear. Why don't I have Billy call Dare on the cop radio? That way you'll be sure he'll answer and if he wants backup or something he can organize it right away."

Rayne paused the search for her phone but shook her head. "He can do that if he wants but I want to talk to Dare as well. He might have questions for Sophie."

"Don't." Tim's command was abrupt and in a completely different tone than his normally easygoing manner. Her heart stuttered and a nervous chill ran through her body. She looked up from her handbag just as Tim pulled a gun from his pocket, pointing it directly at Sophie. "Step away from your purse and put your hands up. Don't make me hurt her."

Rayne raised her hands and took a few steps back. A sob

erupted from Sophie and she pressed her fingers over her mouth. "Tim, what are you doing? Where did you get that gun?"

Tim reached into his back pocket and pulled out a set of handcuffs, which he tossed to Rayne. Pointing the gun at Sophie's head, he didn't bother answering any questions.

"Put the cuffs on Rayne, sweetheart. Behind her back, if you please."

Rayne's pulse roared in her ears but she took a few breaths to try and stay calm. She needed to keep her wits about her and not do anything stupid. Stupid was how people ended up dead.

"How did you get the gun?" she asked as Sophie snapped the cuffs on her, the metal cold against her flesh. "Did you have it when you came here? I don't remember seeing it."

Tim gestured for Sophie to go back and sit at the table. "It's Billy's gun and handcuffs. By the time he wakes up with a headache we'll be out of here."

At least Billy wasn't dead, but that was small comfort when there was a gun pointed at her heart.

"And where are we going?" Rayne asked, although she had a pretty decent idea.

Tim smiled as he held the gun on the two women, looking as if he didn't have a care in the world. He probably didn't since she and Sophie had just solved his problem about the drawing.

"To the cave, of course, but you knew that didn't you, Rayne? You're a pretty smart lady and quite talented. Too bad I don't have time for some ink."

"What is wrong with you?" Sophie whined, tears still coursing down her cheeks. "Why are you doing this? Tim, it's not too late. We can call my brother and work all this out."

"Honey, that's the last thing we're going to do. And I'm doing this for the money, of course. Lots of it. Duke and I will be rich and we can leave this piece of shit town behind."

"You're one of the bank robbers," Rayne said, her fingers gripping the kitchen counter behind her as if holding it would keep her sanity in check. How many times did a human being get to cheat death? Someone had already tried to burn her to death; now Tim Wallace had a gun and she was probably just collateral damage. "But I don't understand why you needed the drawing. You are the one that broke into my shop and home, correct? And mugged me?"

Trying to fit the puzzle pieces together kept her mind preoccupied and not thinking about how much fucking trouble she was in at the moment. Things didn't look good for her or Sophie and a wave of responsibility ran over Rayne as she gazed at the sad and terrified young woman. She had to get them both out of this alive and as unscathed as possible.

She needed a plan but subterfuge wasn't one of her strengths. She'd spent most of her life dealing with people as straightforwardly as possible.

Tim nodded in agreement. "I am, although I had help from Duke. I mugged you while Duke broke into your place. It was easy to trail the sheriff since I was dating his little sister."

"You jerk," Sophie spat, her eyes red-rimmed and her face pale. "Why would you do this? What's in it for you?"

"Money, my sweet, although dating you wasn't the hardship I thought it might be. You were perfect for keeping tabs on the sheriff and you were a decent fuck as well. I'm tired of living paycheck to paycheck and being a joke in this town. I want what other people have. You were just a means to an end." Tim grinned and brandished the handgun. Hatred and anger burned in Rayne's gut as Tim smirked in victory. If her hands had been free she would have happily slapped the crap out of him for hurting Sophie. "Now it's time for you to be a good little girl and get in the utility room."

"What?" Sophie was shaking her head and another sob tore from her throat. "I'm not going in there."

"Actually, you are. I noticed that the room locks from the outside. They probably put the door on backwards but it will come in handy today. With no windows and a solid wood frame it should keep you out of the way until I retrieve the money and get out of town."

"You think the money is in the cave?" Rayne asked, hoping to distract and delay as she pulled at the metal cuffs. If she could keep him talking Dare might show up before Tim left. "How did you not know where the money was? That doesn't seem like good planning."

Scowling, Tim stepped closer, the muzzle of the gun only a few feet from Rayne's heart.

"The money started out at the mine house but then Patrick got paranoid and moved it. Ernie and Milo confronted him about it but Patrick just said he was making sure nothing happened to the money."

A thought hit Rayne and she shook her head in disgust. She should have known before now. "You asked me about dating Dare before anyone knew. But you knew because you were following me."

"True," Tim conceded. "Although Duke helped too. I knew Dare was going to be an issue after last night but I didn't think I'd get a lucky break this quick. He'll be gone for hours for the autopsies."

Tim grabbed Sophie's arm so hard she yelped and tried to twist away, but he was so much larger and stronger he was easily able to overcome her struggles and toss her into the utility room. Rayne assumed she was next but instead he slammed the door shut and locked it, a satisfied grin on his face. He slid one of the chairs under the knob with a grunt before banging on the door.

"You be a good girl in there. I hope you're not afraid of the dark."

The sounds of heartbroken sobs could clearly be heard through the door and Rayne had to restrain herself from kicking Tim in the groin. Sophie was learning a hard and terrible lesson about men today and she wouldn't forget it very soon.

"You just used her and now you're tossing her away."

Tim leaned forward as if to tell her a secret. "Just between you and me I kind of liked her. But I knew she could never deal with this. She's too much like her tight ass brother, all law abiding and shit. Now you, my dear Rayne, you're something completely different. You're a woman that understands nuance. I'm not sure what you see in that Gomer of a sheriff."

Rayne could spend the next twenty-four hours extolling Dare's virtues but that wasn't what Tim wanted to hear at the moment, so she tried to ask him more questions.

"There were only four bank robbers, but you've talked about five people. Were you there at the bank?"

Tim just laughed and reached for her, his fingers digging into her arm. She had to bite her lip to keep from crying out in pain, but she didn't want to scare Sophie on the other side of the door who couldn't see what was happening.

"I think we're done with the question and answer period of the evening. It's time to go."

He practically dragged her to the front door, pausing there to hold the gun to her temple.

"Don't make a fucking sound. No screams for help, nothing. If you want you and Sophie to come out of this alive you'll do exactly what I tell you. I'm not a murderer but I can be."

She nodded, pressing her lips together as sweat began to pool at the base of her neck. Keeping her gaze away from Tim's face, she was able to control her breathing enough that she didn't shake with fright. Wanting to believe what he said was true, she didn't try and pull away or scream. For now, she'd play along and wait for an opportunity to escape.

Swallowing hard, she let him escort her to his truck, shoving her into the passenger seat. He swung into the driver's side and fired up the vehicle, kicking up some dust as he pulled away. She craned her neck to peer into Billy's car and saw him slumped over the wheel unconscious. She prayed Tim was correct and the young deputy would have nothing more to remember this than a nasty headache.

Her arms and shoulders ached and her heart pounded against her ribcage. It made her sick to think she'd defended this man to Dare.

It was all about survival now.

CHAPTER THIRTY-SEVEN

D are turned the SUV into his neighborhood, fatigue lying heavy on his shoulders and mind. It had been a damn long day and he was anxious to have a hot shower and a cold beer. He wouldn't mind some tender loving care from the woman in his life either, if she was offering. A neck rub sounded like heaven after the crap he'd been through at the coroner's office.

He'd shown up thinking that they were going to perform the autopsies but there'd been a paperwork snafu, so instead he'd stopped at the station to have them start running the prints before heading back home.

To Rayne.

It felt right having her in his house, his bed. She made even the everyday things like making coffee or watching television better, and he had a sneaking suspicion he was going to want her to do those things with him for the foreseeable future. And beyond.

He passed Billy's cruiser and was pulling up into the driveway when Billy and Sophie came barreling out of the house right in front of Dare's truck. He slammed on the brakes and threw the vehicle into park before jumping out to see what was going on. Sophie's face was red and tearstained while Billy's forehead had a trickle of blood between his eyebrows.

Dare's chest felt heavy and he had trouble exhaling as he desperately looked for Rayne as well. He ran up to Sophie and wrapped his arm around her waist, supporting her slight weight. She was still crying and he had a hard time making out her words between sobs. He turned to his deputy who was holding a dishtowel from the kitchen to his head.

"What the hell happened here? Where's Rayne?"

Billy's breathing was labored and he seemed to have trouble getting the words out with a couple false starts. "Tim knocked me out and stole my gun. Then he locked Sophie in the utility room." Billy paused, his eyes wide with fear. "He's got Rayne and he's on the move."

Dare half coughed and half gasped, feeling like he'd been punched in the gut. Tim had Rayne? Did that mean Tim was part of...

Son of a bitch. He'd known that pissy little bastard was trouble.

Dare placed his hand on Billy's shoulder to get his attention. "Radio for backup and an EMT. You need someone to look at that bump on your head. Then radio Tanner Marks in Springwood and tell him to get his ass over here. He's going to want to be in on this. Go."

Stumbling down the driveway, Billy made it to his vehicle and Dare turned his attention to his weeping sister. He lifted her quivering chin so she had to look up at him and brushed at her wet cheeks. "Baby girl, I need you to tell me what's happening here. Are you hurt?"

Sophie shook her head, hiccuping as she scrubbed at her swollen eyes.

"Do you know where Rayne is?"

She nodded but her breathing instantly sped up. Not a good sign. "Can you tell me where Tim took Rayne? Can you do that for me?"

"He–he took her to the caves outside of town. The symbol on the design is spray painted on the side of one of the caves. That's where the money is." More sobs shook her slight frame. "He robbed that bank and he dated me to keep an eye on you."

Holy fucking hell, when Dare got his hands on that prick, Wallace was going to wish he'd never been born. No one touched his sister and his woman.

He didn't have all the details he'd like to have but there was no time for a long interrogation. He needed to get to Rayne as soon as possible. He guided Sophie back into the house and set her down on the couch. "I need you to stay here with Billy, okay? I'm going to get Rayne and then we'll be back and you can tell me all about this."

Sophie nodded, tears still flowing, but she wiped her face with the hem of her shirt and put on a brave face. "Go get her, big brother. She has to be so scared. He made me handcuff her so she can't defend herself."

Dropping a kiss on the top of her head, Dare strode out of the house to his SUV. Protecting his woman was uppermost in his mind and he wouldn't falter from his task.

Because he fucking loved her.

He hadn't said it yet but he did. It was what the entire relationship had been leading up to and he desperately wanted a chance to tell her. Prove to her how he felt even if her feelings weren't the same.

Tim Wallace had made a grave error and was about to pay the price.

✧ ✧ ✧ ✧

"You'll never get away with this."

Rayne wasn't sure why she was even bothering to speak, especially a cliché such as this one, but she couldn't seem to control her mouth. Something deep inside was forcing the words out as if talking affirmed her continued state of…aliveness.

Tim's old truck pulled to a halt at the end of the dirt road. "I think I will. Your hero Dare is going to be caught up with those autopsies for hours so there's no one to come to your rescue."

That's exactly what she was afraid of. Until Deputy Billy woke up or Sophie managed to get out of the utility room, Rayne was up a creek without the proverbial paddle. There was only herself to depend on and the last time she'd been in a life or death situation she hadn't saved her own life. It had taken Jason and his father to drag her butt out of that burning building, and they were in a completely different state at the moment. She had to blink away the tears that were welling up in her eyes and swallow the lump that had taken residence in her throat.

The outlook was bleak.

If Tim meant what he said about leaving Rayne alive he would probably abandon her here once he found the money. She could die of exposure while waiting for rescue and she had a feeling that was a particularly nasty way to go.

If Tim was being honest…

He exited the truck and came around to her side, pulling her out and to her feet. His fingers gripped her arm as he dragged her toward the cave, a flashlight in one hand. She stumbled over the uneven ground trying to keep up with his longer legs but he didn't slow his gait, clearly anxious to recover his money. As they moved closer, Rayne could make out the spray painted image on the rocks that matched the drawing.

"Slow the hell down. If the money's here it's not going any-where."

"What do you mean if it's here? It has to be here."

Tim's brows pulled down and his eyes narrowed, not liking her statement at all but then she hadn't said it to make him more comfortable.

"It doesn't have to be," she countered, sweat sliding down her back, making her shirt stick to her skin. Rising fear kept her heart galloping, but she tried to ignore it by keeping up a steady dialogue. "Moulson could have been using the tattoo as a red herring. Maybe the money is in some offshore account in the Cayman Islands."

His head whipped around and he jerked her up close so she was looking into his blazing eyes. "It's fucking here. It has to be here."

"I'm sure it is. I was just conjecturing."

Rayne used her most soothing tone but he didn't appear mollified. He yanked her over to a large rock at the mouth of the cave and pushed her down onto it, adding a few more bruises to her already sore body.

"Sit the fuck down and shut up. Don't try and run or scream, either. Not that there's anyone here to help you. We're all alone, baby." Tim ran his finger down her cheek and she shuddered in revulsion. "Maybe after I get the money you and me can celebrate. I bet you'd like that. I always thought you'd be hot in the sack. I can count your tattoos and piercings."

I'll see you in hell first.

"Fuck you."

Tim laughed as he reached for Rayne's foot, tugging off first one tennis shoe and sock and then the other.

"Fuck you too, sweetheart. I'll just take these shoes to make sure you won't go anywhere. It would be suicide to run even with them. You'd die of exposure before sunup but this will make sure you stay put."

Stuffing the socks into the shoes, he reared back his arm and tossed a shoe into the darkness. She heard a thud in the distance before he threw the other one.

"Those were my favorite Chuck Taylors."

Cold was already beginning to seep through into her toes. Tim Wallace was a true bastard extraordinaire. He was going to leave her to freeze to death in all likelihood.

"Women love to shop. Now stay here and be a good girl."

"Fuck you."

"I think we've been through this once already but luckily for you I don't hold a grudge."

The moon was high in the black sky and Rayne shivered as the cold breeze dried her damp skin. Tim went deeper into the cave until she couldn't see him anymore but could hear his heavy boots stomping on the packed ground.

As soon as he was out of sight, Rayne struggled to her feet. Her heart pounded wildly and her mind raced with possibilities, each one more dire than the last. Her odds weren't good either way but staying with him was surely a death sentence. Best case scenario she'd be raped and left for dead. Running was a lousy option but it felt like the only one she had. That little voice in her head that had saved her ass too many times to count was chattering away in her ear, urging her to get away. Run. Move. Anything but stay here like a fly caught in a spider's web.

Her gaze darted in every direction, calculating the most advantageous place to run or hide. She wanted to run toward the main road but that direction was too exposed and Tim would easily spot her even from a distance. Running away from the road didn't make much sense either, as she would be moving farther from civilization and a human being that might help her. To her right was rocky terrain that would be hell on her now freezing bare feet.

To the left then.

Not wasting any more time, she took off running into the dense trees and bushes, hoping against hope that Tim couldn't see her in the dark. It wasn't a full moon but there was enough to light her way until she was in the dark shadows of the large pine trees. It was then that the reduced visibility played havoc and she found herself stumbling and falling to her knees a few times.

She struggled to stand without the use of her arms and pushed forward, only to hiss in pain as rocks cut into the soles of her feet. Her vision blurred with tears and she didn't have a hand free to wipe them away. Staying and enduring the tender mercies of Tim Wallace hadn't been a good idea but this one didn't seem any better. She was quite likely going to perish out here and they'd find her body in the spring.

Because she was an idiot who didn't know how to survive in the woods.

She'd been too busy living in cities and using plumbing and air conditioning, ignoring the lessons her adventure loving parents tried to teach her. She'd been so smug and now she was going to die because she was stupid. Sniffling, she awkwardly bent her head and tried to wipe her nose on her shirt but she couldn't reach. She had no doubt she made a pathetic as hell picture. Her shoulders, arms, and wrists ached, her feet burned, and she could barely see a foot in front of her face. Goose-bumps were raised on the flesh of her skin and the rapidly chilling air made a cloud of fog in front of her face with every ragged breath.

Finding a large clump of trees, Rayne huddled behind them, trying to bury her feet under the bed of pine needles hoping they would keep her from losing her toes. A sob rose up in her throat choking her as she swallowed it down, hesitant to make a sound when Tim was so close. Once he had the money, he might come after her.

Crumpled into a ball on the frigid ground, Rayne could hear the beat of her heart like a freight train in her ears, the whooshing sound drowning out any other noise. Feeling more tears leak down her face, she concentrated on breathing in and out, not allowing fear to swamp her common sense. If there was any moment she needed to be smart, it was now. Right now. And that voice in her head was telling her to lie low and hide. Stay quiet and hope the curtain of darkness cloaked her whereabouts.

She didn't know how long she sat there, the scent of sweat mixing with pine. Time drifted on without meaning and she only counted each breath, one after the other. Each one meant she was still alive and kicking.

Lost in that fog, she jumped when she heard the sound of gunshots. Two. Then three. Then two more. Had Dare arrived? He should have been back at the coroner's office but if Billy or Sophie got free...

Silence.

She heard shouting in the distance and her body trembled with hope. Had the cavalry arrived or had the gunshots been fired by someone else?

Holding her breath, she waited...listening...praying...

If I get out of this alive I'll never complain about anything ever again. And I will tell Dare that I love him. Because I do, and if he wants to be grouchy every day for the rest of our lives that's okay with me.

When she heard his familiar voice she collapsed into a heap, relief suffusing every fiber of her being. Despite all the odds, he'd fucking found her and she wasn't going to die a miserable death out here, cold and forgotten.

It took every ounce of energy she had to call to him, her voice coming out as a croak.

"Dare! I'm here!"

She waited and could hear his calls more clearly. Crawling out from behind the trees, she somehow managed to stand on her shaky knees. "Here! I'm here!"

This time the words came out stronger and she heard him call back that he was coming. Her legs gave out underneath her, and she sat there waiting for Dare as tears of relief and happiness replaced those of fear and anger.

"Baby, I've got you. You're safe now."

His dear voice was hoarse with emotion as he scooped her up in his arms. She'd been alone just moments before but now there were people everywhere. An EMT covered her with a blanket and walked beside them as Dare's long legs ate up the distance quickly. She huddled closer to his warm, strong frame and let him be the stronger one. Just this once, she'd allow herself the luxury of letting a man take care of her. She'd be okay in a little while but right now allowing her head to rest on his shoulder felt undeniably wonderful.

Placing her on a stretcher next to an ambulance, he ran his hands up and down her arms and legs, coming to a halt at her ankles. "Baby, where are your shoes? Jesus, your feet are frozen."

His hands began to massage her numb toes and she winced as the feeling returned to her extremities.

"Sophie? Tim?" She hated to ask the question but she had to know.

"Sophie's fine. She has friends and Deputy Billy back at the house taking care of her. Tim's been taken into custody, although not willingly. Tanner has men looking for his brother Duke. I'm guessing he was the mastermind behind all of this."

The word mastermind was spoken in an ironic tone but Rayne understood. No one had thought the two brothers would be able to do something this elaborate…or deadly.

Rayne reached out and brushed her fingers over Dare's cheek as he worked on her feet.

"He threw my shoes away so I couldn't run."

Wrapping her legs in another blanket, Dare pulled a small key from his back pocket and held it up. "He doesn't know you at all, does he? A little thing like bare feet wouldn't keep you from escaping. Now let's get you out of those cuffs."

Rayne groaned when the cuffs were removed and she could stretch her arms forward, wriggling her fingers. The EMT that had been hovering finally stepped forward.

"Sir? We really need to check her over. If you would just step aside…"

That scowl that she now loved so much crossed his face but she patted his shoulder and leaned down to briefly press her lips to his. "I'm okay, but let's let them do their jobs. Then I want you to take me home. Will you do that for me?"

He nodded but was reluctant to let her go. "I'll be right here. I'm not leaving you for a second."

The EMT crowded in and finally Dare took a step back but still held onto her hand. As her adrenaline drained away, she found herself shaking uncontrollably and her teeth chattering despite the fact that they'd wrapped her up in several blankets and Dare had even taken off his coat and slipped it over her shoulders. This was the second time she'd been in deadly danger and it wasn't getting any easier. In fact, this time was far worse. She'd be having nightmares about running from Tim Wallace for a long time.

After instructions from the EMTs as to how to care for the cuts on her feet that they'd carefully cleaned, Rayne once again found herself scooped into Dare's arms and carried to his SUV. He tucked her into the passenger seat, the interior already toasty from the blasting heater, and stretched the seatbelt across her body.

"We're going home."

She caught Dare's hand before he could close her door. "Wait. What happened? I—I don't know what happened."

"I'll tell you everything when we get home, baby. Trust me."

The door slammed shut and she watched as he gave one of his deputies a few instructions. Then he swung into the driver's seat and put the truck into reverse.

She was going home. Alive.

CHAPTER THIRTY-EIGHT

Dare doubted if Rayne had ever enjoyed a hot bath and clean pajamas more than she had tonight. She'd soaked until the water was tepid before letting him lift her out of the tub and dry her off with a soft towel. She'd sat almost submissively as he'd helped her into a plaid flannel pair of sleeping pants and a black t-shirt before carefully bandaging her tender feet. He'd stayed close as she ran a comb through her hair and rubbed lotion on her arms and legs.

Of course, before she would consent to a bath she and Sophie had hugged each other tightly, tears running down their faces. Dare's chest had tightened at the sight of the two most important people in his life safe and sound in their home and he'd had to clear his throat several times before he was able to speak.

It hit him then and there how lucky they all were. This could have gone a much darker way and it had been a guardian angel who had messed up the autopsy paperwork so that he'd returned home early. He'd be forever grateful.

The entire way to the caves he'd been bargaining with whatever divine entity would listen.

If I can just find Rayne safe and sound I'll never give her a hard time about her dancing in the rain ever again. I'll smile more and I'll damn well tell her I love her. She's my future and I'll do anything to win her love.

Now Sophie was tucked upstairs in her room with three girlfriends who had brought ice cream and were commiserating about boys and love. As much as Dare hadn't liked Tim Wallace, he hoped this wouldn't color Sophie's image of relationships too badly. She deserved to be happy but by someone better. A boy who wasn't a bank robber, for example.

Dare had wrapped Rayne in a flannel blanket and placed her in front of the fireplace while he fixed them both a brandy. He could use the alcohol and he was sure she could as well, if only to help warm her up after her ordeal.

"Here you go, baby. This will heat you up from the inside out."

She frowned but accepted the glass, taking a tentative sip. Her nose wrinkled and she coughed a few times. "Strong. What is it?"

"Brandy. Never had it before?"

Dare settled on the end of the couch and pulled her feet into his lap, picking up the ankle massage where he'd left off at the caves.

"We didn't have such fancy liquor in our house. Mom and Dad were a beer and wine kind of couple. I didn't really have you pegged for a brandy guy either, to tell you the truth."

Chuckling, Dare sipped at the liquid, feeling the fire race down to his belly. "I'm full of contradictions. I'll guess you'll have to stick around to learn them all."

Pink stained her pretty cheeks. "I guess I will. Will you tell me what's going on now? Will you tell me what happened? The curiosity is killing me."

Settling more comfortably in the cushions, Dare contemplated where to even begin. The case was a strange one, convoluted to even experienced lawmen such as himself and Tanner Marks. He and Tanner had spoken while Rayne was soaking in the tub and the details were beginning to become clearer now that Duke was in custody.

He set the brandy on the end table. "Tim was one of the bank robbers but it was his brother Duke who was running the show. He didn't personally rob the bank with the others but it was his plan. The other three were friends of his apparently, although I use that term loosely as he had no problem double crossing all of them and eventually putting bullets in their chests."

"So he's the murderer, not Tim?"

"That's the latest from Duke. Tanner has him at the station and is interrogating him. He just sent a text update a few minutes ago. Maybe Duke is trying to protect his baby brother by taking the rap but I seriously doubt it. I've never known the man to be all that charitable."

Rayne fiddled with the glass, her gaze far away as she pondered his revelation. "So Tim told the truth when he said he wasn't a murderer."

"It was probably the only truthful thing he ever said," Dare growled, anger at the young man still churning in his gut. He'd hurt Sophie and Rayne and for that he would pay dearly. Dare would see to it. "Everything else was just a big con. He admitted that he dated Sophie to watch my movements. They'd planned more bank robberies in the area, including here in Valley Station, although after Moulson was killed that plan was put on hold."

"Poor Sophie," Rayne murmured, her full lips turned down. "She got the shit end of the stick."

This woman never ceased to amaze him. "I'd say you're the one. She may have been locked in a utility room but she was at least safe at home. He dragged you to the caves to get the money. God knows what he would have done to you when he found it. At least you had the good sense to run."

"I thought you'd ream me out about that. I did run into the freezing night with no shoes."

"I'll buy you new ones," Dare assured her. "You were safer out in the woods than you were with him. You knew I would come find you."

"I thought it would be hours and I would die of exposure. You were supposed to be at two autopsies but whatever brought you home early I'm grateful for. But yes, I preferred dying of cold to dying at Tim's hands."

She shuddered and he lifted her up, blankets and all, placing her on his lap. "I don't know if Tim would have really killed you. He says that wasn't the plan but..." Dare shrugged. "I'm not sure he really knows what he would have done. Clearly his first instinct isn't to kill since he left Sophie and Billy here alive."

Rayne tucked her head into his shoulder with a heavy sigh. "So Tim and Duke are in jail. The money is returned. And we're alive. Not a bad day's work, Sheriff. You should take the day off tomorrow for all your good work."

Dare snorted at the thought. "I'll be questioning Duke and Tim tomorrow. They're not going anywhere. A night in a cell might loosen their tongues, not to mention that Tim had to be treated at the hospital tonight for a concussion. It's better to talk to them tomorrow when they've had time to think about all the bad shit that can happen now that they're caught. We're keeping them separate, though. I don't need them plotting against us."

"A concussion? How did he get that? You still haven't told me what happened while I was hiding in those trees."

He'd been putting that off because he knew she was going to freak out when he told her.

"Let's see, I guess the story starts when the autopsies were cancelled due to a snafu with the paperwork. So I turned the truck around and headed back home. When I got there, Billy and Sophie were on the front porch and it was clear something serious had gone down. Sophie was sobbing and Billy had blood on his forehead."

"Tim knocked him out and stole his gun and handcuffs while Sophie and I were inside looking at the drawing. He heard Sophie tell me where she'd seen the symbol before."

That was a little fact Dare hadn't known but he didn't stop to ask what made Rayne decide to study the design tonight.

"So I told Billy to call for backup and Sophie told me where she'd seen the symbol and that Tim had you. I set off for the caves and by the time I got there it was dark and hard to see. I yelled your name a few times but I doubt you heard me. But Tim did."

"Where was he?"

"He was looking around the rocks for the money which we later found shoved in a crevice near the spray paint. I could see his flashlight, which he turned off when he realized I'd shown up. He shot at me a few times and I shot back. Then he climbed on top of a boulder to get a better vantage point and I shot a few more times, but he slipped and fell, hitting his head and dislocating his shoulder. At that point it was easy for me and my men to get him into custody. Almost the first words out of his mouth was that it was all his brother's idea."

Rayne scraped her fingers through her still damp hair. "He fell? That's it? Kind of anticlimactic."

It had been but Dare had been relieved. He didn't need a shootout that endangered men's lives. It was better when it was simple and straightforward even if it wasn't as exciting.

"Personally, I'm thrilled. Nobody got shot and everybody's home with their loved ones tonight. Well, everyone but Tim and

Duke."

Her slow, sexy smile bloomed and he felt his heart lurch in his chest. Damn, he loved her and he needed to tell her. "Am I your loved one?"

Tell her now.

"I love you, Rayne. I was so fucking scared tonight. Believe me when I say I would have gone to the ends of the earth to find you and bring you home safely."

His voice had sounded rough due to the tightness in his throat but she didn't seem to mind. She cupped his jaw and kissed him, running her tongue lightly across his lower lip. Her eyes shone with emotion and everything felt perfectly right.

"I love you too, you big grouchy bear. In fact, I think I love your growly moods the most."

"That's good because I've got a bunch of those." His nose caressed the side of hers before his lips captured hers in a kiss that sent electricity surging through his veins. "I love dancing in the rain with you. When your feet heal that is."

"Next rainstorm we'll do a waltz on the front lawn." Her arms looped around his neck as she smiled up at him as if he was something special. The warmth that suffused every pore of his body reveled in the feeling...of being loved. He'd make sure she didn't ever regret it. "Now kiss me, big bear."

Those were the kind of orders he was glad to follow.

CHAPTER THIRTY-NINE

Rayne opened her eyes and kicked off the bedcovers. Dreams she couldn't remember and frankly didn't want to had invaded her peace and she lay there for several minutes listening to the sounds around her. The rustle of branches against the windows. The even breathing of the gorgeous man lying next to her. The hum of the heating system as it kicked on and off. All strangely comforting as she slowly woke up, leaving sleep behind. She must have moved or made a noise because Dare was beginning to stir.

"Baby, are you okay?" Dare rolled over and blinked up at her sleepily. "Are you sick?"

"I'm fine," she whispered, checking the digital clock on the bedside table. Six in the morning. "Can't sleep. I think I'm awake for the day."

Stretching and yawning, Dare laid on his back and pulled her into his arms, her head tucked under his chin. "Are you upset or scared? Do you want to talk about it?"

"I thought I would be but I'm not. I feel safe with you."

She did feel safe lying next to Dare. His mere presence had made it possible to fall asleep in the first place.

His hand stroked up and down her spine, relaxing her entire

body until she was almost boneless against him. "I'll protect you from the monsters under the bed."

She adored this little seen playful side. Giggling, she pressed a soft kiss to his collarbone. "Great, now I think there are monsters under the bed. That should be good for a nightmare or two."

"Our monsters mind their own business. They're more afraid of you than you are of them."

"I've heard that before and I never believe it. I'm going to hide so they'll never find me."

Pulling the covers over her head, she curled up in a ball and scooted down the mattress.

"Uh oh, I think there's a monster down here. What ever shall I do?"

The comforter lifted slightly, letting in a shaft of light. "What are you up to? Or do I even want to know?"

He'd growled the words, but there was a happiness in his tone that hadn't been there in the past. "I think you'll like the surprise, my grouchy bear. I'm going to vanquish this giant monster."

Dare had woken up with morning wood – the monster – and today she was going to take complete advantage of it. Both of them liked to sleep in the nude so there were no boxers or pajamas to strip off and keep her from her goal. Her fingers wrapped around his cock and she clearly heard his hiss of pleasure as she began to move her hand up and down, using the precum to ease her way.

Allowing herself the luxury she explored him from root to tip, tracing every ridge and vein, loving the steely feel of him under her fingertips. "This monster isn't so scary. I think I can tame him."

Her tongue extended and swiped at the tip, his salty flavor

exploding on her tastebuds. Dare moaned his approval as she engulfed the head in her mouth, tracing the slit and the underside until he was moving restlessly on the sheets.

She straddled his body, part of his cock fisted in her hand while she sucked up and down, licking around the head, her lips wet and tight around his ample girth. In the warm cocoon of the bedcovers, his manly scent was strong and intoxicating, amping up her arousal and dampening her thighs.

Not sure how it happened, she was suddenly lying on her back and Dare hovering above her. The blankets were still pulled over their heads, creating a sort of play fort that blocked out the rest of the world. When they left this room there would be interrogations, autopsies, and forensics, but right now there was only the two of them.

"You woke the monster, baby, and you'll have to deal with the consequences."

Yes, please.

His wet and nimble tongue found her nipples, flicking at them until they were diamond hard and aching. He suckled at first one pink bud and then the other making her writhe underneath his muscled frame. Kissing a wet trail down her abdomen, he pressed two fingers inside of her drenched pussy, drawing a groan of satisfaction as those thick digits found her g-spot.

Her hips arched up off the mattress as his mouth wrapped around her swollen clit, sucking softly and scraping his teeth on the sides while his busy fingers thrust in and out of her slick channel. Her toes curled as pleasure fizzed through her veins like the champagne she drank on New Year's Eve.

"Fuck me, Dare."

This man – her man – didn't make her beg or wait. He positioned himself between her quivering thighs and entered her in one mighty stroke. Crying out with the exquisite pleasure of being so thoroughly filled, Rayne wrapped her legs around his middle, digging her heels into his muscular backside.

In the darkness, she couldn't see his face but she could feel his warm breath on her neck. He nuzzled her ear as he buried his cock in her pussy again and again, faster and hard with each thrust. Rayne swiveled her hips so that his groin rubbed her clit with each stroke. Her orgasm built swiftly and she found herself teetering at the edge but needing something extra to push her over.

Raking her nails down his back, she panted and moaned, her pussy clenching around his cock. So close. "Faster. Harder. Please, Dare. I need more."

She didn't understand what she needed more of but thankfully, her sweet lover did. His thrusts became deeper with an extra grind against her clit to give her the push she desperately needed. Her legs shook as her climax hovered, and her fingers dug into his muscled shoulders as he bit down on the sensitive flesh where shoulder met neck, laving the hurt he'd inflicted.

The bit of pain with her pleasure was exactly the "more" she'd been needing and she tumbled over the cliff, every fiber of her being flush with pleasure. She chanted his name as if it was an incantation and he buried himself in her one last time, his body tense and hard as he filled her with his hot seed.

The collapsed together in a twisted tangle of arms, legs, and blankets, their breathing ragged and their bodies sweaty. Pleasure still thrummed through her veins and she closed her eyes for a long moment to savor it.

Dare pulled the covers down below their chins and the cooler air hit her face, a welcome rush of fresh air. Dawn was starting to peek through the curtains and their pleasurable but brief respite from the real world was coming to an end.

Rayne sighed and laid her head on Dare's shoulder. "It's morning."

He played with her hair, twisting the strands around his fingers. "There's no way that I know of to keep morning from coming. But there's always tonight."

Emotion clogged her throat as she thought of spending every night in this bed. "I guess there is, if it's okay with you. I'm not in danger anymore so I could go back to my place. You might have to help me with the new furniture, though."

"Or you could just stay here."

She couldn't help but tease him. Just a little. "I don't know. What would Sophie think? She's so young and impressionable."

Dare's chuckle rumbled in his chest. "I think after what happened I should upgrade Sophie from a kid to a young woman. Besides, she adores you and would love it if you were here. Frankly, so would I."

Rayne sat up so she could look Dare in the eye. He was completely serious but then he didn't joke about much. "Do you think it's too fast?"

That smile that made her heart flutter appeared and he caressed her cheek with his rough fingers. "Probably, but I don't give a damn. Do you?"

No, she didn't.

"People will talk."

"I daresay they will," he agreed, his grin growing wider. "They'll pity a nice, pretty thing like you being stuck with a grouch like me. I bet you'll play it up for all it's worth too, but I don't mind. I know I got lucky."

She poked his chest with her finger, a naughty smile curving her lips. "I know how to make you happy."

His expression sobered and his hand slid around to her back, pulling her close so their lips were millimeters apart. "You're the only one who can."

There it was. Love. She hadn't even known she needed it and then it found her whether she liked it or not. He filled up all the empty spaces in her heart and she wanted to do the same for him.

Joy.

Glee.

Jubilation.

Elation.

She'd give him all of that and more.

And if he wanted to scowl that was just fine. He didn't have to change.

As long as he danced with her in the rain.

Shivering, Dare locked his SUV before entering the old roadhouse, glad he'd worn his gloves today. It was a damp and cold Sunday morning and the parking lot was deserted except for the vehicles belonging to the other sheriffs. Dare counted six trucks, which meant that everyone had already arrived but him. He would take some shit for this but he'd had a hard time prying himself out of a warm bed with an even hotter woman in it. Rayne had been living at his home for a month now and they'd both had to rush around in the morning more than a few times to make it to their respective jobs on time.

He couldn't get enough of her, and thankfully she felt the same way.

"Sorry I'm late."

Might as well get the ribbing out of the way up front. He poured himself a cup of coffee from the drip maker on the bar and sat down in the only empty chair.

"Trouble getting out of bed this morning?" Reed laughed.

"Now you know what it's like, asshole."

Knox snickered behind his coffee cup. "Stuck in bed with a sexy female? Doesn't sound like a bad problem to have, if you ask me."

Griffin stroked his chin and grinned. "Do you even remember the name of the woman you slept with last night?"

Knox waggled his brows and leaned back in his chair as if he didn't have a care in the world. "Her name was Kate but you should be askin' if she remembered my name. She kept calling me God."

Tanner groaned and pounded his fist on the table to bring the meeting to order. "And on that note, let's get started. I think we'll start with Dare and me giving an update on the bank robbery and triple murder. We now have statements from both Duke and Tim Wallace so we have more details than we had before. Dare, do you want to start?"

Not particularly, but Tanner had been deferring a great deal of authority to Dare on this case. Technically they should have shared it, but the older lawman's wife was having a terrible pregnancy and had been put in the hospital on bedrest so she could be monitored more closely. Tanner was now working half days only, which meant most of the case fell to Dare.

He didn't mind, of course. His friend needed to take care of his wife and child. But it felt strange to lead Tanner, the most experienced of them all, when by all rights it should have been the other way.

One more step in this crazy road to adulthood. He'd been shoved into it reluctantly, coming to Valley Station to take care of his sister when his father died. Now he'd found himself embracing the role of partner with the woman of his dreams living with him.

"Not sure what everyone does or doesn't know so I'll start at the beginning. Duke Wallace planned the bank robbery. The original plan had several to be made in the area but that went to hell when they all turned on each other. Patrick Moulson was a friend of Earnest and Milo so he didn't know Duke or Tim, which I guess turned out to be an issue. Anyway, they all suspected each other of greed and so on, so Patrick decided to have a tattoo designed on his arm that would let his girlfriend know where the money was if he ended up dead. Of course he did, but before he had a chance to get inked. When Moulson thought he had been followed, he slipped the drawing into Rayne's gym bag for safekeeping. When he came back for it sometime later Duke was following him. They argued about the drawing and Duke shot Moulson, then ripped apart the shop looking for it."

Evan's connections had finally paid off and he'd found Moulson's girlfriend, who had gladly spilled the beans on her lover and his friends between bouts of crying. Apparently Moulson didn't like the nine to five grind and was always looking for shortcuts.

He sure as hell found one.

"So Moulson hid the money before he was killed?" Seth asked, grabbing an apple from the bag on the table and shining it against his button-down shirt. "Greed did them all in."

"How in the hell was the girlfriend supposed to know what that tat meant?" Griffin asked. "Experienced lawmen didn't even know what it meant in the beginning."

"She said that Moulson told her he would find a way to communicate with her," Dare replied. "Personally, I think he could have just sent her a text or something. It sounded like they were really into the subterfuge of it all. That somehow being a bank robber was a romantic thing to do."

Knox snorted into his coffee. "Nice girl. She didn't care her boyfriend was a criminal. Her parents must be proud."

"I bet her parents have their hands full with her," Tanner replied with a chuckle, taking up the story, much to Dare's relief. "So once Moulson was dead the other two panicked. They met at the old mine to put together a plan to get rid of Duke but he was one step ahead. He followed them and shot them both. Now he only had to share the money with Tim."

Reed shook his head, clearly disgusted with the story. "Poor Sophie. She really got the shaft with this one, finding out her boyfriend was a bank robber. How is she holding up?"

Amazingly well, with Rayne's help. Dare's sister was stronger than he'd given her credit for.

"She's doing good. She's planning to start school in Denver in January and she'll live in the dorms. A change of scenery will be good for her."

Evan refilled his coffee. "And Rayne? How is she doing?"

Dare felt the smile he couldn't suppress spread across his face. It happened every time he thought about the sexy pixie with the purple stripes in her hair.

She filled him with joy.

"She's fine. She rented her house out and the shop is cleaned up and back in business. She usually has a full roster most days of the week."

Dare's hand automatically went to his left bicep where her latest artistry had created a tat just for the two of them. Their initials were entwined in a fancy scroll along with a couple of strategically placed raindrops. Hers was located on her ankle.

"You should marry that girl." Tanner slapped Dare on the back and grinned. "She's a keeper."

They'd get there. It was only a matter of time and Rayne definitely wasn't the type to push for a ring and a wedding. While some girls had spent their adolescence playing bride, she had spent it drawing and dreaming.

The remainder of the meeting was spent on smaller crimes, mostly drug related. By the time they adjourned Dare couldn't wait to get back to the woman he'd left curled up under the covers. He hurried back to his truck but paused as Evan stood on the sidewalk unlocking his own vehicle with a key fob in his hand.

"Hey Evan, I wanted to thank you again for chasing down Moulson's girlfriend. It helped that she was able to shed light as to why the guy would want to ink what basically amounted to a treasure map on his arm. I do appreciate your help."

Evan smiled briefly and nodded. "No problem. I just made a few calls."

He'd probably done far more than that but Dare didn't contradict his friend. The fact was Evan looked more unhappy with every passing day. Not being a US Marshal was eating away at the man. He wasn't yet forty but today he looked ten years older.

"Is there anything I can do for you? You look...well, you look like shit, my friend."

Evan was a straight shooter himself who didn't take offense at Dare's bald statement. Instead, he actually smiled. "I think that's a step up from how I looked last week, which was 'like hell' if I remember what my sister said correctly. I'm afraid you're going to have to stand in line, Dare, because there are others worried about me as well. My sister thinks I need a woman and my brother thinks I need to go back to the Marshal Service even if all I can do is sit at a desk. What do you think? I'm taking a poll."

The bitter edge of the words weren't lost on Dare but he didn't take the bait. "I think you're a grown man who should do whatever the hell he wants." Dare leaned against the hood of the truck. "But a good woman doesn't sound too bad. Got one in mind?"

"I do not," Evan retorted, slapping his cowboy hat back on his head. "But you're right. I should do whatever the fuck I want. I'm tired of doing whatever people expect me to. Following the rules. I want to live a little bit."

"You sound like Logan and I'm afraid to ask what you mean by living. Should I be scared?"

Evan grinned and pulled open the driver's door. "Everyone should be afraid. Have a good one. Go home and kiss your woman."

Saluting, the lawman climbed into the truck and reversed out of the parking lot before driving away. Dare did the same, heading in the opposite direction. He hoped Evan could pull his life together and find some kind of happiness. He'd been through so much and he was a decent guy, always helping others. But life didn't come with guarantees. If Evan wanted something he had to reach out and grab it.

But he had one terrific idea. Find Rayne and give her a kiss.

He planned on doing that every day for the rest of his life.

Thank you for reading Cowboy Justice Association – Justice Inked

Sign up to be notified of Olivia's new releases:

Newsletter Sign Up: http://eepurl.com/Y6aof

About The Author

Olivia Jaymes is a wife, mother, lover of sexy romance, and caffeine addict. She lives with her husband and son in central Florida and spends her days with handsome alpha males and spunky heroines.

She is currently working on a series of full-length novels called The Cowboy Justice Association. It's a contemporary romance series about lawmen in southern Montana who work to keep the peace but can't seem to find it in their own lives in addition to the erotic romance novella series – Military Moguls and the romantic suspense series – Danger Incorporated.

Visit Olivia Jaymes at
www.OliviaJaymes.com

Danger Incorporated

Damsel In Danger

Hiding From Danger

Discarded Heart Novella

Indecent Danger

Embracing Danger (coming Spring of 2016!)

Cowboy Justice Association

Cowboy Command

Justice Healed

Cowboy Truth

Cowboy Famous

Cowboy Cool

Imperfect Justice

The Deputies

Military Moguls

Champagne and Bullets

Diamonds and Revolvers

Caviar and Covert Ops

Emeralds, Rubies, and Camouflage